MAYHEM IN MIDTOWN

A Novel

DAVID RAINES

Disclaimer: This is a work of fiction. Names, characters, businesses, places, events, and incidents are either the products of the author's imagination or used in a fictitious manner. Any resemblance to actual persons, living or dead, or actual events is purely coincidental.

Published by
DUKE PUBLISHING
NAPLES, FLORIDA

Copyright © 2026 David Raines

ISBNs: 979-8-9940434-0-0 (softcover)
979-8-9940434-1-7 (hardcover)
979-8-9940434-2-4 (ebook)

All Rights Reserved. No part of this book may be reproduced or transmitted in any form or by any means, electronic or mechanical, including photocopying, or by any information storage and retrieval system, without the written permission of the author.

"They have murdered and raped at least three high school girls that we know of. There is no way in hell we're going to let them get out of Midtown!"

—Frank Malone

A NOTE ABOUT THE AUTHOR

David Raines is the author of the thrilling crime novel *The Monster of Midtown,* wherein he created several interesting characters who were readily embraced by his readers. The story introduced a grizzled, big-city homicide detective and his thirteen-year pursuit of a diabolical serial killer. People who read *The Monster of Midtown* enjoyed the characters so much that they expressed a desire to learn more about them.

After publishing his first novel, Raines moved on to an entirely different project. Eventually information from his readers began to filter back to him. He was moved by how interested his readers were in his characters. He had considered writing a sequel but initially shelved the idea. His plan was to go in another direction with a whole set of new characters. Sequels can be problematic in many ways. The author didn't want the first book to be required reading to enjoy the second book. However, at the same time, he wanted the next book to have a connection to the classic original. The result is what many are calling one of the best sequels ever.

So, buckle up again, everyone! Lieutenant Frank Malone and his partner, Eddie Dolan, are back! This time they are after two serial killers who have committed a number of ruthless and horrible crimes. Malone must confront a minefield of obstacles threatening to destroy everything he holds dear. When all said and done, he is left with only his sense of compassion for the victims and his unrelenting quest for justice.

To achieve justice, the detectives must confront powerful forces who are hell-bent on stopping them at all costs. *Mayhem in Midtown* is the quintessential book about good versus evil, right versus wrong. Will Malone and Dolan succeed, or will they be swallowed up in an ocean of malevolence and dastardly deeds? Whatever happens, brace yourself: *Mayhem* is sure to follow.

MAYHEM IN MIDTOWN

CHAPTER 1

Midtown Homicide Lieutenant Frank Malone was preparing for bed when he received a text message from police dispatch. The body of a white female had been discovered on Old Highway 9 near mile marker 77. Malone dressed quickly. He donned his black trench coat over his sport coat and buttoned-down white shirt. He carried a pair of waterproof neoprene boots. He was out the door in fewer than twenty minutes.

Fifteen minutes later he was in the parking lot of Midtown's 9th Precinct. He was waiting for his partner, Detective Eddie Dolan, to pick him up. The headlights of Dolan's black unmarked Ford Explorer appeared quickly as he drove up and parked parallel next to Malone's Explorer. For the past two hours, a horizontal, wind-driven rainstorm had saturated Midtown. Malone jumped out of his vehicle, dashed to the passenger side door of Dolan's vehicle, and got in.

Once inside, Dolan observed the glistening wet sheen on Malone's damp face. "Dreadful night, eh, Frank?"

Malone acknowledged him with a nod. "It's a freaking monsoon out there," said Malone.

Malone keyed his portable radio. "Lieutenant 21 to Dispatch."

"Go ahead 21."

"Show Lieutenant 21 and Detective 119 en route to mile marker 77 on Old Highway 9, reference deceased white female."

"Acknowledge. Lieutenant 21 and Detective 119 en route."

Dolan drove cautiously as squalls of wind and rain pounded the streets of Midtown. Visibility outside the Explorer's bleary windshield was near zero. Sloped streets, gutters, and storm drains were no match for the sheer volume of water being produced by the storm. The foul weather added to the already dismal landscape that constantly draped Midtown. Early November rains were often a warning of the frigid temperatures that would surely follow. Residents readily acknowledged that Midtown essentially had two seasons: the bleak period and the dead of winter. The storm signaled that the bleak period was drawing to a close.

In many ways, Midtown was similar to other urban cities. It had gobs of blighted areas, drug trafficking was evident on practically every corner, gang members patrolled their turf, and prostitutes applied their trade as the sun set. It was also a sanctuary city. A massive influx of undocumented immigrants had caused additional strain on Midtown's already underfunded budget. There was not enough low-income housing available to provide cost-effective shelter for the new residents, nor was there enough space in classrooms to accommodate their children. Crime rates and human-trafficking activity had increased exponentially. The lack of housing would eventually become deadly as dispiriting winter conditions loomed on Midtown's unwelcoming horizon.

In February 2025, just eight months ago, Malone and Dolan had responded to the scene of a deceased female victim near mile marker 77 on Old Highway 9. That victim's name was Tammy Patterson. She was an exotic dancer who performed locally in a strip club called Silver Stilettos. At some point, Patterson had crossed paths with the notorious serial killer known both locally and nationally as the Monster of Midtown. She had been the ninth victim in the Monster's long reign of terror.

The forty-minute trip out to Old Highway 9 conjured up a time for the detectives when all of Midtown was on edge, fearing when and where the Monster would strike next. Dolan strained to see out the windshield of his Explorer. The downpour grew more intense as he navigated the rain-soaked streets. Unrelenting sheets of rain reduced visibility to a mere few feet.

"What a night, Frank," Dolan said as he gripped the steering wheel tighter. "A Hollywood scriptwriter couldn't have picked a more perfect scenario for a murder. I was already in bed when dispatch texted me."

"I was headed that way myself," Malone said with a similar tone.

Up ahead, the detectives saw four sets of flashing blue beacon lights flickering in the Midtown night. In anticipation of venturing out into the harsh elements, Malone buttoned the top button of his trench coat and pulled up the collar.

Dolan parked the Explorer outside the yellow crime scene tape on the shoulder of Old Highway 9. The detectives slipped on their waterproof boots and exited the vehicle. Wind violently whipped against their trench coats and rain pelted their faces as they approached the rippling yellow tape that defined the perimeter of the crime scene. Sergeant Skip Anderson approached Malone and Dolan. He lifted the tape so the two detectives could easily duck underneath.

"What do you have, Skip?" Malone asked, shouting so he could be heard over the howling wind and rain.

"A nude, white female, likely a teenager," Anderson said with a grim expression. "It's a disturbing scene, Frank. Prepare yourself; it is déjà vu all over again."

"What is that supposed to mean?" Dolan asked.

"You'll see."

Anderson led the detectives to the body. As they approached, Anderson's reference became evident. There, lying spread-eagled on the muddy terrain alongside Old Highway 9 was a young, nude, white female. She had been placed on her back. Her right ankle was fastened to her right wrist with a nylon zip tie. Her left wrist was attached to her left ankle in the same manner. Her feet and hands were noticeably discolored, a result of the tourniquet effect the zip ties had on the distal portion of her extremities. The discoloration likely indicated that the zip ties were applied while the victim was still alive. Her torso was riddled with what appeared to be dozens of human bite marks. Her face was grotesquely contorted into a frozen, terrifying scream. Stapled to her forehead was a laminated yellow Post-it note with "#12" written on it. A total of eleven victims had been attributed to the Monster of Midtown.

Malone and Dolan looked at the gruesome sight. Even as experienced detectives, they were shocked.

"Dear G-d, Frank, it's not possible, is it?" Dolan gasped.

Approximately eight months earlier, Midtown's infamous resident, the Monster of Midtown, had dumped his ninth victim in virtually the same desolate location. That victim was posed in the same manner. A Post-it note with "#9" written on it had been stapled to her forehead.

Malone stared at the shocking sight in disbelief. "It can't be," he said. "It just can't be."

The appalling scene was even more disturbing because Malone, Dolan, and Anderson were well aware that Malone had killed Lawrence Joseph Carsdale, better known as the Monster of Midtown, in a subway train shootout back in February.

Malone took a closer look at the victim. She appeared to meet the description of the missing seventeen-year-old high-school student Kerry Hamilton, who had vanished four days earlier. She was last seen leaving school at 3:00 p.m. on Tuesday, November 2. Her disappearance had been headline news in Midtown and throughout the country. The teenager's innocent, fresh face had captured everyone's attention as authorities frantically conducted a twenty-four-hour-a-day search for her.

"Skip, do any of your patrol officers have a brand-new tarp, in its original package in their patrol car?"

"Of course, Frank."

"Please use it to cover the victim."

Malone wanted the victim covered to keep the rain from further washing away any trace evidence that might have been left on the body. The new tarp was called for to avoid an unsavory attempt later by a defense attorney to disqualify any trace evidence that might be collected. An experienced defense attorney could have a field day arguing that a previously used tarp had contaminated the entire crime scene.

"I'm on it, Frank."

Skip ordered a uniformed officer to retrieve a new tarp from the trunk of his police cruiser while Malone and Dolan examined the body closer. The marks on the victim's neck appeared to be indicative of manual strangulation. That was the same method used by the Monster of Midtown to kill his victims. The Post-it note was laminated. That was marginally different from the Monster's modus operandi; however, Malone quickly concluded that it was likely done in this instance to preserve the integrity of the Post-it note. The killer apparently didn't want the rainstorm to wash away his or her message. The killer wanted authorities to know that a newly reincarnated version of the original infamous serial killer was the culprit.

"Who discovered the body, Skip?"

"A state trooper spotted her. He is sitting over there," Anderson said, pointing to a patrol car.

Malone pulled the collar on his trench coat higher. The temperature was dipping as the wind and rain threatened to wash away all potential evidence. The uniformed officer returned with the tarp. Dolan took a picture of it with his phone before it was removed from its original packaging, to visually document that a new tarp was being used to cover the victim. The two detectives searched the area near the body for items that would be difficult for the rain to wash away. They looked for clothing, a cellphone, a purse, shoes, jewelry, a discarded weapon, or anything that could be used to identify the killer. The victim had almost certainly been killed elsewhere and dumped in the current location. Unfortunately, any chance of identifying potential tire tracks from the vehicle used to transport the victim to the scene had already been washed away.

Malone and Dolan headed over to the state trooper's patrol car. As they neared, the trooper got out of his vehicle. He was a tall, slender man with a pockmarked face. After the detectives introduced themselves, the trooper provided his account of how he had discovered the body.

When their conversation ended, Malone gave the trooper a directive: "I need a copy of your dashboard camera video as soon as possible. Especially the portion that demonstrates what occurred prior to and up until the time when you discovered the body."

The trooper nodded, then paused a moment to assess Malone's request. "You don't think I had something to do with this, do you?"

"No, I don't," replied Malone. "But I want to be able to visually demonstrate that to a jury if this case ever makes its way into a courtroom."

"Understood," the patrolman said.

Meanwhile, a CSI team had arrived on the scene. Moments later John Gordon from the coroner's office pulled up. The two detectives ducked under the crime scene tape to meet with the coroner and the CSI team.

"John, I need autopsy results as soon as possible, especially the time of death, cause of death, and whether she was sexually assaulted," Malone said with a sense of urgency.

"I will Frank," responded Gordon, conveying a sense of cooperation.

Malone returned to Sergeant Anderson. "Skip, I want absolutely no leaks from anyone regarding the victim's identification. I want to inform the family myself before the media gets wind of this."

"Consider it done, Frank."

Malone and Dolan left the scene shortly after 4:00 a.m. Malone looked at the dismal skyline of Midtown as they drove back to the 9th Precinct. A bleak new day was dawning, and it brought with it a shocking new murder investigation. The rising sun was beginning to illuminate the wretched urban landscape. Gang graffiti scarred buildings, homeless people wandered aimlessly, and prostitutes completed their "night shift." Dolan parked the Explorer. The detectives hustled around puddles, through the drizzling rain, and up the stairs to the front entrance of the 9th Precinct.

The warm and dry conditions inside were a welcome change. The place was nearly deserted. It would still be a couple of hours before the daily wave of dysfunction made its presence known. Malone and Dolan entered the elevator; their olfactory senses immediately detected the familiar musty smell inside. Malone pressed the button for the fourth floor, where the homicide division was located.

Once on the fourth floor, Dolan headed to the community break room to brew the day's first pot of coffee. Malone went to his office and called the police chief, who had obviously just woken when he answered the phone.

"Chief Parker."

"Good morning, Chief. It's Frank Malone. I'm sorry to call you at this hour, but it's important. I rolled up on a murder scene several hours ago on Old Highway 9. The victim is Kerry Hamilton, the missing high school girl."

"I was afraid her disappearance was going to end up like this," the Chief conveyed.

"That's only the half of it, Chief. She was posed in a

manner that was consistent with the Monster of Midtown murders. She had a yellow Post-it note stapled to her forehead with the number twelve written on it. I suspect that we likely have a full-blown copycat killer on our hands. The Post-it message appears to be an indication that the killer intends to take over where the 'Monster' left off."

"Dear G-d."

"It could be starting all over again, Chief."

"I understand, Frank," the Chief said with a foreboding tone. "Assemble the necessary resources and give it top priority. Put a lid on the details. Just disseminate basic information to the media for now. I don't want to cause a full-scale panic. It will be bad enough without any of the gory details."

"Understood, Chief."

"I'll call the mayor to inform him. You can imagine how that's going to go down."

"I don't envy you, Chief."

"I'll speak with you soon, Frank."

Malone hung up. He mentally revisited everything he had observed at the crime scene, which included informing the Hamilton family. He assessed the possible disturbing ramifications that would likely follow. He was well aware that copycat killers were their own unique brand of psychopath. Unfortunately and predictably, they often possessed many of the same narcissistic traits as the original. They were most often known for their warped aspirations to seek out the same level of notoriety and attention as the criminals they revered.

Midtown residents were certainly not over the Monster of Midtown's thirteen-year reign of terror. The wounds he had inflicted on Midtown's psyche were still raw. For thirteen years an omnipresent sense of danger lurked around every corner in Midtown. Citizens were afraid to leave their homes to patronize local businesses. If they did find the courage to venture out, they were scared to return home in fear of what might be waiting for them when they got there. Political pressure escalated as the community, and its leaders blamed the police department for the lack of progress on the case. Malone had been at the epicenter of the turmoil because he was the lead investigator. The copycat killer would inevitably scrape open old wounds. Malone momentarily stared off into space as he contemplated all the dire scenarios that were sure to follow.

CHAPTER 2

At 7:00 a.m. that same morning, Lucy, Malone's longtime clerical assistant, stuck her head inside his office doorway. "I see you are getting off to an early start, Boss. What's up?" she said, moving into the room.

"Eddie and I have been up all night. A female murder victim was discovered on Old Highway 9," Malone conveyed in his matter-of-fact tone.

"Oh dear, not again."

"I'm afraid so. The victim is the missing Hamilton girl."

"Oh Lord, that is terrible, her poor mother. I was afraid her disappearance would end this way."

"On top of it, it looks like we have a Monster of Midtown copycat killer on our hands."

"Ugh. That's certainly going to get everyone's dander up. I can't believe it's all starting again. Let me know if you need anything, Boss."

"Thanks, Lucy. Keep this under your hat until I have a chance to inform the victim's family."

It was still early in the morning. Malone wanted to wait a bit before he notified Kerry's family of her death.

"You don't need to worry—this information is safe with me," Lucy assured Malone.

Malone got up from his desk and headed down to the break room for a cup of coffee. Dolan and detectives Tommy Jackson, Matt Dillon, Trace MacDonald, and Kinsey Phillips were there, engaging in friendly conversation.

Malone poured himself a cup of java in his personal cup and joined the group. "Good morning, everyone."

"Good morning, Frank," the group responded warmly.

"I hate to interrupt, but please come down to my office for an impromptu meeting," Malone said.

The five detectives followed Malone into his office. Matt, Trace, and Kinsey brought in extra folding chairs so everyone had a seat.

The six detectives sat down. Their sense of concern was aroused by Malone's serious demeanor.

Tommy Jackson was a large African American who had played offensive line in the National Football League. Unfortunately, his career had been cut short by a knee injury. He spent his childhood growing up in Midtown. His athletic prowess as a high school football player was almost legendary around town. It seemed only natural that he would either become a hoodlum or a police officer. Tommy knew every inch of Midtown. Over the years, he had cultivated a network of informants who had proven valuable in solving notable homicide cases.

Jackson's partner, Matt Dillon, was a tall, slender guy who looked considerably less imposing than Jackson. Nevertheless, he was a dogged detective and a spirited interrogator.

The bespectacled Trace MacDonald projected a very studious image. He looked more like a computer technician than a cop. But looks could be deceiving. He was a tenacious investigator and an effective problem solver.

Kinsey Phillips was the newest addition to Midtown's homicide division. The detectives all called her the "professor" because she was the only member of the Midtown Police Department who possessed a doctorate degree in public administration, specializing in advanced criminology. Everyone in the room, with the exception of Phillips, had been on the task force Malone led to track down the Monster of Midtown. Phillips had been a patrol officer at the time. She had replaced Trace MacDonald's original partner, who the Monster had ambushed and brutally killed.

Jackson and Dillon had been assigned to the Kerry Hamilton case when the student first disappeared. Malone and Dolan would have usually taken the case, but they had been tied up in court testifying in a double-murder case.

"I'm sure Eddie has filled everyone in on what we saw at the murder scene last night," Malone assumed. "Kerry Hamilton is likely the victim of a copycat killer emulating the Monster of Midtown. As a result, you can be sure this case is going to get everyone's attention. Therefore, I want to get out in front of this thing early. I'm going to assemble a six-person task force and investigative team. There's no need for you to raise your hand to volunteer. You have already been assigned. For the first order of business, I want Tommy and Matt to bring everyone up to speed on where the Kerry Hamilton case stands at the moment. Please start with her parents."

"The parents have been divorced for seven years," Jackson said. "They have two daughters, Kerry and her younger sister, Melissa. Both daughters were living with their mother when Kerry disappeared. According to Kerry's mother, the father meets all his financial obligations regarding alimony and child support. He is also a very active and conscientious parent in raising their two daughters. There appears to be no animosity between Kerry's mother and father. Neither parent has an arrest record. There isn't any evidence that the parents are substance abusers, nor do either of them have a concerning social media history. Despite their divorce,

Kerry's parents appear to be on the same page regarding the raising of their two daughters. Finally, neither parent received a ransom demand. At this point, we feel comfortable scratching both parents off the suspect list.

"The father has been in a relationship with another woman for the past two years. The mother is also dating someone. Everything appears to be amicable. The mother's boyfriend is an anesthesiologist. He checks out clean. He was married previously and has a twelve-year-old son. Mr. Hamilton's girlfriend is an attorney. She has been employed at the same law firm for the past twelve years. She also appears to be clean. Both of Kerry's parents and their significant others participated in the search for her. Both parents have made public appeals pleading for Kerry's safe return."

"What can you tell me about Kerry, Tommy?" Malone asked after sipping from his coffee cup.

"She was an outstanding student," Jackson said while reading from his notes. "Matt is still working on her social media history. It appears to be quite extensive. We have no evidence so far that would indicate that she was bullied by anyone. She was popular and had a large network of friends. We have compiled a list of them. We've interviewed many of them. At this point, we have only been able to eliminate a handful of them from our potential suspect list. We also spoke to Kerry's five primary high school teachers, but there are other faculty members we still need to contact. Teachers and coaches were certainly in a position to gain Kerry's trust."

"I agree," Malone said. "What about a boyfriend or girlfriend?"

"It appears Kerry was heterosexual," Jackson replied. "She's only had boyfriends in the past. She apparently wasn't seeing anyone regularly when she went missing. The jury is still out on whether she was sexually active."

"What happened this past Tuesday when she disappeared?" Malone asked.

"Matt and I have looked at a good portion of the school's CCTV video. Trace and Kinsey have helped us with that. The school has cameras installed throughout the campus. There are still miles of video material we haven't gotten to yet. However, we did catch a glimpse of Kerry leaving school through the main entrance on Tuesday when classes were dismissed. The cameras initially captured her walking with a group of friends and then ultimately alone in a westerly direction toward her house. Eventually, she walked out of range of the school's cameras. We were able to get CCTV video images of her from home security systems along the route to her house. Unfortunately, in the end, we lost track of her about three blocks from the school. That's when the abduction must have occurred.

"Kerry did have her cellphone with her when she disappeared," Jackson continued. "We cited exigent circumstances and submitted a formal request to her cellphone carrier for her GPS location information. The day after she disappeared, her carrier was able to identify a stationary pinging signal. Eventually we were able to establish the general area where Kerry's cellphone was located. We assembled search teams comprising members from the police department, fire department, and community volunteers. A firefighter noted several storm drains in the area. We called out the Public Works Department. They got us access to the storm drains. That's where we found Kerry's cellphone. As a result, we likely have the location where the abduction occurred, but it obviously didn't give us her location."

"Are there other family members or neighbors we should be concerned about?" Malone asked.

"All of Kerry's grandparents, aunts, uncles, nieces, and nephews live out of state. None were visiting when she disappeared, and none have criminal records. However, we haven't had the chance to interview all of them yet. We are still in the process of checking out the homeowners along the route where Kerry began walking home from the school to where we found her cellphone," Jackson continued. "Also, we have begun checking into the registered sex offenders living in the area. According to the National Sex Offender Public Website, there are eight registered sex offenders living in the immediate area around the Hamilton's residence and Kerry's school. Those numbers are not unusually high, but they are there. Trace and Kinsey have been helping us verify their alibis. There's a lot we haven't gotten to yet, Frank. Our priority at the time was to find Kerry, but that's all changed now."

"Frank, it's only been four days since she disappeared," Matt added. "We have received hundreds of tips after Kerry went missing. There are an overwhelming number of potential suspects in this case. What we have done so far hasn't been conducted with the thoroughness required for a homicide investigation. Our focus and sense of urgency were on finding Kerry alive. We felt we were up against the clock. As a result, almost everything needs to be looked at through the more thorough lens of a murder investigation."

"I fully understand what your priorities were," Malone replied. "I also agree that we will need to virtually restart the investigation. Tommy and Matt, focus on Kerry's school. That means interviewing all faculty members, custodians, landscapers, contractors, counselors, and other relevant personnel. Also, go through every inch of the school's CCTV video footage again.

"Trace and Kinsey, use the list that Tommy and Matt have compiled to track down and interview all of Kerry's closest friends. Pay special attention to any past boy-friends, girlfriends, and other possible sexual partners. Take a thorough look at her social media history and cellphone activity. Locate all CCTV cameras, including those from homes, businesses, and traffic lights in the area. Maybe one of them captured an image of Kerry while she was walking home. Additionally, verify the alibis of all registered sex offenders in the area.

"Eddie and I will focus on Kerry's family. We will reinterview them and their significant others. We will attempt to confirm their alibis from the time Kerry left school on Tuesday until her body was discovered last night. We will also look into Kerry's boyfriend/girl-friend situation from the family's perspective. Also, we will investigate any contractors who may have worked at the Hamilton's residence within the past twelve months. Finally, we will attempt to locate CCTV cameras from businesses and traffics lights along the route to where Kerry's body was discovered. Perhaps a camera captured an image of the vehicle that transported Kerry's body out to Old Highway 9. Finally, I will handle the police chief and mayor. I suspect that will be a job in and of itself. Everyone, keep each other informed via email. We have a lot of ground to cover and only six people to do it. Okay, if there's nothing else"—Malone paused momentarily—"let's get to it."

Dolan remained in Malone's office after the others left.

"Give me a few minutes to update the police chief," Malone said. "I don't want him to get blindsided by any of this. Then we'll go over to Kerry's house to inform her mother of her daughter's death."

"I'm not looking forward to this one, Frank."

CHAPTER 3

Dolan parked in the driveway of the Hamilton residence. Malone dreaded notifying families about the loss of a loved one, especially when the victim was a child. The detectives prepared themselves for the grim task ahead.

They exited the Explorer. A steady drizzle continued to soak Midtown after a week of consistent rain. The Hamilton home was located in a middle-class neighborhood. The houses and landscaping in the area were well maintained. Dolan rang the doorbell. Victoria Hamilton opened the door moments later. The detectives recognized her because she had been all over the news for the past week pleading for her daughter's safe return. She looked exhausted and had been crying. A curious teenage girl peeked out from behind her mother's left shoulder.

"Good morning, my name is Lieutenant Frank Malone. I am from the Midtown Police Department, and this is my partner, Detective Edward Dolan."

The detectives displayed their badges.

"May we come in?"

A look of dread from Kerry's mother and sister conveyed that they had quickly figured out what was coming next. Malone was about to proceed when a wave of tears filled Victoria's eyes and began spilling down her cheeks. Melissa, Kerry's younger sister, began sobbing, then turned and ran away from the front door. Victoria appeared as if she was going to collapse.

Malone stepped in and held her upright before she could crumple to the floor. He assisted her to a chair in the living room. He crouched down and looked into Victoria's eyes. Her facial expression conveyed utter defeat and tragic loss.

"Can I get something for you, Ms. Hamilton, perhaps a glass of water?" Dolan asked, joining them in the living room.

Victoria attempted to gather herself. She took several deep breaths and grabbed a tissue from a nearby box to dab at her eyes. "Kerry is dead, Lieutenant?"

"I'm afraid so. I'm so sorry for your loss."

"I certainly didn't want this ordeal to end this way, but I half expected that it would," Victoria said while wiping away her tears.

"Do you feel up to having a conversation with us?" Malone asked.

"I will try, but please just give me a few minutes to compose myself, Lieutenant."

Somehow, Victoria mustered enough strength to continue her conversation with the detectives. "Was my daughter murdered, Lieutenant?"

"I haven't received official confirmation from the coroner yet, but it appears so. Are you sure you want to continue, Ms. Hamilton? Detective Dolan and I can come back if you don't feel up to talking to us right now."

"It's okay," she said, sniffling. "I want the person who did this to be held accountable. I don't want this to happen to someone else's daughter."

"That's very brave and unselfish of you, Ms. Hamilton," Dolan said in a comforting manner.

"Where did you find Kerry? What happened to her?"

"Her body was found along Old Highway 9," Malone replied.

Victoria shuddered to think about her daughter being left in such a desolate area. A new wave of tears began to flow. She took another deep breath and attempted to gather herself once again. "How was she killed?"

"Likely strangled, but we don't have an official cause of death yet. I want to prepare you for what's to come. Your daughter's murder appears to have been the work of a Monster of Midtown copycat killer."

Victoria gasped. She began to contemplate the level of evil her daughter must have confronted during the final moments of her life. Tears began to flow freely again. "Was she raped, Lieutenant?" Victoria sobbed.

"I cannot confirm that either, but the evidence appears to point in that direction. Ms. Hamilton, are you sure you want to do this right now? We can come back later."

"Please call me Victoria. I'm okay. I want to help you find the person who did this."

Malone stood up from his crouching position. He and Dolan sat on a couch across from the grieving mother.

Victoria studied Malone's hardened face and the prominent deep lines on his forehead and around his eyes. She noted that his eyes appeared to be very observant to every detail around him. His face conveyed a worldly sense of determination and grit. "I recognize you, Lieutenant. You are the police lieutenant who was involved in the subway train shootout with the Monster of Midtown. I have seen you on television many times speaking about the case. You are the person responsible for ridding our community of that horrible person."

"Yes, ma'am, I was involved in the shooting."

"You are very brave, Lieutenant."

"Thank you, ma'am."

Just then, Kerry's sister joined them in the living room. Still weeping, she stood behind the chair where her mother was sitting.

"Again, we would like to extend our condolences to both of you."

"Thank you, Lieutenant. We appreciate that."

"Please call me Frank." Malone looked around the room. The Hamilton home was warmly decorated. Everything was in its place. "You have made a very nice home for yourself and your daughters, Ms. Hamilton."

"Again, please call me Victoria and this is my other daughter, Melissa, Kerry's younger sister."

"It is very nice to meet you, Melissa. I wish this was under different circumstances. However, Detective Dolan and I promise you that we will do everything in our power to find and arrest the person responsible for Kerry's murder."

Melissa shook her head to convey her understanding.

Victoria Hamilton looked totally spent. Her blue eyes were bloodshot, puffy, and watery. Her nose was red and raw. Melissa looked much the same. They had already endured so much. Both Malone and Dolan pulled out their notepads and pens.

"Victoria, would you mind if Detective Dolan spoke to Melissa alone in another room while you and I have a conversation?"

"No, of course not, Frank. Melissa and Detective Dolan can use the den. Feel free to close the door."

Melissa's look conveyed apprehension.

"It's okay Honey, the detectives are here to help," Victoria assured her.

Dolan and Melissa went to the den, and Malone turned his attention back to Victoria. "Once again, I would like to extend my deepest sympathies to you and Melissa."

"Thank you, Frank. . . . This has been a very difficult week. I wish it would have ended differently."

"Of course you do."

"First, I couldn't sleep because I didn't know what had happened to Kerry. Now I will probably never sleep again because I know what happened to her. I often hear people in my situation say, 'At least you have closure.' Apparently, at some point I am supposed to appreciate that. How am I ever going to appreciate anything ever again after what was done to my daughter?" Victoria said, her voice trailing off.

"I don't have any answers to that question. The only thing I can say is we will do everything possible to find the person responsible and hold them accountable."

"As I mentioned, I have seen you on television many times, discussing the Monster of Midtown case. I know you pursued him for a long time. Despite everything you faced, you never relented in your quest to find him. I also know that you risked your life to get justice for all the families involved in that case. I trust that you will do the same for Kerry."

"Rest assured, I will. Victoria, I would like to speak to you about the male members of your family. I understand that you are divorced from Kerry's father."

"Yes, Frank, that is true. We have been divorced for seven years."

"Was your ex-husband actively involved in Kerry's life?"

"Yes, Evan is a very good father. Obviously, we had issues in our marriage, but I have never doubted his commitment to being a father for our daughters."

"Has there ever been a time when you suspected that your husband might be acting inappropriately with your daughters?"

"I know where you are going with this. I can assure you that Evan had nothing to do with Kerry's abduction and murder. There is just no way. I've known him for almost twenty years. Unfortunately, we both fell out of love, and our marriage ended. But I know Evan. He is a good person, an excellent provider, and a dedicated father. We just couldn't make our marriage work. He would never do anything to harm either of our daughters."

Malone continued to question Victoria about the male figures in Kerry's life.

"Victoria, did Kerry have a boyfriend?"

"She has male friends, but she didn't have what I would classify as a boyfriend at the moment."

"This is going to be an awkward question, but I must ask it. Was Kerry heterosexual?"

"I saw no indication that she wasn't."

"Do you know if Kerry was sexually active?"

"Not to my knowledge, Lieutenant. However, she was a seventeen-year-old high school girl. I am not sure she would have shared that with me if she was. I didn't see any obvious signs that she was sexually active."

Malone knew from his initial investigation notes that Victoria was a real estate agent. He questioned her about her coworkers, especially her male coworkers. Did they stop by the house occasionally? Was Kerry ever alone with any of them? What about Kerry's uncles and male teachers? Was Kerry involved in sports, and if so, what about her coaches? Did all their actions appear to be appropriate? Did she know if Kerry had ever used illegal drugs or alcohol? Did Kerry have any enemies? Did she ever complain about being bullied?

Victoria mentioned that Kerry took ballet classes on Mondays and Thursdays. She informed Malone that in all the confusion following her daughter's disappearance, she had forgotten to mention that to detectives Jackson and Dillon. But she added that Kerry's ballet instructor was a well-qualified married woman whom Kerry was very fond of.

Meanwhile, Dolan was in the den questioning thirteen-year-old Melissa. Dolan asked her about Kerry's sexuality, her male friends, did she have a boyfriend, did she know if Kerry had ever been intimate with anyone, or whether Kerry ever used illegal drugs or drank alcohol. Dolan asked her about the male adult figures in her life. Were there any teachers, coaches, family members, neighbors, or other adults who came onto her or made her feel uncomfortable? Did Kerry keep a diary?

"No, she didn't keep a diary," Melissa said.

Back in the living room, Malone was going through a litany of questions with Kerry's mother. He asked about the existence of a home CCTV security system, to which Victoria said there was none. Both sets of questioning went on for well over an hour. Finally, Dolan and Melissa reconvened in the living room with Malone and Victoria. Malone handed them business cards with his contact information.

Before the detectives left, Victoria added one more insightful comment about Kerry: "Frank, my daughter was a very beautiful and intelligent young woman. She had an obvious sense of maturity about her. Physically, she definitely fit the mold of someone who could attract a predator. She was an attractive young lady. However,

I don't think she could have been easily deceived. With that being said, I think the person involved in this must have had Kerry's trust or was in a position to easily gain her trust. I don't think she was forcibly snatched. I don't see that happening on a street corner in broad daylight. She was very strong and athletic. I know she would have put up a fight. Also, I am sure that none of our family members are involved in this. Don't waste your time spinning your wheels in that direction."

"I understand what you are saying. I ask you to be patient with us. A homicide investigation is often a process of elimination," replied Malone. "That's just how it works. It can appear to be an exercise in futility, especially for the victim's family members. We have to keep checking the boxes. Just keep reminding yourself during this process that we will never rest until we get justice for you and your family."

Victoria nodded her head. "I understand you have your way of doing things, Frank. Keep in mind we're just trying to survive here. I appreciate your efforts, and I understand the reality of the situation."

CHAPTER 4

The detectives left the Hamilton house and proceeded to Dolan's Explorer in the drizzling rain. Once inside, they stared ahead for several moments. Finally, Dolan turned to Malone.

"Did you ever notice that ninety-nine percent of the murder cases we investigate generally start in the same place? With us posing a series of uncomfortable questions to the grieving members of the victim's family? I could throw up thinking about some of the questions I had to ask Melissa. She's just a kid. She's younger than both my daughters."

All Malone could do was nod in solemn agreement.

"Where to next?" Dolan asked.

"The Classic Ballet dance studio. Victoria said Kerry took ballet classes on Mondays and Thursdays. She mentioned that she forgot to tell Tommy and Matt about the classes in the aftermath of Kerry's disappearance. The studio is located on the way back to the office. Let's stop by there and check it off our list."

The detectives observed the dreary conditions on the way to the dance studio. They drove through a section of Midtown where many Italians and Irish had settled prior to World War II. It was a place where factories and textile mills once thrived. They passed an old cemetery that provided the final resting place for Civil War veterans, World War II heroes, famous innovators, Industrial Revolution leaders, junkies, prostitutes, and cops.

"Another Chamber of Commerce day in Midtown, Frank," Dolan uttered sarcastically.

"Eddie, you need to be more appreciative of the current dank, rainy conditions. You'll be longing for these days in a month when you're freezing your ass off."

"I can always count on you to put things into the proper perspective, Frank."

Dolan parked the Explorer in the parking lot of a strip mall. The dance studio was one of many tenants in the plaza. Malone and Dolan hustled through the raindrops to the dance studio's front door and entered. Soft classical music played inside.

Malone and Dolan observed a woman across a wide-open wood floor holding on to a barre, a stationary handrail providing support for dancers. She was wearing black dance tights that clung to every inch of her fabulously taut athletic figure. She had her back to them, standing on the toes of her right foot and repeatedly raising her pointed left foot high above her head and pressing her leg against her face. She had marvelously graceful, long, lean legs; superbly defined slender, muscular arms; an exceptionally thin waist; and a headful of dangling blonde curls that rested on her shoulders.

Malone and Dolan stood by silently, watching her incredible display of flexibility and elegance as she moved rhythmically to the music.

Finally, she noticed her visitors in one of the many wall mirrors. She walked over to a table, picked up her cellphone, and used it to turn off the music. She strolled over to greet the two men. "May I help you, gentlemen?"

She was beautiful. She appeared to be fully made up for a pending dance recital. Her plump lips were high-lighted with glossy red lipstick. Her face was covered with a generous amount of foundation. Her high cheekbones were subtly tinted with a hint of rouge, and her vibrant green eyes were outlined with long lashes and thick mascara.

"Yes, ma'am, we are homicide detectives from Midtown's 9th Precinct. This is Detective Dolan, and I am Lieutenant Frank Malone."

"My name is Annette Rousseau. It is nice to meet you both." She possessed a sophisticated voice with a distinctly Eastern European accent.

"We would like to speak to you about one of your students, Kerry Hamilton," Malone said.

"Yes, I am aware that Kerry has been missing for several days. She is a wonderful and beautiful young lady. Please follow me to my office where we can sit down and be more comfortable."

Malone and Dolan followed Annette to a minimally furnished office. She sat behind a desk and motioned for the detectives to sit in the chairs across from her.

"First, I must inform you, Ms. Rousseau, that Kerry is now deceased. We believe she was murdered. Her body was found along Old Highway 9. We are investigating her death," Malone stated.

"That's awful!" Rousseau gasped. "I am so sorry to hear that. Kerry was a charming young lady."

"It certainly is a terrible situation. We would like to ask you a few questions about Kerry."

Rousseau's dazzling green eyes glistened from developing tears. "Yes, of course. I will try to help you in any way I can."

Dolan took out his notebook and pen from his inside coat pocket. "Ms. Rousseau, did you happen to observe who drove Kerry to the dance studio on the days when she had lessons?" Dolan asked.

"I believe her mother dropped her off."

"Was it always her mother?" Malone further probed.

"Yes, as far as I can recall. However, I certainly didn't notice every time. It wasn't where my focus was."

Malone continued his questioning.

"Was Kerry ever accompanied by a man or perhaps a boyfriend?"

"No, I don't think so. I only recall seeing her mother."

"Did a male friend ever visit the studio during her dance lessons?"

"No, I don't recall seeing anyone like that."

The dance instructor was distractingly gorgeous. She was quite aware of her alluring physical qualities. How could she not be? Nevertheless, the detectives were determined to concentrate on the matter at hand.

"So as far as you know, it was always her mother who picked her up after her dance lessons?" Malone questioned.

"Yes, I believe so."

"Did Kerry ever confide in you about male figures in her life or perhaps she commented on a boyfriend?" Dolan interjected.

"Not that I recall. There are approximately twenty-five young ladies in Kerry's dance class. I exchange greetings and pleasantries with all of them. However, my relationship stays strictly within the confines of me being the instructor and them being the students. It has to be that way. Teenage girls can become easily distracted without strict professional rules and guidelines. If I don't make the rules clear and enforce them, the girls will get little to nothing out of the classes. My job is to teach them ballet. I take that very seriously. As a result, I only know Kerry as an attractive, pleasant girl who possessed moderate dancing skills."

Malone and Dolan continued to question Annette for another thirty minutes. Malone ended their conversation by handing her a business card with his contact information. "Please call me if you think of something later that might be helpful to our investigation."

"I sure will, Lieutenant," she said seductively.

Malone ignored her alluring tone.

With that, the detectives left. They hustled through the pouring rain to Dolan's Explorer. Once inside, Dolan stated the obvious. "She didn't provide much, Frank, but maybe we should come back again and interview her a couple dozen more times just to make sure," Dolan said jokingly.

"You better let me handle Ms. Rousseau, Eddie," Malone replied with a smirk. "I don't want you getting sidetracked."

"I always appreciate your concern for me, Frank." Dolan said while laughing.

Meanwhile, Tommy Jackson was attempting to go through all the CCTV video footage at Kerry's school. The head of security and the school's IT person, Irene Richards, provided assistance. Richards replayed the footage whenever Tommy requested it. She zoomed in on images when asked and ran the video in varying degrees of slow motion when Tommy requested it.

Tom Howard, the school's head of security, provided a wealth of information. He gave Tommy a copy of the school's formal written security procedures and a copy of the work schedules for the entire staff. He also handed over documents detailing the various means of electronic surveillance that the school had in place to track the activity of visitors, students, faculty members, and support staff. In addition, Howard provided Tommy with a list of the guests who visited the school on the day Kerry went missing.

Simultaneously, Matt Dillon was collecting information from contractors and their employees who worked on the school's property. He was especially interested in driver's licenses, social security cards, passports, green cards, and work visas. He would use the information to see if any of them had been previously arrested. Matt was particularly keen to learn of prior felony arrests for crimes like rape, kidnapping, child molestation, assault, battery, domestic abuse, and possibly murder.

While Tommy and Matt were working on matters within the confines of Kerry's school, Trace and Kinsey were knocking on the front door of a registered sex offender. Robert Susskind lived in an apartment building three blocks from Kerry's school. He was initially sentenced to fourteen years in a state penitentiary for molesting a twelve-year-old girl. He was released after serving just over five years. He was required to check in with his parole officer every other week and to attend regular sessions with a licensed mental health therapist.

Trace and Kinsey immediately noticed when Susskind opened the door how thin and pale he was. He had the appearance of being undernourished. His hair was greasy and unkempt. His clothes appeared to need laundering.

"Mr. Susskind, my name is Trace MacDonald, and this is my partner, Kinsey Phillips." The detectives flashed their badges.

"We are homicide detectives with the Midtown Police Department. We would like to have a word with you."

Susskind sighed. "Has another girl been molested? I swear, every time a girl pulls her pants down in this town, the cops come knocking on my door. What the hell, don't you cops have any other suspects in this godforsaken town besides me? I have served my time. The constant questioning of my whereabouts is bordering on harassment."

"Mr. Susskind, do you mind if we come in? We would like to have a private conversation with you," Kinsey asked.

"Yeah, sure, whatever, I have nothing to hide."

Susskind's apartment was as unkempt as his personal appearance. There were two computers on a table, both screens were running, an iPad was open, and two televisions were mounted on the wall. Both were turned on. Paper wrappers and cups from a local fast-food restaurant were scattered about.

"May we sit down?" Trace asked.

"Be my guest," Susskind said with a wave of his hand.

Kinsey was uneasy about the whole setup in Susskind's apartment. The electronic equipment had her wondering what he was using it for, considering his criminal background. She wasn't exactly excited about sitting on Susskind's furniture either, but she followed Trace's lead, sitting on a couch while Susskind sat in a nearby chair.

"Mr. Susskind, we are investigating the disappearance of Kerry Hamilton. She's the missing high school girl who has been in the news," said Trace.

"I've heard about her. She's very cute."

"Where were you this past Tuesday, Mr. Susskind?" Trace asked.

"Oh, here we go again with the questions. Do you actually think I'm involved with her disappearance? I can assure you I had nothing to do with that."

"Just answer the question. Where were you?" Kinsey demanded out of frustration.

"Right here in my apartment."

"Was anyone here with you?" Kinsey asked again.

"No, I was alone."

"What were you doing?"

"I wasn't looking at kiddie porn if that's what you're insinuating."

"Just answer the question, Robert," Trace insisted. He too was getting frustrated.

"I do a podcast from my apartment. I also play stocks and gamble online."

"What is your podcast about?" Kinsey inquired.

"I discuss a variety of subjects."

"Is that what you were doing this past Tuesday?" Kinsey asked.

"Yeah. Why do you guys always come here when something like this happens? I've done my time. I have been rehabilitated," he said, smiling.

"You're a registered sex offender, Mr. Susskind," Trace said with disdain. "You were convicted of an awful crime involving a child. People who are convicted of such crimes are seldom rehabilitated. A murder investigation is always a process of elimination. You live in the immediate area where a high school girl was abducted, and likely raped and murdered. You have a related criminal history. I know she was probably a bit too old for your tastes, but we still need to account for your whereabouts this past Tuesday," Trace said with a sense of cynicism. "If you don't cooperate, I am going to start wondering why."

"I haven't done anything! I told you I have been rehabilitated. I'm off little girls. I'm more into grown women these days, like your cute little partner here." Susskind leered at Kinsey. "What do you say, detective? Would you like to go on a date with me?" he asked. "I'll let you pick the wine."

"I'm afraid my schedule is full, Mr. Susskind," Kinsey responded quickly.

"But I haven't given you a time and date yet."

"I'm afraid my schedule is full for the rest of my life."

"Mr. Susskind, let's get back to the matter at hand if you don't mind," Trace interrupted. "Late last night, Kerry Hamilton's body was discovered in a desolate area off Old Highway 9. As I previously stated, she was likely murdered."

"Hold on a minute," Susskind responded nervously. "Don't tell me you're trying to pin a murder rap on me?"

"I'm not trying to pin anything on you, Mr. Susskind. We're just asking for your cooperation. A seventeen-year-old girl is dead. We want to find out who killed her."

"Well, it wasn't me."

Thirty minutes later, after going through dozens of questions about his whereabouts on Tuesday, Trace and Kinsey finished their interview with Susskind. They walked back to Trace's unmarked Explorer in the damp, misty conditions.

"It's not every day, Kinsey, that you get an offer like that from such an upstanding citizen," Trace joked. "You might want to reconsider. He does have a certain perverse sense of charm about him."

"I feel like I need to be sprayed down with a fire hose after sitting on that dude's furniture," she said after giving Trace's shoulder a backhand swat. "His apartment and that audio/video setup he has gave me the creeps. I have no idea what is going on in there."

"He seemed like just your type to me," Trace said with a hearty laugh.

"Yeah, his body odor and his pasty skin were a real turn-on."

CHAPTER 5

As the detectives made their way back to the 9th Precinct, Malone's cellphone rang. He answered. "Frank, it's Lucy. Will Sutton from the *Midtown Times* is in the lobby. He wants to speak to you. Are you coming back to the office any time soon?"

"I'll be there in five minutes. Tell the front desk sergeant to have him wait for me in the lobby."

"Consider it done, Frank."

Malone turned to Dolan. "Will Sutton is at the Ninth Precinct," he muttered. "He must know something already."

Willford Sutton was the *Midtown Times'* longest-tenured and most capable reporter. Following the conclusion of the Monster of Midtown investigation, he wrote a book detailing the case. He had interviewed Malone and Dolan many times during the writing of his book, seeking facts and anecdotes to ensure its accuracy and to make it engaging. Malone had read the final manuscript before it went to publishing and was quite impressed by the thoroughness of Sutton's research and his writing prowess.

The detectives entered the brightly lit lobby of the 9th Precinct. The walls were adorned with police memorabilia and old black-and-white photographs of police officers performing their duties from decades past. The 9th Precinct was over a hundred years old. It was an ancient relic in its own right. It was a venerable sentinel, constantly standing guard. The floors were covered with linoleum tiles worn by years of endless foot traffic. Midtown's police department was established in 1905, but it wasn't until the era of prohibition that it really got its footing. During that time, most of the personnel were comprised primarily of World War I veterans and the sons of Irish immigrants.

The department experienced a well-needed boost to its reputation during the Great Depression. Midtown's men in blue earned tremendous respect from its citizens during the heyday of organized crime when they confronted some of the era's most infamous bank robbers. Many of the pioneers in Midtown's police department were famously involved in memorable shootouts with legendary gangsters.

Will Sutton was sitting on a bench along a wall opposite the dais where the front-desk sergeant was perched. Sutton immediately stood up when he saw the familiar faces of Malone and Dolan.

"Hello, Frank, Eddie; it's good to see you both again."

"You too, Will. What can we do for you?" Malone asked.

"May I have a word with you, Frank?"

"Sure, let's go up upstairs to my office."

The two detectives and the reporter took the elevator to the fourth floor. Eddie veered off toward his cubicle while Sutton followed Malone to his office. Sutton sat in one of the two familiar guest chairs while Malone slid into his chair behind his desk.

"What's up, Will?"

"First, I want you to know that my book goes on sale tomorrow," Sutton said proudly.

"Congratulations, Will. You did a great job with a difficult subject. Good luck with it," Malone responded sincerely.

"Thank you, Frank. Second, I want to thank you for your assistance on the project. Any success the book might have will be because of your willingness to be open and honest during our interviews. I can assure you that I will never forget that," Sutton said gratefully.

"I hope it will be a terrific seller, Will. You deserve it. I really enjoyed reading the manuscript."

"Thank you. The third issue I'd like to discuss with you is regarding Kerry Hamilton's disappearance. I heard that she was murdered and her body was discovered last night on Old Highway 9."

"Unfortunately, that is true. Kerry's body has been found. But I can't confirm that she was murdered just yet. I have yet to receive the results from her autopsy."

"A seventeen-year-old girl doesn't go for a voluntary casual walk, naked, down a desolate strip of highway in the pouring rain, Frank. I think we can both agree on that."

"I'm not agreeing to anything right now, Will, and you, of all people, know why. How did you come across this information? I would be interested to know."

"Frank, you're not the only S.O.B. in this town who knows how to do his job. I have my ways."

"I suppose you have a point."

"Anyway, Frank, I'll get to why I am here. I've heard you have a copycat killer on your hands, similar to the Monster of Midtown. Is that true?"

"Just because a body was discovered on Old Highway 9 doesn't mean we have a copycat killer on the loose. I wouldn't print that if I were you, Will."

"I heard the body was found by mile marker 77. That's the identical location where that Patterson girl's body was discovered earlier this year. Can you confirm that?"

"Yes, I can, but I would appreciate it if you didn't print that right now."

"Why?"

"I'm trying to avoid a mass hysteria situation. The nerves of our citizens are still raw."

"Then give me something I can print, Frank."

"I was tied up testifying on another case when Kerry first disappeared. I'm less than a day into this thing, Will. Besides, you know how this works. I can't speak about an ongoing investigation."

"You are going to be forced to speak at some point, Frank. I'm not the only reporter who has information on this. I'd like to be the first to get the real story."

"Please sit tight for the time being, Will."

"Frank, if somebody from the Midtown Police Department doesn't speak about it soon, rumors and conjecture are inevitably going to run amok. That will not be good for anyone, and it won't help you catch the killer. I don't want to print something that is not true."

"I will likely be able to release more information once I get the autopsy results. Until then I can't make any promises."

"My readers want more than just the autopsy results."

"Give me a chance to get some footing on this case, Will. Like I said, I have been on this thing less than twenty-four hours."

"Okay, Frank. As usual, you're a tough nut to crack. I look forward to hearing from you."

"Good luck with the release of your book tomorrow. I wish you the best with it."

"Thanks, Frank."

With that the two men shook hands and Sutton left. It was getting late, and Malone hadn't slept for over twenty-four hours. He looked in his email inbox. Tommy had sent an email indicating that Matt and he had finished preliminary interviews with all the faculty members and counselors at Kerry's school. He also said they would follow up on those interviews to confirm their statements and alibis over the next several days. Kinsey had sent an email indicating that Trace and she had interviewed all the registered sex offenders in the immediate area but were still verifying some of their alibis. Everyone needed more time to finish their assignments. Malone responded to both emails with a simple "understood."

Malone often suffered from insomnia when he was overtired. Sometimes a cocktail and stimulating conversation did him a world of good. His girlfriend, Sarah Summers, was a bartender at a staple Midtown tavern called the Last Stop Saloon. He had met Sarah during the final weeks of the Monster of Midtown case. They hit it off immediately. Sarah's mane of unruly dark hair, her captivating gray eyes, her shapely figure, and her charming wit had instantly captured Malone's attention.

They fell in love right away. But since then, their work schedules had begun to drive a wedge between them. A homicide detective often worked long and irregular hours. That was the primary reason Malone had never been able to maintain a meaningful relationship in the past. Sarah worked nights. She could change her schedule, but there was no reason for her to do so because Malone wouldn't be around anyway. Eventually, they reached the point where they thought they might need to take a break from their relationship, but neither was willing to entirely give up on it. Without question, they were crazy about each other.

Malone was even considering retirement to make the relationship work. He called a lawyer friend of his in Naples, Florida. His firm needed a private investigator. The job would require about thirty hours of investigation work per week, most of which Malone could do from home on his computer. That kind of schedule would be better suited for a long-term relationship. Malone had his pension, and Sarah could get a bartender's job just about anywhere. It could work. The only thing left was for him to convince himself he could live without being a Midtown homicide detective. It was practically all he had ever known. It was his identity.

Eddie had left for home about an hour earlier. Malone donned his trench coat and took the elevator downstairs.

Another day of lively activity in the 9th Precinct lobby was over. He headed outside to find himself once again in a steady drizzling rain. He navigated the puddles in his rubber boots while he carried his dress shoes in a plastic bag. A definite chill was stirring in the air. Malone raised the collar on his trench coat. He walked briskly to his Explorer.

He once again navigated the dreary streets of Midtown for the umpteenth time. Prostitutes, junkies, and other street dwellers were nowhere to be found. The weather had driven them to seek refuge in various unknown crevices. Midtown was like a ghost town—deserted, except for a few cab drivers and police cruisers patrolling the otherwise vacant streets. Up ahead, Malone's destination was indicated by a blinking neon **OPEN** sign in the window of the Last Stop Saloon. A single floodlight dimly illuminated the parking lot. Malone parked his unmarked Ford Explorer.

The construction of the Last Stop Saloon pre-dated World War II. It was a place for the hopelessly unemployed and bored retirees during the early and midmorning hours. Later it transitioned into a quirky happy-hour destination for Midtown professionals who sought stiff highballs, conversation with coworkers, and perhaps an occasional impromptu sexual encounter. The fedoras, gray-flannel suits, pin curls, pencil skirts, and World

War II veterans that once occupied the old place were long gone now. However, faded black-and-white photographs hanging on the walls kept their memories alive. Pictures of iconic sports heroes and legendary film actors conjured up memories of a simpler time.

Inside the Last Stop Saloon, Sarah Summers was pouring hopes and dreams into thick rocks glasses filled with ice. She engaged in idle chitchat with men seeking to get the attractive brunette's attention. In addition, she mixed a variety of concoctions for women seeking female conversation. She listened intently and spoke when needed. She had an engaging sense of humor and a wealth of fine feminine qualities that captured everyone's attention. Her charming attributes often had her admiring customers wanting more.

Sarah was putting cash in the register when she heard the saloon's front door swing open. The heavy rain outside sounded like a runaway locomotive. She looked in the mirror facing her and saw the familiar tall figure of the broad-shouldered cop reflected behind her. The distinctive carved deep lines around his eyes and on his forehead could belong only to one person. He removed his trench coat, causing water to puddle on the concrete floor. Malone was wearing Sarah's favorite brown herringbone sport coat, a white button-down dress shirt, and a dark maroon-and-gold striped tie.

He zigzagged around chairs and tables on his way to the last stool on the east end of the bar. He made eye contact with Sarah as she glided down the bar toward him. She produced her familiar seductive smile. His grizzled face returned his own welcoming smile.

Sarah loved Malone's face. Sure, he looked a few years older than his fifty-two years. But it was a great face, one that seemed to strike the perfect balance between gruffness and compassion. His eyes were attentive, and he was constantly observing his surroundings.

Sarah flipped a coaster on the bar, leaned in, and softly kissed his lips. "What'll be, Frank? Irish whiskey on the rocks?"

"Of course, I have no reason to change at this point."

She reached over and caressed his face along his jawline. "You look tired, Frank."

"I am, but I'm also afraid I won't be able to sleep again. I thought a special cocktail made by my favorite bartender might be just what I need to put me to sleep."

Other men in the bar slumped in disappointment as they observed the pretty bartender affectionately address the tall man with the distinctive hardened face. He definitely looked like someone to steer clear of, especially in a physical confrontation.

"You sure are a comforting sight for these tired eyes," he said.

"Hold that thought and let me make your drink."

Sarah sauntered over to the Irish whiskey bottle, scooped up a rocks glass full of ice, and poured the amber liquid over it. She was wearing tight jeans, black ankle-high boots, and an ivory white sweater. She returned with Malone's drink, placing it on the coaster in front of him. "I heard the Hamilton girl's body was discovered last night. Is that what you have been working on?"

"Yeah, it was awful. I spoke to her mother today. She is devastated."

Sarah shook her head. "That's some job you have, Frank."

"It's definitely not for the weak at heart. Aside from addressing my insomnia, I needed to see a kind face to maintain my sanity."

Sarah examined Malone's rugged countenance. She shook her head. "I don't know how you do it, Frank. I know I've said it a hundred times, but I still don't know. You live in a world completely different from mine." She looked down the bar and saw a few empty drink glasses. "I'll be back. I have to make a couple of drinks."

Sarah sashayed back down the bar and surveyed her customers, asking them if they wanted another drink. As she mixed their cocktails, she looked down the bar at the solitary figure of Frank Malone. In many ways, her relationship with Malone was frustrating. They both seemed to be in desperate need of something from the other, but they were flailing aimlessly to make it happen. She loved Malone. She wanted more from him, and she wanted to give more. She knew that underneath his rough, austere exterior was a compassionate man who possessed a wealth of kindness. She walked back down the bar. Malone once again greeted her with a smile. She returned it with one of her own.

Malone loved the way the bridge of her nose crinkled when she smiled.

"Frank, why don't you go home, take a warm shower, and get into bed. It's slow in here tonight. The rain has scared everyone away. I'll close up early and come over to tuck you in."

Malone's eyes and countenance brightened.

"That's if you are in the mood for company."

"I'll leave the door unlocked for you."

"No need to, Frank. I still have a key."

"I don't ever want it back," he insisted.

CHAPTER 6

Malone navigated a torrential rainstorm to get home. He entered his apartment and flicked a light switch on. His apartment had become a lonely point of refuge without Sarah's regular presence. He went to the refrigerator and retrieved half a leftover sandwich from yesterday's dinner. All those years he had never given much thought to what was for dinner. He never really cared if his apartment was a quiet, empty place. He had become accustomed to solitude. Being a homicide cop was his life. He never considered he might need more. But now he missed the tasty, healthy meals Sarah prepared for him when their schedules allowed.

Malone had had relationships before Sarah, but they were superficial and often centered on satisfying his own needs. Now, he was more concerned about another person's needs, likely for the first time. Truth be told, he was happiest when Sarah was happy.

He opened a can of beer and sat at his kitchen table. He took a bite of the sandwich. He thought about the audacity of Kerry Hamilton's killer. Her assailant must have meticulously read all the news accounts and listened to the hours of television coverage of the Monster of Midtown case. Kerry appeared to have been killed and subjected to the exact same sadistic torture as the Monster of Midtown victims. It was all very frightening, to say the least. Malone was anxious to get the autopsy results. Perhaps, there, they would find something that would distinctly separate the copycat killer from his predecessor. As in most cases, Malone hoped that someone out there might come forward with information that would lead him to the killer.

Malone finished the sandwich. He left a light on in the living room so Sarah could find her way. He took a steaming hot shower. While drying off, he could hear the howling wind and driving rain outside. He was concerned about Sarah's safety driving in such nasty weather conditions. He got into bed and began combing through emails on his cellphone. His persistent insomnia was giving way to sleep. Perhaps knowing that Sarah was on her way had provided just enough comfort for him to fall asleep.

Almost an hour later, Sarah quietly slipped into Malone's apartment. She went into his bedroom and found him sleeping, sitting up in bed. She stealthily removed her wet clothes and turned on the shower. She looked back into the bedroom; Malone was still sleeping. Perhaps he was able to fall asleep knowing her comforting presence was on the way. She hoped that was the case. She knew his mind needed a peaceful respite from all the ugliness in the world.

She entered the shower. The warm water washed away the chill from her wet clothes. She turned off the water and dried herself with the fresh towel Malone had laid out for her. She looked in the bedroom. Malone was still sleeping. He had never changed his position. Midtown's top detective hadn't detected her presence as she moved about his apartment while he slept. She lifted the bedcovers and slid in underneath. She wrapped her arms around him and pressed her naked body against his. She smiled; he was naked too.

Sarah's warm, gentle touch stirred him. They kissed passionately. Malone drew back and looked into her vibrant gray eyes. "I thought you would never get here."

They made love as if it were the first time. In fact, it always seemed like the first time.

Later the two lovers held each other under the bedcovers and looked out Malone's bedroom window. Distant lightning and rumbling thunder provided a meteorological fireworks show.

"Sarah, I like when we're together. I don't like our current arrangement. We are apart too much."

She looked at him and kissed his lips. "I don't like it either. What are we going to do about it?"

"We'll figure something out. I know we will. Just stick with me."

They held each other until they both dozed off.

In the morning Sarah put on a lightweight robe Malone had bought for her to keep at his place. She put her wet clothes in the dryer and rummaged through his kitchen to find something to make him for breakfast. The cupboard was pretty bare. She was able to make coffee and find a few eggs to scramble. She immediately made plans to buy groceries for him later in the day.

Malone came out of the bedroom wearing sweatpants and a white T-shirt.

"There's not much around here to whip up for break-fast, Frank. You live on the bare minimum."

"I haven't had much time to grocery shop. There are some protein bars in the cabinet above the stove. I would have shopped if I knew you were coming."

"I swear, Frank, if you don't start eating something nourishing, I'm going to . . ."

"You are going to do what?" he asked.

Sarah hesitated and then smiled. "I guess I'll just have to love you to death."

"I'm going on a hunger strike, starting right now," he said, smiling.

After breakfast, Malone went into the bedroom to change into his work clothes. Sarah cleaned the dishes, cups, and frying pan and wiped down the countertops. She poured herself another cup of coffee and sat at the kitchen table. A few minutes later, Malone came out of the bedroom clean-shaven, wearing a sports jacket, a white shirt, a shoulder holster, and a tie. He was carrying his trench coat. Sarah stood and walked over to him to receive a warm embrace. She straightened his tie and looked into his observant eyes.

"Midtown's top homicide cop should have his tie straight. Don't you know that?" she said, smiling. "You be careful out there today, Frank. You don't live in a very nice world."

"You know I will. I love it when you're here with me, Sarah." He smiled, kissed her, and then he was gone.

Sarah decided to clean Malone's apartment. While doing so, she got lost in her thoughts. She reflected on their relationship. There had to be other couples with conflicting schedules. Just because she didn't have everything she wanted from their relationship now didn't mean that it would never happen. Of course there were no guarantees, but wasn't it better to have a portion of what she wanted than nothing at all? Malone was a homicide cop when they fell in love. There was no reason she shouldn't be able to stay in love with him. He was still the same person. Malone hadn't changed. Then she realized that she was the one who was changing. She was the one who wanted more. Was it so wrong to want more?

Sarah had been on her own since age nineteen. She left home with a boyfriend who had a job opportunity in Midtown. Shortly thereafter, the relationship ended. She didn't want to return home defeated, so she stayed in Midtown. That decision required her to grow up fast. She had to nix her aspirations of becoming a nurse. She began working as a waitress and bartender. That proved to be the best way for her to quickly support herself. She scrimped and saved until she had enough money to buy her own apartment. She was so proud of herself the day she moved into her own place.

For obvious reasons, it had always been easy for Sarah to garner attention from men, but that eventually became just background noise. It wasn't until she met Malone that she realized that she could have so much more. He wore his compassion for the victims and their families on his sleeve every day. His integrity was unshakeable. She respected him so much. She was sure that he was the one. Yet, if he was the one, why were things becoming so difficult? The conversation she was having with herself had come full circle. It was her. She knew the real shift in their relationship was taking place inside her.

CHAPTER 7

Malone got off the elevator on the fourth floor in the 9th Precinct. He went into the break room. He poured himself a cup of hot coffee in the mug Sarah had given him for his birthday. He greeted Lucy warmly on the way to his office.

"Good morning, Boss. You're running a little late this morning. Is there anything going on?"

"I ran into traffic," Malone said, covering for the extra time he had spent with Sarah.

Malone sat behind his desk and sipped his coffee. He began scrolling through his emails when Dolan entered his office.

"Good morning, Frank, you're running a little late today."

"Yeah, I ran into traffic."

"Have you heard from the coroner on the cause of death yet?"

"No, I haven't." Just then Malone's desktop phone rang. He looked at the caller ID; it was the coroner. "Speaking of the devil."

Eddie closed Malone's office door as Malone picked up the phone. "Good morning, John. Eddie Dolan is in my office. I'm going to put you on speaker."

"Good morning, guys."

"What have you got, John?"

"Several curveballs, I'm afraid."

"What do mean?"

"The victim was deceased about six hours prior to the discovery of her body. She apparently died of asphyxiation. However, it's not what you may think. The victim's hyoid bone was intact."

"What does that mean, John?" Malone asked.

"It means," John said and cleared his throat. "The victim was gently strangled to death. She sustained injuries but not from a struggle, at least not a violent struggle. Let me clarify. There were some indications that she may have initially struggled with her assailants. However, at some point, she was sedated with heroin. I found traces of the drug in her system. Of course, we know about the zip ties and how she was posed on scene. There were indications that her restraints were applied while she was still alive. The combination of the intoxicating drug and the restraints likely ended her desire to struggle. I'm sure at some point, despite being intoxicated by the heroin, she likely concluded that resisting was a hopeless endeavor."

Malone shook his head in disgust.

Then Dolan chimed in. "John, did you say assailants, like in plural?"

"I did. The victim was raped. There are signs that she engaged in rough sexual intercourse prior to her death. There might also have been other means of vaginal penetration aside from conventional heterosexual sex. I have identified three DNA contributors and several DNA methylation differences. I found saliva and seminal fluid from an unknown male contributor present and the presence of saliva and vaginal fluid from an unknown female contributor. The remaining samples I collected were from the victim."

Malone and Dolan were shocked.

Malone gathered his thoughts. "I thought the rain would have washed away the DNA evidence."

"A lot of it was washed away. Fortunately, I was able to gather evidence from areas where the rain hadn't washed it away yet."

"John, let's go back to the hyoid bone and the fact that it is intact. What do you think that means?" Malone asked.

"Apparently, a nonabrasive material, approximately one inch in diameter, was wrapped around the victim's neck. It was likely tightened many times and then released before she was ultimately asphyxiated."

"Do you mean the victim was intentionally deprived of oxygen for the erotic pleasure of her assailants?"

"It appears that's the case. There is every indication that is what happened, up until the time she was killed. Most times, deaths related to this type of activity are generally not intentional. When they are intentional, it's often the result of some elaborate suicide attempt. However, keep in mind; some of my conclusions are speculation. Examining the murder scene plays an integral part in making the determinations I am suggesting. Unfortunately, we don't know where any of this activity occurred. It certainly wasn't where her body was found. Nevertheless, I am certain that a male and a female assailant were involved in the victim's murder."

Malone shot a wide-eyed glance at Dolan, who simply shook his head in disbelief.

Then Dolan chimed in again. "What about the bite marks, John?"

John cleared his throat, again. "I was going to get to that. Keep in mind; I am not a forensic odontologist. However, just a cursory examination of the bite marks indicates they were inflicted by two different assailants. Moreover, considering the sheer size difference between the two bite radii, the configuration of the teeth, and DNA evidence, I have determined that nineteen bites were inflicted by a male assailant and thirteen by a female assailant."

A long pause ensued as Malone and Dolan processed the statement.

Malone broke the silence. "Have you entered the DNA evidence into CODIS (Combined DNA Index System)?"

"Not yet, but I will when I get off the phone."

"One last thing, John. What are the chances that Kerry was the first victim of these monsters?"

"Frank, people who engage in this type of behavior have a starting point. Typically, their behavior invariably progresses over time. It takes more and more stimulation to get them aroused and keep them aroused. This type of behavior probably started with just the two assailants as willing participants. Gradually, they likely brought in a third person who was willing to partake in their activity. Once that lost its edge, they eventually decided to bring in a third noncompliant person to heighten the arousal factor. That's when they had to resort to murder, likely for two reasons: one, to send their sadistic sexual gratification factor through the roof, and second, to cover their tracks to conceal their behavior. Most disturbing is that on top of all this aberrant behavior, they decided to adopt the modus operandi of an infamous serial killer. So, to answer your original question, is there any chance Kerry Hamilton is the first victim of these two monsters?

There's not a chance in hell. I don't know what rock these two crawled out from underneath, but you have a couple of serial killers on your hands with some real deviant impulses."

Malone shot Dolan an ominous look. "Thanks for the update, John. Please let us know the results of your CODIS search."

"Will do."

Malone hung up the phone. He could only shake his head.

"I can't imagine how poor Kerry Hamilton crossed paths with two animals," Dolan muttered.

"I don't know, but I am sure as hell going to find out," said Malone. "I was planning to talk to Kerry's father today, but let's nix that. I want to focus on any CCTV video we can find along Old Highway 9. You take the first three entrances and exit ramps north of mile marker 77 where Kerry's body was found. I'll take the first three south. Check traffic light intersections, fueling stations, convenience stores, coffee shops, ATM machines, and any place else where you can find a camera."

"It makes sense to focus on a four- to five-hour window, Frank. The state trooper said he discovered the body at 10:32 p.m. It's unlikely the victim was dropped there in broad daylight. It gets dark out there around 6:30 p.m."

"Good point; we'll narrow our focus to the hours between 6:00 p.m. and midnight. That should adequately cover the timeline leading up to when the body was dropped and a sufficient amount of time thereafter."

"That's potentially a lot of video, Frank."

"I know. Once we collect the videos, I'll pull the others off their assignments. We can go through it all systematically. If we don't find anything, we'll have to expand our search farther north and south. One thing is for sure. The vehicle used to drop Kerry's body off at mile marker 77 entered Old Highway 9 at some point and then exited somewhere later. We need to identify that vehicle."

CHAPTER 8

Malone and Dolan went their separate ways to find security cameras that had captured the image of the vehicle and the occupant or occupants who drove Kerry Hamilton's body out to mile marker 77. Malone spent the entire day speaking to people who managed businesses on Old Highway 9. People were willing to cooperate and anxious to help. He also saw several traffic intersections with cameras. He would submit formal requests to the county's traffic division to obtain those videos.

At 5:00 p.m., after successfully collecting a number of videos, Malone decided to call it quits. He hadn't had anything to eat since Sarah had made him breakfast. He headed to his favorite Jewish deli for a sandwich. As the sun was setting, it started to rain again. Malone parked his vehicle and hustled into the deli. He was standing in line to receive a sandwich he had ordered when he heard a familiar voice.

"Well, if it isn't Midtown's top detective. Long time, no see, Frank. What have you been up to?"

It was Alexandra Martin. Malone had befriended Alex during the Monster of Midtown case. Alex was an exotic dancer in Silver Stilettos strip club. Her roommate was the Monster's ninth victim. Despite her occupation, Malone saw Alex as an innocent, mixed-up kid. She was a victim of a dysfunctional childhood. That misfortune set her on a path filled with bad choices and dubious results. Malone liked her and tried to be a role model. She was constantly surrounded by bad characters and unfortunate circumstances tugging her in the wrong direction. Malone constantly urged her to get out of the stripping business.

Alex had jet-black hair. Her face was covered with an abundance of makeup that she didn't need. She was naturally pretty. Her heavy coat was open. She had on skin-tight blue jeans with strategically "torn" holes, knee-high boots, and a black sweater that barely covered her ample bosom. Her chest seemed poised to burst out the top of her sweater at the slightest awkward movement. Curiously, she was wearing sunglasses in a town where the sun rarely ever shined.

"Hello, Alex. How have you been?"

"I'm okay."

Malone noticed a black-and-blue bruise emerging from underneath her sunglasses. "What happened to you, Alex?"

"Oh . . . I fell."

Malone reached out with both hands and gently removed Alex's sunglasses. "You didn't get that from a fall, Alex. What happened?"

"Please don't hassle me, Frank. I don't want to talk about it."

"Spill it, Alex. What happened?"

Alex sighed. She knew Malone would not relent until she gave in. "Okay, if you must know, I was seeing this guy named Miguel. I met him at work. Anyway, he started out being nice and really cool, but after a while, he became possessive and jealous. He doesn't like it when I give customers attention at work. I mean, what the hell, Frank? That's my job . . . right. He knows I'm a dancer; that's how we met. He knows the place is filled with guys who want attention."

Malone made a calculation of Alex's situation. "I suppose it is."

"Anyway, after work about week ago, he starts slapping me around. That's how I got the black eye. So, I tell the dude I'm done with his act, and I don't want to see him anymore, but he doesn't take 'no' for an answer. He's been coming around the club ever since, threatening to beat my ass if I don't start screwing him again. He's turned out to be a real nutcase. The dude won't listen to anything I tell him. I don't know what to do. I just know I'm sick of him."

Alex and Malone received their order and sat at an open table.

Malone listened to Alex intently while chewing a bite of his sandwich. His reaction was seemingly no reaction at all. "So, basically the dude is stalking you, is that what you are telling me?"

"Kind of, I guess. He comes to Silver Stilettos every night and he won't leave me alone. He's scaring off all my regular customers. I'm afraid to tell the bouncers because he might cause trouble and get me fired."

Alex continued to drone on about Miguel.

"Alex, I thought you were going to get out of the stripping business. There's nothing good that's going to come out of you working in that place."

"I need a job, Frank. I need to eat and keep a roof over my head. Dancing pays well."

"You can't dance forever. You're not always going to look like you do now. The years will go by fast. It's not a good life, Alex. I bet you have been partying hard too."

"No, not really, I've been trying to make some changes."

"Alex, you're a smart kid. You can do something else. Guys are not going to respect strippers. That's just the way it is. You're never going to get the respect you deserve if you continue dancing."

"What am I supposed to do, Frank? I don't want to

live on the streets. Everyone wants me to get high with them and get in my pants—men and women. I live in a crazy world."

"You need to get out of it. The hard part is taking the first step. I don't want to roll up on a scene one day and find out you're the victim."

"I should have never left home when I was sixteen, but I had to. My stepfather was abusing me. My mother was pissed at me because she said I was egging him on by the way I dressed. Now she wants nothing to do with me because she knows I'm a nude dancer. I thought I met a pretty decent guy, and the next thing I know he starts kicking the shit out of me. I don't know what the hell to do, Frank."

Malone took another bite of his sandwich and put the rest back into the white paper bag it came in. "Come on, Alex, follow me."

"What, where are we going?"

Malone stood, made his way around the table, and abruptly pulled Alex's chair out. "Come on, follow me."

Alex followed Malone out the deli's door and into a steady rain.

"Get in the car, Alex."

"Why, Frank, tell me where we are going?"

"Just get in the car, Alex."

They both got into Malone's Explorer.

"Where are we going?"

"Just sit tight."

Although annoyed, Alex calmed down as Malone drove over the soggy streets of Midtown. Tears began to stream down her face. "I know I probably disappoint you, Frank. I wish I didn't. You're a really good guy. I really respect you. You have been a good friend to me." Alex wiped her nose with the sleeve of her coat. "You know, Frank, you're about the only person who doesn't want anything from me. I've offered you a no-strings-attached piece of ass many times and you always turn me down. Why is that, Frank?"

Malone remained silent and kept his gaze forward. "Is it because of your girlfriend? You know I wouldn't tell her, Frank. I would never snitch on you."

Malone still remained silent.

"Man, you're a real boy scout, Frank. I've never met anyone like you."

A few moments of quiet ensued. Alex looked over at Malone. "How is your girlfriend, Frank?"

"We're going through a rough patch right now."

"Why?"

"It's a long story."

"All I have is time."

"Our schedules aren't matching up. We don't see each other enough to move the relationship forward. We're both frustrated right now, but I'm sure we'll figure it out."

"I hope you do, Frank. I really do. However, if things don't work out, you always have me. I'll treat you really nice."

Malone smiled. "I'll keep that in mind."

Malone drove into the parking lot of Tommy D's Italian Restaurant. It was generally known as the best place for Italian food in Midtown.

"What's this about, Frank? We just ate."

"You're getting out of the stripping business today, Alex, before you really get hurt. The guy who owns this place is a friend of mine. He needs a waitress and you're it."

"I don't know how to wait on tables. I have a job, Frank!"

"You sure do, and this it. Get out of the car, Alex."

Alex reluctantly followed Malone up to Tommy D's front door, and they both entered.

A loud voice suddenly erupted. "Yo, Frankie! What's up!"

"Tommy, what's going on? I trust you're doing well." Malone genuinely hoped.

"Why don't you come in more often? You don't like Tommy's food?"

"I love your food, you know that."

The two men hugged each other.

The owner and chef of Tommy D's, Tommy was a pudgy, thick-necked, dark-haired Italian. He had a towel draped over his shoulder that he used to dab at the perspiration on his brow. "You need a table for two, my friend?"

"No, no, I just ate. May I have a word with you somewhere in private?"

"Of course you can. Follow me."

Malone turned to Alex. "Wait here. I'll be right back."

Malone followed Tommy into the kitchen where employees were moving about making red gravy, frying breaded chicken cutlets, and chopping green peppers and onions.

"What's up, Frank?"

"Are you still looking for a waitress?"

"Yeah, why?"

"I'd like you to give that girl who came in here with me a shot."

"Geez, Frank, I don't know."

Tommy stepped around Malone and looked out through the glass window in the swinging door that divided the kitchen from the dining room. He looked at Alex. She was twirling her hair with her fingers. "What's her story?"

"She's in the middle of a rough stretch. She needs a break. I was hoping you could give her one."

"Frank, you know we're friends, and I'd like to help, but this is a family restaurant. She has a black eye . . . and that cleavage. She's bursting out the top of her sweater . . . and those jeans, with all the holes everywhere. My two teenage daughters work in this restaurant, Frank. I have to consider that."

"I'll make sure she wears something appropriate if you hire her. She's a good kid, Tommy. She just needs a break."

"How did she get that black eye?"

"Her ex-boyfriend knocked her around."

"Frank, I don't want him coming around here making trouble. I can't have that. This is my livelihood."

"I'm going to take care of the boyfriend. He won't be coming around, I promise you."

Tommy looked at Malone and shook his head.

"What do you say, Tommy?"

"This is a big ask, Frank."

"I know it is."

Just then Tommy's wife, Rita, came through the swinging door. Rita was all Italian. Her wide-open chocolate-brown eyes were her most prominent facial feature. She immediately gave Malone a big hug. "What's going on, guys? This looks like a serious conversation."

Tommy looked at his wife. "Frank wants me to hire that girl in the dining room, the one with the big boobs and the black eye."

"Rita, she's a really good kid in need of a break," Malone said sincerely. "She's been a dancer at Silver Stilettos for the last couple of years. Her ex-boyfriend roughed her up. I'm trying to get her out of the dancing business. She left home when she was sixteen because she was being abused by her stepfather. She's been out on her own ever since. She has a kind heart, and I think she could do really well in the right environment."

Rita peered through the glass window in the swinging door at Alex. "She's a stripper, huh? That's some figure she has. Her boobs look like they are going to tear the buttons off her sweater."

"I'll make sure she dresses appropriately when she comes to work. What do you say, Rita? How about it?"

"I guess everyone could use a helping hand. Okay, she can start tomorrow. Make sure she's here at four o'clock. I'll train her myself."

Malone reached out, hugged Rita, and kissed her on the cheek. Then he looked at Tommy. "Thanks, buddy. I owe you one."

Tommy and Rita followed Malone into the dining room. The three approached Alex.

"Alex, this Tommy and Rita, they own the restaurant. They will be your bosses. You start tomorrow at 4:00 p.m. sharp. Don't be late."

Tommy and Rita gave Alex a warm smile.

"Thank you for hiring me," Alex said humbly.

Rita reached out and hugged her. "I'll see you tomorrow, Alex. You'll do fine."

With that, Malone and Alex left the restaurant. They were unsuccessful dodging raindrops on the dash back to the Explorer.

Once inside, Alex looked at Malone. "I know you're trying to help me, Frank, you always try to help me. But I don't know if I can wait on tables. I don't want to mess things up for them. They seem really nice."

"They are really nice, and you can wait on tables. Working for them will give you a second chance. You need a sense of normalcy in your life, Alex."

Malone turned on the windshield wipers and put the Explorer in drive. He silently drove through the persistent rain. Neither spoke for a while. Finally, Malone broke the silence. "Alex, you'll need to wear a top tomorrow that covers your cleavage, all of it. And don't wear pants or jeans that have holes in them everywhere."

"But that's how I roll, Frank," Alex said, smiling.

"Yeah well, you're going to roll in a whole new

direction from now on. Where can I find Miguel? I'd like to have a word with him."

"Frank, that's not necessary."

"You broke up with him . . . right?"

"Yeah."

"You don't want to see him anymore . . . right?"

"Yeah."

"Okay then, I don't want Miguel coming around Tommy's place looking for you and causing trouble. Where can I find him, Alex?"

"He tends bar in a tavern on Forty-Second Street."

"What time does he get off work?"

"Usually, around 9:00 p.m."

Malone looked his watch. It was quarter past eight. He drove through the waterlogged streets of Midtown to the tavern's parking lot. He parked and tilted his seat back.

"Frank, I must tell you Miguel has a really bad temper, and he's a really big guy," Alex said with concern about Malone's safety. "He works out all the time. He's very strong, and he doesn't like people telling him what to do."

Malone looked over at Alex. "I'm going to close my eyes for a few minutes. If I doze off, wake me at five minutes before nine."

Malone didn't want to start a physical confrontation

with Miguel. He just wanted him to know that he was in Alex's corner and that she didn't want to see him any-more. However, Malone was confident in his ability to defend himself. He had been a state wrestling cham-pion in high school. That success earned him a college scholarship, and he went on to win 134 matches. He later took Judo classes, learned striking, and eventually became a self-defense instructor at the police academy.

"Why are you doing all this for me, Frank?"

"Because we're friends . . . right?"

"Yeah, we're friends. I've never had a friend like you before. I owe you big-time."

"The only thing you owe me is to show up at Tommy D's tomorrow on time, dressed appropriately, and try your best."

"Oh, look, Frank, that's Miguel right there!" Alex said with a sense of trepidation.

Malone saw a muscular shadowy figure walking between cars in the parking lot. He looked over at Alex. "You stay here."

Alex sat up in her seat. She watched with wide eyes as Malone got out of the Explorer and approached Miguel. At first Miguel didn't seem to see Malone emerging from the darkness. Malone called out to him, "Hey, Miguel!"

Miguel turned and saw the silhouette of a tall figure

wearing a trench coat approaching. "Who are you? I don't know you. How do you know my name?"

"I'm a friend of Alex Martin. I just wanted to inform you that she doesn't want to see you anymore."

Miguel gave Malone a curious look. "Who the hell are you?" he asked.

"Who I am is not important. Alex doesn't like the way you have been treating her. She doesn't want to see you anymore, so stay away from her, and there will be no trouble."

Miguel began to laugh. "What is this? Alex sends Father Time here to deliver me a threatening message. You have to be kidding me, old timer."

"No, Miguel, I'm not kidding."

Miguel stepped in close and looked Malone up and down. Malone sensed that Miguel was sizing him up. Meanwhile, Alex leaned even more forward on her seat in the Explorer. She was concerned about Malone's safety as she anticipated a physical confrontation. She had heard from others about Miguel's prowess as an accomplished street fighter.

Miguel smirked and feigned like he was going to walk away. He balled his fist and took a swing at Malone. Malone adeptly blocked his punch, clamped onto his arm with a basic self-defense arm lock maneuver, and then struck Miguel with a brachial chop that immediately dropped him to his knees. Malone grabbed a handful of Miguel's hair and drove his face into the side panel of an adjacent parked SUV, breaking his nose. Blood flowed freely from both his nostrils. Miguel slid down onto the parking lot's surface, stunned and barely conscious. The confrontation was over in less than ten seconds.

Alex had witnessed everything. She was astonished by how quickly it had all happened.

Malone squatted down, grabbed a handful of Miguel's hair again, and pulled him up to a sitting position, bringing him face-to-face with Malone. "Listen to me, Miguel, and listen to me good. If I ever hear that you are within ten miles of Alex Martin, I am going to come back here and kick your pathetic ass all over Midtown. Do you understand me, Miguel?" Still grasping a handful of Miguel's hair, Malone shook his head in an attempt to keep him conscious. "Do you understand me, Miguel?"

With blood freely running down his face and neck, the only thing a dazed Miguel could do was marginally nod his head to convey his understanding. Malone let go of Miguel's hair, and he slid down the side of the parked SUV and back on to the wet parking lot surface. Malone stood up and returned to the Explorer.

Alex's mouth was agape as Malone got in. "Holy shit, Frank! I have never seen anything like that. I was afraid he was going to hurt you. Where did you ever learn to fight like that?"

Malone looked over at her with a stoic expression. "How do you think I have survived on the streets of Midtown for the past thirty years?"

"Man, Frank, you are a certifiable, bad-to-the-bone badass."

Malone smirked at Alex's comment. He put the Explorer into drive and drove out of the tavern's parking lot. Alex had to give Malone directions because she had recently moved to a new apartment building. He parked in front of an old redbrick four-story colonial-style building. He looked over at Alex. "Make sure you're at the restaurant on time tomorrow."

"I'm very grateful for everything that you have done for me. Why don't you come up to my apartment? I'll open a bottle of wine."

Malone's silent look conveyed he wouldn't come up to Alex's apartment.

"I don't understand you, Frank. Don't you think I'm pretty?"

"Yeah, I think you're pretty."

"Practically everybody in the world wants to get in my pants. It's the only thing anyone cares about, except you. Why are you so different? You're the only person in the world who doesn't want anything from me. Why is that?"

Malone turned and looked away from her.

Alex stared at his profile for several moments. She contemplated the current situation further. "You're too loyal to that girlfriend of yours, or too by the book. Which is it, Frank? Is it because you're the big bad Midtown detective who only goes by the book? Or is it just your thing to go around rescuing women in distress? Which is it, Frank?"

Malone looked over at her. "Alex, I can't come up to your apartment for a lot of reasons. First and foremost, I'm too old for you. I'm old enough to be your father."

"Miguel doesn't think you're too old," she said with a wry smile. "At least he doesn't think so anymore."

"I'll see you around, Alex. Stay out of trouble, and one other thing. Try to polish up your boyfriend selection process. It needs a little work."

Alex smiled, reached over the Explorer's console, and kissed Malone softly on the side of his face. "You can't hide it, Frank. I know you like me. Thanks for everything. I'll do my best tomorrow."

"Make sure you do."

CHAPTER 9

alone woke up early the next morning. His apartment felt empty without Sarah there. She had cleaned his apartment the day before and bought him eggs, apples, spinach, cheese, whole-wheat bread, and sliced turkey. Malone was touched by her thoughtfulness. He sensed that her growing frustration with their relationship was getting worse. He had to make some changes to accommodate for her feelings or he was going to lose her. He certainly didn't want that.

Malone wore his exercise clothes to work. He carried his sport coat, corduroy slacks, tic, and white shirt on two hangers. He arrived at the 9th Precinct twenty minutes later. He went to the second floor, which had a gym. In the past, working out had always been a way for him to clear his head. It didn't work this time. After his workout, he showered, dressed, and went up to his office. He emailed his investigation team, calling for an 8:30 a.m. meeting in conference room one. He wanted to disseminate the thumb drives and disks containing the CCTV videos that Dolan and he had collected the day before.

At the appointed time, he walked into conference room one. Dolan, Tommy, Matt, Trace, and Kinsey were drinking coffee and engaged in a lively conversation. Malone went to the front of the room. "Good morning, everyone. Yesterday, Eddie and I collected a number of surveillance videos from businesses along Old Highway 9. Eddie, do you have yours with you?"

"Yes, I do." Eddie pointed to the thumb drives and disks laid out on the table in front of him.

There were a total of twenty-four in all. Malone divided them up evenly between each member of the team. "There will be more to review once I get the traffic light videos from the county. At the very least, we're looking for any vehicle that is capable of transporting a body. We are especially looking for a vehicle that travels in one direction and then back in the other during the relevant time frame. If you spot such a vehicle, pay particular attention to the driver and any occupants who might be inside. Obviously, we know for sure the vehicle that transported Kerry Hamilton's body entered Old Highway 9 at some point. What we don't know is if a camera captured that image. Please be very meticulous in your review."

"Remember, we think we're looking for a male and a

female suspect," Dolan interjected. Several of the detectives nodded to confirm their understanding. With that, Malone went to his office. The others went to their cubicles to review their assigned videos. He was at his desk for about fifteen minutes when the coroner called. There were no CODIS hits on the DNA specimens he had collected from Kerry Hamilton's body.

Five hours later, Malone was still reviewing his first video when his phone rang.

"Malone."

"Detective, this is Victoria Hamilton. Do you have a moment to speak?"

"Yes, of course," Malone replied with a reassuring tone.

"Have you made progress with your investigation? I know you were going to speak to my ex-husband today, but Detective Dolan called him to cancel your meeting. I was wondering if you canceled because you had made some progress elsewhere."

"In a way we have," Malone attempted to explain. "The autopsy results, some of which I can't share with you at the moment, have led me to believe that your ex-husband is not a suspect in Kerry's murder. You were right about that. Currently, we are focusing on CCTV videos from cameras belonging to businesses along Old Highway 9. Obviously, a vehicle was used to transfer

Kerry's body to the location where it was eventually dis-covered. We're hoping a camera caught an image of that vehicle and perhaps the driver."

"That sounds extremely labor intensive," Victoria thought aloud.

"It is, but I have all the detectives assigned to Kerry's case reviewing videos. It is going to be a time-consuming task, but I am hopeful it will produce some valuable results."

"Understood, I appreciate everything that you are doing. I am praying for you. Please keep me informed. It's the only thing I have to hold on to right now."

"I sure will."

Malone hung up the phone. He had heard the pain in Victoria's voice. It made him even more resolute to get justice for her. Just then, Dolan bounded into Malone's office.

"Frank, I found something interesting on one of the convenience store videos I have. You need to see this."

Dolan handed Malone a thumb drive. He plugged it into his computer.

"Fast forward to 9:47 p.m., Frank," Dolan said with a tone of anticipation in his voice.

Malone followed Dolan's instructions. Dolan came around Malone's desk and stood behind him. Malone began playing the video.

"Do you see that white Silverado pickup truck right there?" Dolan pointed to the vehicle on Malone's computer screen.

"Yes, I do."

"Keep your eye on that."

Malone watched the truck carefully.

The driver parked in a space directly in front of the convenience store. A woman exited the vehicle on the passenger side. She entered the store. The video was blurry and lacked clarity. She was wearing an unbuttoned long black coat. She appeared to have on black leggings and a tight black top that left her midsection exposed. She turned to the right and disappeared from the camera's view. Several minutes went by before the woman reentered the screen in full view, carrying two cups of coffee. The woman's hair was blonde with loose, dangling curls. She possessed a sleek athletic figure. It was the unmistakable body of Kerry Hamilton's ballet instructor, Annette Rousseau!

Malone pushed pause to stop the video and looked at Dolan. "What the hell is she doing there?"

"I asked myself the same question. I can only come up with one answer."

Malone contemplated his own question for a moment. He looked at Dolan. "Kerry's ballet instructor is a serial killer?"

"Her and whoever else is driving that pickup truck."

Malone returned to playing the video. Annette Rousseau paid for two cups of coffee with cash. She reentered the pickup truck. The license plate on the vehicle never came into view. The driver backed out of the parking space and drove off.

Malone looked at Dolan. "This likely means the ballet instructor lured Kerry Hamilton into a situation that led to her rape and murder. Or is this some type of impossible coincidence?"

"I don't believe in coincidences, Frank. The pickup truck fits too. It could have easily transported Kerry's body out to mile marker 77. I think Kerry's bombshell dance instructor has just become our primary suspect."

"Let's take a ride to the dance studio and have another talk with Ms. Rousseau," Malone said.

Thirty minutes later, Dolan pulled in to the strip mall parking lot where the dance studio was located. There were a number of cars parked directly in front of the studio. There was a lot of human activity going on.

Dolan selected a parking space removed from the studio's front entrance. He didn't want the detectives' presence to draw attention. "It looks like class is ending and parents are there picking up their kids."

"Yeah, let's wait here until things settle down a bit. I don't see the white pickup truck anywhere," Malone observed.

"Maybe the truck belongs to her boyfriend or husband," Dolan surmised.

Malone looked out the Explorer's windshield, staring at the dance studio. He was trying to convince himself of the idea that Kerry Hamilton's ballet instructor was a serial killer. "Over thirty years in this business, Eddie, twenty-five in homicide; none of it prepares you for what might be going on with this woman."

The last of the cars in front of the dance studio had left. Things had calmed down. It was raining again. The two detectives trudged across the parking lot, their trench coats flapping in the wind. They entered the studio.

Annette Rousseau was standing on the far side of the open dance floor. She saw the two detectives walking toward her. "Detectives, you're back. What can I do for you?"

"Ms. Rousseau, we would like to have another word with you," Malone said.

"Of course, how can I help?"

"Do you own a white Silverado pickup truck?"

"Excuse me?"

"Do you own a white Silverado pickup truck?"

Rousseau appeared momentarily taken aback by Malone's question. "No, why?"

"What type of vehicle do you drive?"

"A black 2023 Land Rover. It's in the parking lot. Why do you ask?"

"Are you married or have a boyfriend, Ms. Rousseau?"

"Yes, I'm married. What is this about?"

"Does your husband own a white Silverado pickup truck, Ms. Rousseau?"

"He has a white pickup truck," she said hesitantly. "I'm not sure what brand or model it is. That's not something I pay attention to."

"Did you and your husband go out for a drive last Tuesday night?"

The confident, sexually provocative quality that Annette Rousseau constantly projected had disappeared. "I'm not sure. We go places in his truck. Again, what is this about?"

"Ms. Rousseau, were you and your husband out for a drive in his white Silverado pickup truck this past Tuesday night?"

"I don't remember."

"It should be an easy question to answer, Ms. Rousseau. It was less than a week ago."

"I'm not sure I want to answer your questions if you're not going to tell me what this is about."

"Ms. Rousseau, did you and your husband stop at a convenience store on Old Highway 9, last Tuesday night, at 9:47 p.m.?"

Annette's eyes darted back and forth. She was searching her thoughts for a reason why she and her husband would drive out to Old Highway 9 on Tuesday. She couldn't think of one. "I don't want to answer any more of your questions, Lieutenant."

"Did you buy two cups of coffee in a convenience store, Ms. Rousseau?"

"I am not going to answer any more of your questions," she said defiantly.

"That's unfortunate, Ms. Rousseau. A student of yours has been raped and murdered. I would think you would want to help us find her killer."

"I do, but I don't like your tone or inference, Lieutenant Malone. I want to know, where is this conversation heading? What are you insinuating?"

"Please provide us with your home address and your husband's cellphone number. We would like to speak to him."

"You can speak to our lawyer, Lieutenant."

"Who is your lawyer?"

"Wait here."

Rousseau hurried to her office. She returned moments later with the name and phone number of her lawyer scribbled on a piece of paper. She handed it to Malone. She placed her hands on her hips to convey a silent message of defiance. Malone reviewed the paper. He placed it in the chest pocket inside his coat.

"Ms. Rousseau, an innocent seventeen-year-old girl has been murdered. She was drugged, physically abused, and then raped before her death. She was left on the side of the road, posed in a disturbing manner, reminiscent of how an infamous serial killer had left his victims. The medical examiner found over two dozen bite marks on the victim's body. The bites were inflicted by a male and a female assailant. Kerry Hamilton was a student of yours. Your husband owns a white pickup truck. We have CCTV video from a convenience store located on Old Highway 9. That video captured images of you getting out of a white pickup truck on the night Kerry's body was discovered. We saw you enter the convenience store. You bought two cups of coffee. Unfortunately, for some inexplicable reason, you cannot remember any of this, even though it occurred less than a week ago. I find that very concerning. Do you have a reasonable explanation, Ms. Rousseau?"

"Am I under arrest, Lieutenant?"

"Not, yet, Ms. Rousseau, but we're heading there."

"Then I am going to end this conversation and ask you to please leave the premises."

"Have it your way, Ms. Rousseau. However, I must tell you that I find your behavior quite peculiar. I assure you, we will be speaking to you again in the near future. Good day."

With that, Malone and Dolan turned and marched away. Once again, they had to cross the parking lot in the rain.

"She's guilty as hell, Frank. She doesn't have an answer for anything you asked her. I think we should sit on her for a while and see what she does next."

"I agree. I want to rattle her cage."

The detectives knew Annette Rousseau's eyes were on them as they sat in the Explorer. Rousseau emerged from the dance studio an hour later and entered her Land Rover. She drove west on 36th Street. Dolan followed her. She continued for about fifteen minutes before entering the driveway of a house located at 17 North Columbus Drive. The garage door opened. A white Silverado pickup truck was inside. She pulled into the garage next to the pickup truck. Then the garage door closed.

"It looks like her husband is home, Frank."

Malone nodded.

Dolan parked on the swale across the street from the house. The rain outside continued to fall. "What next, Frank?"

"Let's stay here awhile and give her a chance to speak to her husband. Let's see what he does."

Thirty minutes later a tall, well-proportioned Caucasian man, presumably Annette Rousseau's husband, emerged from the house. He had long, wavy brown hair and a bushy mustache. He strode across his damp lawn toward the Explorer. The detectives watched him carefully. He approached the Explorer and knocked on the closed driver side window.

Dolan pushed the button to roll down the window. "May I help you, sir?" he asked.

"Why are you parked in front of my house?" the man asked. He didn't have Annette's accent.

"Enjoying the scenery," Dolan replied.

"Why are you harassing my wife?"

"That's an easy question to answer Mister Rousseau," Dolan responded flippantly. "First, she has a hellacious body. Second, we think the two of you were involved in the rape and murder of a local seventeen-year-old high school student."

The man stared at Dolan with contempt.

Dolan smiled back at him. "Is there anything else I can help you with today, sir?" he asked.

"You clowns are barking up the wrong tree," he said angrily. "You are going to wish you never crossed paths with Bobby Rousseau."

"Is that so?"

"Yes, it is, because if you don't back off, I am going to

drop a load of bricks on your ass. You have no idea who you're dealing with."

"You know, that's kind of funny, because we were thinking about dropping a truckload on your ass."

Bobby Rousseau stared intensely at Dolan for several moments.

"Is there anything else?" Dolan asked.

"Don't say I didn't warn you, smart ass."

Rousseau stomped off. Dolan and Malone could see he was incensed by his quick-stepping gait. They watched him reenter his home.

Dolan looked at Malone. "How do you think that went, Frank?"

"Rather well. Let's get out of here."

Meanwhile, Alex showed up at Tommy D's at 3:45 p.m. She had on jeans, without holes, and had ditched most of her makeup. She was wearing a top that discreetly covered her voluptuous chest. Rita greeted her warmly. She handed her an apron and immediately had Alex accompany her to wait on several tables. Tommy watched the two women through the service window. Several other waitresses, including one of Tommy's daughters, were also waiting on tables. An hour later,

Rita and Alex seemed to be getting on well. Tommy was pleasantly surprised.

Rita made a quick determination that Alex was a fast learner. Eventually, Rita gave her an opportunity to work on her own.

During a lull in the action, Rita asked Alex to sit with her. "You're doing well, Alex. I am very pleased. I think you will be ready to work solo tomorrow night."

"I am really enjoying the work. Thank you so much for hiring me."

"Alex, do you mind if I ask where you got that shiner?"

"No, I don't mind at all. I was seeing this guy named Miguel, a real macho dude. He started pushing me around to show me he was boss. Anyway, one night he just decides to let me have it, and hit me, several times. That's how I got the black eye."

"That's terrible, Alex. Does it hurt?"

"It was sore for few days, but it's alright now."

"Alex, Tommy and I are concerned about Miguel. Is there any chance he might come around here and make trouble for us? We're afraid something like that could happen. We don't want anything to happen that would upset our customers or any of our employees."

"Don't even think about it. I'm very sure he won't be coming around."

"Really, why are you so sure?"

"Well . . . yesterday, after we left here, Frank wanted to have a word with Miguel. So, we drove over to where he works. After Miguel got off work, Frank confronted him in the parking lot."

"How did that go?" Rita asked curiously.

"Actually, it went really well. After smashing Miguel's face into a parked car, Frank told him that if he ever hears he's within ten miles of me, he's going to come back and kick his pathetic ass all over Midtown. So, I am very sure Miguel won't be coming around here anytime soon." Alex's eyes darted to a table in the corner. "Uh oh, I better go. The couple sitting at table four wants two more glasses of wine."

Alex stood up and rushed away, leaving Rita speechless and slack-jawed.

CHAPTER 10

Once back in his office, Malone took screen shots from the CCTV video of the white pickup truck and of Annette Rousseau while she was in the convenience store. He emailed still pictures to his investigative team with the following message: "Please examine the attached pictures. Look for this pickup truck and this woman in the videos you have. There appears to be a male driver in the truck. I'm assuming it's her husband, Bobby Rousseau. Finding a clear image of him is a top priority."

All the detectives responded, confirming their understanding.

Malone began searching social media and the Web for anything pertaining to Annette or Bobby Rousseau. Meanwhile, Dolan was attempting to locate Annette's and Bobby's driver's license records. Generally, a police officer would scan the bar code on the reverse side of a driver's license with readable hardware in their patrol vehicles to capture such information. Dolan wasn't afforded that luxury because he wasn't in possession of the Rousseaus' driver's licenses. Searching the Web and governmental databases was a much easier task when the searcher had the person's name, their date of birth, or their social security number. Dolan only had Annette's and Bobby's name to work with, and even that information was contingent upon their level of honesty. In regard to Annette, records on women could be more difficult to locate because they often change their last name after marriage.

An hour later, Dolan entered Malone's office frustrated. He slumped in a chair across from Malone's desk. "Frank, I can only find DL records going back three years on an Annette, and a Robert Rousseau. Is it possible they recently immigrated to the United States?"

"I'm sure it's possible. Her accent suggests that she came from somewhere outside the US, maybe he did too. The only thing I can find on the Web or social media is related to her dance studio."

"How do you explain that, Frank? You would think Annette would be credentialed in some way regarding her dance business."

"Check with the building department. See what information they have on her occupational license application and any building permits issued for the dance studio. Also, the strip mall landlord may have something on her."

"Those are good ideas. I'll check them out."

Malone picked up his phone and dialed Kinsey Phillips. She was well versed in following internet and social media trails.

"Hey, Frank. What's up?"

"You saw the pictures I sent of the woman in the convenience store?"

"Yes, I did."

"Eddie and I have done some preliminary searching on her and her husband, Bobby. We haven't found anything worthwhile. I know this is one of your areas of expertise. We believe her name is Annette Rousseau." Malone gave Kinsey the ballet instructor's home and work addresses. "See if you can find anything on an Annette, a Bobby, or a Robert Rousseau."

"I'll get on it right away."

Malone hung up.

"What's next, Frank?" Dolan asked, expressing concern. "They know we are on to them. They might decide to make a run for it."

"They could, but that would be paramount to an admission of guilt. Running doesn't fit with Bobby's threat to drop a load of bricks on us. I think he's sticking around, at least for the time being."

"I wonder what that 'ton of bricks' comment means."

"I don't know." Malone sighed. "Let's shelve it for now. It's late. We'll get back at it first thing in the morning."

Malone and Dolan took the elevator down to the lobby. It was dark outside. They buttoned their trench coats and walked out into the windblown rain. They went down the stairs, across the street, and into the parking lot. Suddenly, a pair of high-beam headlights sprang on directly in front of them. The detectives stopped in their tracks. The headlights illuminated the falling raindrops immediately in front of them, but their brightness obscured everything else. They squinted, their hands shielding their eyes. They heard, rather than saw, the vehicle's doors open.

Two dark figures in trench coats stepped in front of the vehicle. The lights behind the figures created a silhouette, obscuring any identifying features. Both appeared relatively tall. The detectives strained their eyes to make out more detail. Both sensed they might need their weapons. Their 9mms were wedged in their shoulder holsters. Their coats were buttoned to the collar. They didn't have immediate access to them.

"Get ready to move, Eddie," Malone whispered.

"Are you Lieutenant Frank Malone and Detective Edward Dolan?" the figure on the left called out.

The detectives didn't answer as they continued to

assess their situation. Malone eventually responded, "Who's asking?"

"We are from the United States Justice Department. We came here to inform you that the Justice Department is going to take over the Rousseau investigation. Therefore, you two will stand down."

Malone took a moment to process what he had heard.

"Since when does the Justice Department take over a local homicide investigation?"

"That's not important right now. What is important is that you immediately stand down, Lieutenant. Mr. and Mrs. Rousseau are a special case. We will handle the case from here."

"What are your names?" Dolan asked.

"That's not important either."

"Let me get this straight," Malone responded. "You show up here in a dark parking lot. You don't provide a name or any identification. This case obviously falls under the guise of the local jurisdiction. That happens to be us. You can't possibly think your little visit here is going to convince us to back off a homicide investigation involving a seventeen-year-old girl? If you do, you're out of your mind."

"Lieutenant, I can assure you the Justice Department is not out of their mind. Please don't make this difficult.

We are asking for your cooperation. We will conduct the Rousseau investigation vigorously, I assure you."

"First, I don't know who you are," Malone responded. Second, I am not going to ignore my responsibilities to investigate a murder that occurred in Midtown. You're making a request that is ridiculous on its face."

"I was hoping we could handle this off the record. This case involves national security. That's all I can share with you at the moment. We can't go on the record because of the aforementioned national security concerns. We will mitigate any threat the Rousseaus may pose toward Midtown residents. This matter will be dealt with expeditiously. Please, Lieutenant, let us handle this informally between us. Don't force me to go over your head."

Malone assumed a defiant posture. "This is a homicide case, gentlemen. The Midtown Police Department has jurisdiction. Therefore, you can't go over my head. So, turn around, get back in your vehicle, and I'll try to forget this ever happened."

"Have it your way, Lieutenant . . . for now. You'll be hearing from us."

"You're not threatening me, are you?"

"No, Lieutenant, this is not a threat. It's more like a reality check. You will be removed from this case, one way or the other. My hope is we can do this the easy way. You are eventually going to regret that you didn't cooperate with us. Then, the only thing you will have left is to contemplate your stupidity in this matter."

The strangers turned to walk back to their vehicle.

"Wait a minute, fellas, one last thing before you leave."

The strangers turned back.

"Yes, Lieutenant."

"If you ever show up here again using this cloak-and-dagger routine to threaten me, I'm going to ship your ass out of Midtown in the back of an ambulance."

The mysterious figures reentered their vehicle. They pulled out of their parking space and drove away. Their rear license plate was blank.

Dolan looked at Malone. "What the hell was that all about, Frank?"

"I'm not sure, but I suspect it might have something to do with Rousseau's 'ton of bricks, threat."

CHAPTER 11

When Dolan left, Malone sat in his Explorer for a moment to digest the recent development. He decided to call the police chief. He answered his phone right away.

"Chief, it's Frank Malone. I called to fill you in on the status of the Kerry Hamilton investigation. We have identified two very viable suspects, a male and a female."

"I didn't see that coming, Frank."

"Neither did I, but that's just the half of it. Eddie and I were leaving the precinct a few minutes ago. We get a mysterious visit from two guys in the parking lot, claiming to be from the Justice Department. They already know who our suspects are in the Hamilton case. They ordered us to back off our investigation. They said they are going to take it over."

The Chief was incredulous. "What the hell is that supposed to mean, Frank?"

"I have no idea, Chief."

"I've never heard of such a thing. Who are these guys? What did they look like? Did they show you ID?"

"The headlights were in our eyes, it was dark, and the vehicle's license plate was blank."

"Well, none of that makes any sense. But I can tell you this. No one is coming into Midtown and ordering us to back off a murder investigation. Stay on it, Frank. I'll see if I can find out something on my end."

"Understood, Chief."

Malone put the Explorer into drive. The rain outside continued to fall. The streets of Midtown were nearly deserted. The prostitutes, the drug dealers, the homeless, and the gang bangers must have determined it was best to shelter in for the night. The seedy side of Midtown's nocturnal activity was sitting this one out. Malone decided to drive over to the Last Stop Saloon. He hadn't heard from Sarah since she had spent the night at his apartment.

On the way, images of blinking neon signs were blurred by the relentless downpour. A garbage can had been tipped over and its contents lay scattered in the street as Malone passed by. It was probably the result of a homeless person searching for an elusive morsel of food. A large rat scurried in front of Malone's Explorer and disappeared into a storm drain. Streetlights struggled to illuminate the path forward. Up ahead, Malone saw the bleary image of the Last Stop Saloon. He pulled into the parking lot. The single floodlight illuminated iridescent horizontal raindrops that darted through its solitary beam of light. Malone buttoned his trench coat, raised his collar, and stepped out into the rain.

Sarah heard the rain and wind outside when the saloon's front door swung open. In trudged a soggy Malone. He removed his trench coat. He made eye contact with her. She smiled, but it wasn't her normal warm smile. He selected a stool at the far end of the bar.

Sarah strolled over to Malone and flipped a coaster on the bar. "Hi, Frank, what'll it be, Irish whiskey on the rocks?"

Malone detected a difference in Sarah's tone. She walked away, made his drink, and then returned. "How was your day, Frank?"

"Is something the matter, Sarah? You don't seem like yourself."

"I'm fine, just a little down . . . that's all."

"That's not like you. What's making you feel this way?"

"I don't think this is the time or place to discuss it."

"You have to tell me something. I'm concerned about you. I won't be able to sleep a wink if you don't give me something."

Sarah sensed Malone's frustration. She decided to reveal her concerns.

"If you must know, I cried all the way home after leaving your apartment the other day."

"Why, did I do something wrong?"

"It's complicated."

"Well give me the uncomplicated version."

"It's us . . . our relationship. I love you with all my heart, but what we have right now is not enough for me. I feel like a carrot is being dangled out in front of me—what I want is always just out of reach."

"What do you want?"

"I want you, Frank. I want more of you. We're stuck in neutral. It makes me sad that were not moving forward."

"I love you, Sarah. I want more too. We'll figure things out, just stick with me."

"I want to, but how? You work virtually all the time. You're constantly inundated with all the ugliness in the world. Your life is nothing but dead bodies and murder. Every day is a struggle for you to maintain any sense of humanity. I can see it. The Monster of Midtown case almost killed you. You literally shot it out with a serial killer at point blank range. You live your life in a dreadful place. I can see you cherish the moments we have together. It gives you temporary relief from the awful place where you live your life. But the next day, you go right back to it. That is no way for us to live. How can our relationship flourish while you're in that environment? We're stagnant, Frank."

"I'm sorry you feel that way. I want to make it better."

"I don't know if you can."

"I don't want to lose you, Sarah. Please tell me what I can do to save us. I'll do anything, I promise."

"I want everything. I want a life with you. I want all of you, and I want to give you all of me."

The two lovers stared into each other's eyes. Malone finished his drink.

"It's going to work out, Sarah. Please hang in there; don't give up on us."

Sarah's piercing gray eyes softened a bit. "I swear, Frank Malone, sometimes I wish I didn't love you so much," she said with a hopeful smile.

"But you do, and I love you. Please be patient. I'm thinking about making some big changes. I want to give you everything you want . . . I promise."

A warm, more enthusiastic smile made its way onto Sarah's face. "Frank Malone, you're a real conundrum," she said, shaking her head. "Do you want another drink?"

"No, I better not."

Sarah sighed. "Why, because you're working the Kerry Hamilton case?"

Malone couldn't think of a better answer that would assuage Sarah's feelings.

She shook her head out of exasperation. "You see where you are, Frank? Every day of your life is the pursuit of some monster that would kill an innocent seventeen-year-old kid. What you do is a noble endeavor, but what does it do to your soul . . . and to us? For thirty years your life has been inundated with mayhem and murder. The worst part is it keeps you from being all in on loving someone. But that's not even the worst of it. It keeps you from being loved by someone else."

"I'm sorry you feel that way, but somebody has to get justice for Kerry Hamilton."

"Let somebody else do it, Frank. You have put your time in. Hand the baton off to someone else." Sarah stared into the observant eyes of Frank Malone. She felt a wave of tears coming on. She tried to conceal her anguish.

Malone abruptly stood up and put enough money on the bar to cover his bill and Sarah's tip. He put on his trench coat. He looked at her. "Thank you so much for cleaning my apartment and stocking the refrigerator. That was very kind of you. I appreciate it."

Tears began to spill onto Sarah's cheeks. Malone turned to leave.

"Wait, Frank, stop."

Malone turned; Sarah conveyed a look of exasperation. "Frank, I never meant Kerry Hamilton didn't deserve justice."

"I know that." With that, he walked out of the saloon and into a howling rainstorm.

Sarah regretted bringing up the subject.

While driving to his apartment, Malone conceded that Sarah had a valid point. She wasn't a kid. She had a right to feel the way she did. He wasn't fulfilling her needs. He knew he had to make changes, or he was going to lose her. He certainly didn't want that. He had spent virtually his entire life getting justice for victims and their families. He never regretted it, but it had personally cost him a lot. No matter how he spun it in his mind, that was an irrefutable fact.

Inside his apartment, Malone removed his soggy trench coat and hung it on the coatrack by his front door. He went into his bedroom, stripped off his damp clothes, and took a hot shower. Its soothing streams of hot water couldn't wash away the frustration he felt. Afterward, he dried off and started thinking again about his conversation with Sarah. She was right. Their current arrangement was no way for her to live. Malone was accustomed to grinding his way through life. He couldn't expect Sarah to live like that too. She was a beautiful and intelligent woman. She was certainly capable of attracting someone else who could fulfill her needs.

Malone was wired from their conversation. He was feeling frustrated and down. He feared an inevitable bout with insomnia. He lay in his bed and stared at the ceiling. Sometime later, he heard a quiet knock at his front door. It was 2:30 in the morning. He hopped out of bed, put on his robe, and went to the door. He opened it. It was Sarah. She had a devilish smile on her face.

"Do you want some company?" she asked.

CHAPTER 12

Malone's cellphone rang the next morning on his way to the 9th Precinct. It was the police chief. "Good morning, Chief."

"Frank, the mayor just called me. He wants to meet with us at 9:00 a.m. in his office. It must be about the Hamilton case."

"Understood, I'll see you there."

Malone called Dolan to inform him of his meeting. Then he drove directly to City Hall. He parked on the third floor of the Governmental Center parking garage. He raised the collar on his trench coat and made the walk to City Hall. The old nine-story building was located among archaic structures housing financial institutions, law offices, and other iconic images of Midtown's business district. Once inside, he took the elevator to the ninth floor, where the mayor's office was located. Police Chief John D. Parker was sitting in the waiting area. He stood when he saw Malone.

Malone and Parker had gone through the police

academy together. Parker was the department's first African American police chief. The two cops shook hands.

The chief's expression was grim. "I'm sure this meeting will be another cluster . . ."

The mayor's office door abruptly opened. Two men in dark suits, white shirts, and ties came out. Malone examined them closely as they passed by. Although he couldn't be sure, he thought they could be the two men who had confronted him and Dolan the night before. Neither man made eye contact with Malone. The receptionist's phone rang, and she answered it. She hung up and informed the police chief and Malone that the mayor was ready to see them.

The walls in the mayor's office were covered with magnificent oak paneling. An American flag hung in the corner. A variety of oil paintings depicting fox hunt scenes and men in red coats on horseback hung on the walls. The chief and Malone sat in the two chairs across from the mayor's desk.

The mayor was a distinguished-looking man with well-groomed, prematurely gray hair. "Good morning, gentlemen," he said.

The chief and Malone acknowledged his greeting with a wary nod.

"I want to speak to you about the Kerry Hamilton case. I have been informed that the federal government is going to take charge of the investigation. Therefore, Lieutenant Malone, prepare to step away from the case. Please turn over any evidence you may have gathered and give it to the FBI. They will assume responsibilities for investigating the case. "

Malone sat forward in his chair to rebut the mayor. The police chief extended his arm to restrain him. Malone settled back in his chair.

"Mayor, by charter, murders that occur in Midtown's jurisdiction shall be investigated by Midtown's Police Department. There are no exceptions in the charter," said the police chief.

"I am aware of what the charter says, JD. However, this is apparently a special case involving national security. The Feds are adamant about this. Therefore, I am directing the police department to stand down. The FBI has the resources to handle it."

"I don't give a damn about resources. This smells like a federal pile of shit, Mayor," the police chief countered.

"Nevertheless, JD, despite your olfactory senses, I am directing the police department to stand down."

The police chief was incensed. He tried to contain himself. "Mayor, respectfully, why would you want to do this? Kerry Hamilton's murder occurred in our jurisdiction. I don't know what the FBI is up to, but I can assure you their priority is not so solve this case expeditiously. This doesn't make any sense."

"Even so, you have heard my directive, JD."

"And you can hear my response, Mayor. The FBI can take a hike. Midtown's police department has jurisdiction in this case. I'm not about to hand over my responsibility to the federal government. What happens when the media and our citizens want a status update or want us to comment on the case? What happens when Kerry Hamilton's mother wants answers from the Midtown Police Department about her daughter's murder? What the hell do I tell her? 'I'm sorry, Ms. Hamilton, despite the fact that you pay taxes in Midtown, your chicken-shit police department can't handle this case, so we are handing it over to the FBI'? Like hell I'm going to tell her that. I won't do it, Mayor."

"Listen, JD, we have no choice. Midtown can't operate without federal grant money. We also have consent-decree provisions that Midtown is currently not up-to-date on. Some of those provisions involve your department. Finally, we don't need the IRS crawling all over the place looking into Midtown's financial records, my personal tax returns, your personal tax returns, and everything else. They have the ability to make our lives miserable; besides, the FBI is more than capable of conducting a murder investigation."

"Mayor, are you saying the Justice Department is engaging in extortion by threatening to take away Midtown's grant funding?"

"JD, they want our cooperation. It boils down to one law enforcement agency cooperating with another."

Malone interjected, "Mayor, two federal agents threatened my partner and me last night in the Ninth Precinct parking lot. I can assure you, if they are making a play like this, it's not because they want to solve the Hamilton murder case. There's something else going on. We have identified two very viable suspects. We may be able to make an arrest in less than a week. No law enforcement agency in the country would turn their case over to another agency at this juncture. It's unheard of."

"Nevertheless, stand down, Lieutenant."

"Mayor, Victoria Hamilton is preparing to put her daughter in a grave," Malone continued. "The suspects in this case are likely serial killers. This couple has almost certainly murdered before. They won't stop until we stop them. We can't turn this case over to an agency that has an agenda other than making an arrest as soon as possible. Something else must be going on."

"You're making assumptions, Lieutenant. I don't expect you to appreciate the potential financial ramifications of all this. That's my job to do that. This is a dollar-and-cents issue."

Chief Parker stepped in. "Mayor, I don't want to be at odds with you on this."

"JD," the mayor interrupted, "we don't have the tax revenue to fund all of the services that Midtown's government is required to provide by city charter. Your police department included. The grant money helps fund your training classes, purchase patrol cars, build facilities, and pay for other capital expenses. Midtown needs two new snowplowing trucks, a fire engine, a dozen police cars, and two hundred new computers. I want your cooperation on this, JD."

"Understood," replied the police chief. He stood abruptly. "You have my cooperation on this. Come on, Frank, we'll have to make arrangements for the FBI to take over the case."

Chief Parker and Malone left the mayor's office and took the elevator down to the lobby.

The chief grabbed Malone's arm, facing him. "Frank, go through the motions with the FBI. Drag your feet until we can figure out what the hell is going on. Don't hand over anything that is material to your investigation. I'll work this thing from my end. Do you have enough evidence to take your case to the DA?"

"Not yet, but we're getting close."

"Push it, Frank, and let me know if you find out why the hell the Feds are so interested in this case."

Malone drove back to the 9th Precinct in the pouring rain. A windblown cold front was moving into Midtown. Dolan greeted Malone when he got off the elevator on the fourth floor. They walked down to Malone's office.

Dolan could tell Malone was seething. "What happened in your meeting with the mayor and the chief?"

"The Justice Department is threatening to hold back federal funding to squeeze the mayor. They are demanding that we step aside and let the FBI take over the Kerry Hamilton case."

"What the hell is that about, Frank? They can't do that."

"I'm not sure why, but they're ramping up the pressure. The mayor insinuated that they are threatening to deploy the IRS on us personally, take away federal grant money, and revisit Midtown's consent-decree compliance."

"That's crazy, Frank, all to protect a couple of serial killers? That doesn't make any sense. Why is the federal government so invested in protecting these people?"

"I don't have the answer for that right now, but I do intend to find it."

Lucy knocked on Malone's open office door. "The front desk sergeant downstairs just called. There are two FBI agents in the lobby who would like to speak to you."

Malone looked at Dolan. "That didn't take long."

Malone opened the Kerry Hamilton murder investigation folder. He extracted the cover sheet, the autopsy report, and several other innocuous sheets of paper. He was careful to not include information garnered from interviews, CCTV videos, photographs, or any physical evidence they had collected. He handed Lucy the immaterial papers.

"Please make copies of these and put them in a new folder. Label it 'K. Hamilton Investigation' and use the incident number from the original folder. Then tell the desk sergeant to send them up here. When I ask you for the Hamilton file, bring me the new file, not the comprehensive original."

"Okay, Frank. I'll have everything ready when you ask for it."

Dolan gave Malone an amused look.

Ten minutes later, the two FBI agents, wearing dark suits, white shirts, ties, and a serious demeanor approached Malone's open office door. Malone cordially waved them in. Dolan had retrieved an additional chair from the conference room, so everyone had a seat. The men introduced themselves as special agents Michael Morris and Al Hogan. Hogan was tall and broad shouldered. He exuded confidence. He passed himself off as the senior of the two. Hogan appeared to present himself as a tough guy. Morris was also tall, but thinner, and seemingly more reserved.

"What can I do for you, gentlemen?" asked Malone.

"I assume you have spoken to Mayor Daniels about the Kerry Hamilton case?" Hogan asked.

"I have."

"Then you are aware that the FBI will be taking over the investigation?"

"Yes, I'll get you the file."

Malone dialed Lucy's extension. "Hi, Lucy. Please bring me the Hamilton file."

Moments later, Lucy entered Malone's office and handed him the new file. Dolan watched Malone's performance with continued amusement. Malone handed the file over to Special Agent Hogan. Hogan opened it. Morris leaned in to examine the contents of the file. Hogan quickly perused through the documents.

"What is this, Malone? You're telling me this is your entire investigation file on the Kerry Hamilton case?"

"Yes, is there a problem?"

"I've seen more comprehensive files for jaywalking violations. This is ridiculous. This case has been going on for a week. This is all you have? You're holding back on me, Malone."

"I'm sorry Agent Hogan, Detective Dolan and me are

just two dumb city cops who have been directed to turn our local investigation over to the FBI."

Hogan looked at Malone with a blank stare and then turned his attention to Dolan.

Dolan found it difficult to contain his glee behind a blank expression.

"Detective Dolan, Lieutenant Malone is obviously not complying with a directive from Midtown's mayor. Unfortunately, Lieutenant Malone may be too stupid to realize the pile of shit he's about to step in. However, now is your opportunity to separate yourself from such idiocy. You have been investigating a murder. Please turn over any documents you have generated regarding evidence, interview notes, pictures, videos, or anything else you have collected. Lying to the FBI and withholding evidence is a serious crime. I assure you the Justice Department is prepared to prosecute both of you if you don't cooperate."

Malone interrupted. "Why is the FBI so interested in this case, Agent Hogan?"

"Lieutenant, you'll be much better off if you don't ask any questions and just accommodate our request. I know we have gotten off on the wrong foot. That's my fault. Let's start over. We should have never approached you and Detective Dolan like we did in the parking lot last night. I apologize for that mistake. I am dealing with a very sensitive matter involving national security. I would appreciate it if you would please turn over everything you have on the Hamilton case. Once we have it, we will get out of your hair."

"How does a local murder investigation affect national security, Agent Hogan? Please help me understand that."

"Don't concern yourself with that, Lieutenant."

"Let me decide that Agent Hogan."

"I'm sorry, Lieutenant. I can't. But what I can do is assure you that any potential threat caused by the suspects in this case will be mitigated by the end of the month."

"Mitigated? What the hell does that mean?" Dolan asked.

"It means the suspects in your case will no longer pose a threat to the residents of Midtown."

"I can appreciate that," Malone said. "But I'm not in the threat mitigation business. I am in the arrest and conviction business."

"Not on this case, Lieutenant. We are asking for your cooperation. Take my word for it. You're not prepared for what the federal government will unleash on you to get their way in this matter."

"That sounds like a threat, Al."

"Take it however you want. I am just trying to help you see the light on this."

"You have our file, Al. Take that however you want."

"What is that supposed to mean?"

"I am just trying to help you see the light, Al."

Hogan turned and looked at Dolan. "Is your position the same as Lieutenant Malone's, Detective Dolan?"

"It is," Dolan said, nodding his head.

Hogan shook his head in disgust. "That's a pity, Malone. It doesn't have to be this way."

Morris and Hogan stood up. Hogan looked straight at Malone. He put a business card from his inside coat pocket on Malone's desk.

"Please call me, Lieutenant, if you change your mind in the next twenty-four hours. For your sake, I hope you do." With that, the FBI agents left.

Dolan looked at Malone. "That's the strangest conversation I have ever had with someone from the FBI. What do you make of it, Frank?"

"It wreaks politics," Malone replied, sensing ominous ramifications. "How or why, I don't know yet."

"I'm thinking we need to get out in front of this, Frank. We can't wait for them to make the next move. If we do, we might get steamrolled."

"I agree. I have an idea; let's reach out to our old friend Jack Mizell. He may be able to provide us with some answers."

CHAPTER 13

Jack Mizell was a retired FBI agent who had previously worked with Malone and Dolan on several murder cases that overlapped with federal jurisdiction. The most notable was a double murder committed in 2019 during a bank robbery. Another case involved the kidnapping and ransom demand for a well-known commercial real estate developer in Midtown. That case eventually ended in murder. After his retirement, Mizell opened his own skip-tracing business. He now used the skills that he had acquired in the FBI to track down missing persons, deadbeat dads who skipped out on their child support, and people who had defaulted on a debt. It wasn't a glamorous occupation, but it did prove to be a profitable one.

Malone knew from experience that Mizell had his demons, but he also knew he was an honorable straight shooter. Many times, that was the characteristic that had gotten him into trouble with his superiors in his former occupation. Over his thirty-plus years of service, he had earned the reputation of being a renegade. Mizell often laughed at that characterization of him. He frequently said, "Only in the federal government when you do things the right way do you earn a reputation as a renegade."

In addition to skip-tracing, Mizell's other primary activity after retirement was drinking. Malone was certain where he could find him on a weekday afternoon at 5:00 p.m.

Dolan parked his Explorer near the front entrance of Midtown's VFW pub. The detectives once again raised their trench coat collars and trekked through the drizzling rain to the pub's front door. Once inside, it took a few moments for their eyes to adjust to the darkness.

Sure enough, Jack Mizell was sitting on the same barstool where Malone had last seen him. He was a bit pudgier since then. He was also wearing the same tattered sport coat. His face was flushed red, resulting from years of smoking cigarettes and consuming alcohol. He had also missed his morning shave. Malone and Dolan approached him from behind.

"Jack Mizell, you certainly are a creature of habit," Malone said.

Mizell turned slowly, his eyes already bleary from consuming several Kentucky Bourbon Old Fashioneds. "Frank Malone, I'll be damned . . . Eddie Dolan! Pull a stool up fellas; the next drink is on me. What are you guys drinking? Is it still Irish whiskey on the rocks, Frank? And, Eddie, is it still vodka and soda?"

Both detectives nodded. Mizell ordered the drinks, and the bartender delivered them promptly.

"Is this a social visit or are you here on business?"

"Actually, do you mind if we move to a table away from the bar? I think our conversation requires a little more privacy," said Malone.

Mizell gave Malone and Dolan a concerned look. He knew the detectives well enough that what they wanted to discuss must be serious. "Sure, sure, guys. Let's sit at the table in the corner."

The three carried their drinks over to the table and sat down.

"What's going on, guys? How can I help?"

Malone took the lead. "I'm sure you've heard about the recent rape and murder of a high school student in Midtown. Her name was Kerry Hamilton."

"Of course, it has been all over the news for almost a week. The result of that case is a damn tragedy, Frank. I hate hearing about that kind of stuff."

"I agree, Jack. The reason we are here is because we have identified two viable suspects in the case . . . a man and a woman. Eddie and I have approached the two suspects just to rattle their cages and let them know we're on to them. The male suspect threatened us, like he has some kind of juice to make our lives miserable. The next thing we know, we get a visit from two of your former colleagues. They approached us last night in the precinct parking lot and came to see us earlier today. They basically ordered us to back off the Kerry Hamilton investigation. They are insisting that they take over the case."

Mizell was incredulous. "What, take over a local murder investigation? That doesn't seem right. They can't do that."

"That's what we think."

"Who are these guys? What are their names?" Mizell asked.

"They said their names were Special Agents Al Hogan and Michael Morris."

Mizell took a moment to digest the information. "I have never heard of those guys. You must be on to something really big. I'm willing to bet a lot that those two guys aren't actual FBI agents. The Bureau generally has two options when it comes to this sort of thing. They use their counterparts in foreign nations, or they hire independent contractors. They most often use NGOs and a nondescript line item in the federal budget to fund these types of projects. Whichever way they choose, ultimately, some faceless bureaucrat will be channeling your tax dollars to fund a program to work against you. This type of clandestine activity often starts in the deputy director's office. I know that clown well. I'll guarantee you his fingerprints are all over this."

"What do you think this all means, Jack?" Dolan asked.

"The FBI, at some point, has apparently decided to circumvent the Constitution to accomplish what they want in this instance. Typically, they do this when they want to wiretap someone's phone without a warrant or enter into places they shouldn't without a warrant, or gather intelligence by some other means in violation of the Constitution . . . something like that. Once they collect the requisite intelligence, they use it to change the trajectory of upcoming events. Their most common methods to carry out such an operation are sabotage and blackmail."

Now it was Malone's and Dolan's turn to pause and consider what Mizell was saying.

"Back to my original question, do you have any idea what this could be about, Jack?" Malone asked.

"Who are your suspects?"

"As far as we know, their names are Bobby and Annette Rousseau."

Mizell took a moment to contemplate the names. "They sound vaguely familiar. They were certainly not central figures in any of the cases I've ever worked on. I would remember them if they were. But I think I may have heard those names from somewhere. I just can't place where or in what context. Give me a few days to make some calls and sniff around. I'll try to find out something for you."

"Thanks, Jack. I appreciate that."

"In the meantime, we need to take precautions, Frank," Mizell said using a cautious tone. "The fact that operatives like these Hogan and Morris are involved makes me think it is something really big. That means the resources allocated to fund this project will virtually be unlimited. We will need to take precautions to protect ourselves. I'm already on the agency's shit list. They don't like me. I've held their feet to the fire far too many times. As a result, it would be wise for you not to call me directly, or email me, or text me, or come by my house or office. Keep looking over your shoulder. Make sure you're not being followed, especially when you come to see me. If you hear something shocking about me or my reputation in the next few days, you can count on it being bullshit. And, by all means, if I wind up dead, know that I didn't commit suicide."

Mizell had effectively raised Malone's and Dolan's concern. He had their full attention.

"I suggest you two do the same when you communicate with each other. Assume all your means of communication have been compromised. Only speak to each other in person. If you're cheating on your wives or significant others, assume it will come out. Beware of a new 'friend' coming into your life or some sexy broad coming out of nowhere who comes on to you like gangbusters. The agency obviously wants to steer you off this case. They will be seeking to gain leverage any way they can. That's their primary modus operandi. They may attempt to destroy you or someone close to you to get your attention. They may use their influence to turn someone close to you against you. Trust no one. Basically, they have an endless bag of dirty tricks to work from. This is likely going to get real ugly, real fast. These guys play for keeps, Frank. Even the mafia left wives and kids out of their business, but they won't."

"We fully understand where you're coming from," Malone confirmed. "How should we communicate with you, Jack?"

Mizell considered the question.

"I'll reach out to you. Give me your clerical assistant's office phone number. When I have something, I will call her. I'll let her know the time and place where we can meet. You will need to prepare her for my call. Tell her when she gets my call to only communicate my message to you in person. She should not convey any of my messages by any other means than a face-to-face conversation. I'll give your assistant twenty-four-hour notice prior to our next meeting time. That way she won't feel pressured to contact you via electronic means. Make sure she understands all this."

Malone and Dolan began to digest the scope of what they could be dealing with. Mizell had convinced them that they were likely up against forces that were insisting on getting their way and had unlimited resources to do it.

"Jack, are you sure I'm not asking for too much from you? You're retired. I was just looking for some information. I didn't expect you to get involved. I don't want to put you in harm's way."

"Forget it, Frank. You know I love this kind of shit."

Malone smiled. The detectives finished their drinks, stood, and shook hands with Mizell.

"We'll look forward to hearing from you, Jack."

"Remember what I told you, guys. Hogan and Morris are likely two foreign agents or contracted assets. I doubt they are actual Bureau employees. That will make their actions difficult to track. They likely have the indirect support of the director. Considering the potential magnitude of something like this, I doubt the deputy director is alone on his own."

"Understood, thank you, Jack."

Malone and Dolan turned to leave.

"One last thing, guys; remember . . . don't ever underestimate how ruthless this may get. These guys play for keeps."

The deep lines in Malone's face expressed a steadfast determination. He looked around to see if anyone was eavesdropping on their conversation, then he looked back at Mizell. "Yeah, well, we play for keeps too, Jack."

CHAPTER 14

Rain pelted the Explorer as the detectives returned to the 9th Precinct. They were quiet during the ride as they contemplated their situation. Dolan eventually interrupted the silence. "Frank, the Rousseaus are likely depraved killers. The thought of the federal government getting involved in a murder investigation for all the wrong reasons is a terrible idea at best. They wouldn't do it unless they know those two are guilty and want to run interference for them. That's the only way this all makes sense. What is your take on it, Frank? What do you think we should do?"

"We'll do what is right, like we always do. A seventeen-year-old girl is dead. I'll be damned if I'm going to let anything get in the way of justice for Kerry, Victoria, Melissa, or anyone who loves them. We'll just have to watch our backs."

Dolan dropped Malone off in the precinct parking lot. Malone walked back to his Explorer in the rain. He looked around and thought, *Has it always been this way?* Malone saw things with a vivid sense of clarity. It was so easy for him to see what the right thing was to do. Why is it so difficult for others to see it?

As Malone drove through Midtown he was in deep thought. He wondered why he never saw children playing in Midtown in the streets, even during the summer months. The temperature outside had dipped into the low thirties. The rain continued to fall. It made for a raw night. Sarah was right; his life had been reduced to nothing more than murder scenes and the endless flow of grief that followed for the victims' loved ones. How did moral clarity become such an elusive concept? Malone had fought all the good fights. Maybe it was time for him to bow out. Perhaps Sarah had a point: "Let someone else do it."

He had what he thought was the perfect woman, and he was failing to make it work with her. They were always in sync when they were together. Their main problem was they spent so little time together. He was in his early fifties and showing wear. He was fortunate that a woman like Sarah was attracted to him. He often wondered why. Perhaps it was time for him to put his sword down. He knew he would always have regrets if he let Sarah slip away.

He parked in front of one of Midtown's finest jewelry stores. Once again, he stepped out into the pouring rain. It was significantly warmer, dryer, and much brighter inside the store. Diamond rings, necklaces, bracelets, watches, and earrings shined luminously under well-crafted lighting.

An impeccably groomed man wearing a finely tailored suit immediately approached him. "Come in, come in. What a dreadful night. Business has been slow tonight. I was about to close up. My name is Paul. May I help you?"

"Yes, I want to look at engagement rings."

"Congratulations! We have a great selection to choose from. Follow me."

Malone followed Paul to a glass case where dozens of diamond engagement rings were displayed.

Paul studied the hardened, grizzled face of Frank Malone. "Do I know you from somewhere?" he asked. "I think I have seen you before. Where do I know you from?"

"I'm not sure. I don't think we have met previously."

"What is your name?"

"Frank Malone."

"Yes, yes, I do remember you now. You're a homicide cop with the Midtown Police Department. You were involved in a shootout with that awful serial killer, the Monster of Midtown. That son of a bitch terrorized our community for over a decade."

"Yes, sir; that was me," Malone said hesitantly.

"I saw you on the news many times speaking about that case. That son of bitch almost put me out of business. I've been here thirty years. He was destroying commerce in this town. People were afraid to leave their homes to patronize local businesses. Those were some real lean years. I have been through economic downturns, recessions, a pandemic, and half a dozen incompetent mayors and commissioners in this town. I have survived it all, but that son of bitch came real close to doing me in. However, business has been wonderful ever since you killed that bastard. Thank goodness you did. This whole town owes you a debt of gratitude. Pick out anything you want. I will give you fifty percent off on anything you choose."

"That's not necessary."

"Nonsense; you saved my business. I will always be indebted to you. What's the lucky girl's name?"

"Sarah, her name is, Sarah."

"That's a wonderful name for a new bride. Take your time, Frank. Pick out something you really like."

"I don't know what size ring she wears."

"That's okay, that's very common. Pick out whatever you want and bring her in later to have it sized. I can't believe you're in my store. They should have built a statue of you down at City Hall. You've done more to boost business around here than any half-assed politician or Chamber of Commerce organization ever did. I can tell you that."

"I appreciate your kind words, sir. I'm not good at selecting these types of things. Can you recommend something?"

"Yeah sure, how old is Sarah, Frank?"

"She's forty."

"Has she ever been married before?"

"No, she hasn't."

"Your safest bet is to choose a simple classic design, one that has endured over time. That way her ring will always remain in style."

"That makes sense."

Paul showed Malone a number of rings of similar design. Most were a solitary diamond of various shapes and sizes. Malone examined them all and eventually made his selection.

"That's a great choice, Frank. Sarah is going to love it."

Paul cleaned the ring until it shone brightly. Then he put it into a black velvet box and placed the box in a bag. Malone paid with his credit card.

"Thank you for coming in. Come back with Sarah any time, Frank, when you're ready to have the ring sized. Remember, I have some great wedding band designs. Make sure you come back here when you're ready to make a purchase. I'll give you the same fifty-percent-off deal. And I'll give Sarah fifty percent off too . . . on your ring."

"You're very kind."

"Nonsense, you're damn hero, Frank."

Malone chuckled.

After thanking Paul, Malone left the jewelry store. He decided to stop at a smoke shop on the way to his apartment. He bought ten high-quality cigars. He put two in the chest pocket inside his trench coat. He would save the rest for a celebration with his fellow officers. The rain outside was still falling, and the temperature continued to plummet. Nevertheless, for once Midtown didn't seem so dreary. Malone was happy with the decision he had made.

At 9:00 the next morning, Victoria Hamilton heard her front doorbell ring. She went to the door and looked through the peephole. She saw two well-dressed men wearing dark suits, white shirts, and ties.

The Feds were about to begin a systematic character assassination campaign. Their goal was to persuade Malone and Dolan to back off the Kerry Hamilton murder investigation . . . at all costs.

"Who is it?" Victoria Hamilton asked,

"Special Agents Hogan and Morris from the FBI; we would like to have a word with you, ma'am."

Victoria opened the door. The men examined her strained, exhausted face and her bloodshot blue eyes. The funeral for Victoria's eldest daughter was scheduled for later in the day. She was in the middle of an emotional firestorm. One minute her daughter was there, the next minute she was missing, and now she was preparing to say goodbye to her forever.

"Good morning, Ms. Hamilton."

"Good morning. What is this about? Are you assisting the Midtown Police Department with their investigation of my daughter's murder?"

"Yes, we are. Our agency is looking into your daughter's murder. However, we are here on a different matter."

Victoria was perplexed. "What matter is that? The most important thing right now is to get justice for Kerry."

"We understand that. May we come in and sit down, ma'am? We would like to have a conversation with you. It may take some time for you to fully comprehend what we have to say."

"Yes, of course, come in."

Victoria led the agents into her home and offered them a seat on her sofa. She sat in an adjacent chair. "Now what is this about?"

"Ms. Hamilton, the Midtown Police Department has asked the FBI to conduct an internal affairs—like investigation. The target of our investigation are the actions of Lieutenant Frank Malone."

Again, Victoria was confused. "First, I don't have any idea why you would be investigating Lieutenant Malone. He is a competent detective and a good man. Second, doesn't the Midtown Police Department have their own internal affairs division? They are a very large department."

"Yes, ma'am, they do," Hogan said. "But Lieutenant Malone has been with the Midtown Police Department for over thirty years. He has a lot of friends and influence in the department. In addition, he can be a very intimidating figure. City officials don't think their Internal Affairs Division is capable of conducting an unbiased investigation into his actions. Therefore, they have asked us to step in."

"This seems awfully strange to me. I would think the State Police would be next in line to conduct such an investigation if Midtown PD wasn't capable of doing it. I don't understand why the FBI is involved."

"That's a very astute observation, Ms. Hamilton, but . . ."

Victoria assessed his words. "What exactly are you investigating?" she asked.

"Lieutenant Malone's conduct while on duty. It is our understanding that he came to your home to interview you in regard to your daughter's murder. Is that true?"

"Yes, and he was with Detective Dolan. They were both very professional."

"Ms. Hamilton, Lieutenant Malone has been involved in hundreds of murder investigations over the years. It has come to our attention that he has made inappropriate comments and advances toward grieving mothers just like you. He seems to have developed a pattern of taking advantage of defenseless grief-stricken females. It has been alleged that he comes on to vulnerable family members of victims in a sexual way. Did you have that experience with Lieutenant Malone?"

"Absolutely not," Victoria declared with certainty. "This must be some kind of a mistake. I believe he is a very sincere man who is trying his best to find the person, or persons, involved in murdering my daughter. Frankly, I am skeptical of your intentions. None of this sounds right to me. My daughter was murdered in a most heinous way. I want the focus to be on finding her killer, not investigating Lieutenant Malone. This all seems like a needless distraction."

"I can understand why you feel that way, Ms. Hamilton," Hogan responded in an even tone. "Your daughter's murder case is being actively investigated by the FBI as we speak. However, our agency is capable of doing two things at once. We don't want a bad cop compromising a murder investigation. Malone appears to be concentrating his energies on seducing traumatized female family members of victims. The FBI and the Midtown Police Department want all the focus to be on finding your daughter's killer. You were apparently fortunate that he didn't direct his unprofessional intentions toward you. I understand Kerry has a sister. Perhaps he was more interested in your other daughter, Ms. Hamilton. Did he interview her?"

"No, Detective Dolan interviewed Melissa. This is outrageous, Agent Hogan. I'm aghast at your assertions. What you are suggesting is reprehensible behavior. Melissa is only thirteen years old. You should be conducting a criminal investigation if what you are saying is true, not an internal affairs investigation. I don't believe the man I met would engage in such behavior. Is Chief Parker aware of this? He had nothing but praise for Lieutenant Malone on television during the Monster of Midtown case. The residents in Midtown are very grateful that he was able to stop that monster's killing spree. None of this is making any sense."

"It is understandable that you can't make sense out of this," Hogan said while trying to get ahead of Victoria's emotions. "It's difficult for a normal person to comprehend such disgraceful behavior. We're embarrassed by Lieutenant Malone's actions. It gives law enforcement a bad name. It's especially disturbing because we share similar professions with him. The citizens of Midtown should be able to trust their police officers. Our mission is to regain the public's trust in their police department. I want to thank you for sitting down with us. We will stay in touch with you. I will personally inform you about the results of our investigation, once it has concluded. Thank you again for your time."

The FBI agents stood. Victoria Hamilton followed suit. Hogan reached out to shake hands, but Victoria didn't offer hers.

"Wait! May I see your FBI credentials before you leave?"

"Yes, of course," Hogan responded.

The men retrieved their identifications from their wallets and handed them to Victoria. She examined them closely and then handed them back. Victoria watched them leave from her front window.

Later that same day, Alex was wiping down tables in Tommy D's Restaurant when FBI agents Hogan and Morris entered. Rita was performing hostess duties. She greeted the men warmly and sat them in Alex's service station. Alex handed them menus and asked what they wanted to drink.

The men took note of Alex's curvaceous figure.

"Are you Alex Martin?" Agent Hogan asked.

Alex hesitated. How would two men in suits she had never met before know her name? Nevertheless, the defiant side of her personality took over. "Why, who's asking?"

"I'm Special Agent Hogan, and this is Special Agent Morris. We are from the FBI."

Morris nodded at Alex.

She evaluated the men closely. "Yeah, so what? What does the FBI want with a waitress in an Italian restaurant in Midtown?"

"It's not you we're interested in, Ms. Martin. Are you familiar with a Midtown police officer named Frank Malone?"

"Maybe. What's this about?"

"Are you familiar with Malone or not, Ms. Martin? Think your answer through before you respond. It is illegal to misrepresent the truth to a federal agent. Do you know Frank Malone or not?"

"Yeah, I know Frank."

"We have information that Lieutenant Malone has been making illicit sexual advances toward a number of female witnesses and family members of murder victims. We have been assigned to investigate those allegations."

Alex started spontaneously laughing.

"I assure you, this is no laughing matter, Ms. Martin. These are serious allegations," Hogan insisted.

"Let me see your identifications," Alex said, holding out the palm of her hand.

The agents showed their FBI identification cards to her. She took them. Like Victoria Hamilton, she examined them closely. "You two must have picked these ID cards up at some costume shop. You dudes are barking up the wrong tree. Frank Malone is old-school. He's the straightest shooter I have ever met. He would never do anything like you're describing. None of this sounds kosher to me. I don't believe anything you are saying. In fact, I'm not going to serve you. You two should take a hike and beat it." Alex used her thumb to emphasize the point.

"Ms. Martin, your rudeness has been duly noted," Hogan responded. "We have received a number of complaints about Lieutenant Malone, and they are very serious. His behavior may have violated a number of his department's Code of Ethics Regulations. In fact, some of his violations may actually rise to the level of criminal activity. Again, this is a very serious matter."

"Don't try to buffalo me with all your legal talk. I

know plenty about the law. Lord knows, I have screwed enough lawyers in this town over the years to prove it."

"Was Malone one of your conquests, Ms. Martin?" Hogan asked, thoroughly amused with himself.

"Sadly no, I told you he's not that way. I know for sure Frank Malone would never do anything close to what you are accusing him of. I think you're making this whole thing up. I don't believe a word you are saying."

"I am officially warning you not to cover for him, Ms. Martin. You could find yourself in big legal trouble if you are lying to a federal agent."

"I ain't covering for anybody," Alex insisted.

"You were a witness in the Monster of Midtown case, weren't you?"

"Yeah, so what?"

"Malone worked that case. You're a very attractive young woman. You're just the type that Malone tends to prey upon. Did he ever come on to you, Ms. Martin? Did he coerce you into bed? Did you sleep with Lieutenant Malone, Ms. Martin?"

"I don't know where you clowns came from, but take a look at me," Alex said confidently. "Do you see what I have going on here?" Alex waved her hand across her sexy figure. "In my previous line of work, I had half the married men in Midtown turning over a week's pay in fifteen minutes, just to cop a feel on me. I have offered Frank Malone a no-strings-attached piece of ass at least a dozen times. He has always turned me down."

"Maybe you're right, Ms. Martin," Hogan responded. "I guess you're not his type."

"No, Mr. FBI Agent, that's not it at all. I am everybody's type. I could have notches all over my panties to prove it, but I don't because I don't wear panties, Mr. FBI Agent. Frank Malone could have me anytime he wants, but he doesn't do it. You want to know why?"

Alex didn't wait for an answer.

"Because he's my friend, that's why. That's just the way the dude is. I don't know what you two are up to, but I know you're up to no good. I don't appreciate you coming in here and spreading lies about Frank. So, grab a hold of your toy badges and take a hike. Oh, and one last thing. I can assure you he is not going to like what you are saying about him . . . when I tell him."

Alex snatched the menus from the men.

"You heard me. Take a hike. I ain't serving you."

As Hogan and Morris were leaving Tommy D's, a female FBI operative dialed the Dolan residence from a separate location.

Eddie's wife, Doreen, answered the phone. "Hello."

"Is this the Dolan residence?"

"Yes, it is. May I ask who is calling?"

"Are you Detective Ed Dolan's wife?"

"Who is this?"

"I'm a friend of your husband, Mrs. Dolan. I called you because your husband has been screwing my ass off for the last six months. That son of a bitch has been promising me for three months that he was going to ditch your ass. He also promised me that he would keep paying my rent. Now I'm two months behind, and my landlord is all over my ass. Aside from that, my mattress and box spring are in a shambles, and my period is two weeks late."

"Who the hell is this?" Doreen demanded.

"I'm the woman who has been screwing your husband for the last six months, Mrs. Dolan. That son of a bitch has the sexual appetite of an undersexed, rabid mountain goat. You should try to make yourself more available to him, Mrs. Dolan. Maybe then he wouldn't be constantly knocking on my door."

"If you don't tell me what your name is, I am going to hang up this phone."

"I told you who I am. I'm the chick who has been banging your undersexed husband for the past six months. Now, I need money to pay for an abortion."

Doreen Dolan hung up the phone.

Malone and Dolan were staking out the Rousseau residence when Eddie's cellphone rang.

"Hi, Honey. I can't talk for long; I'm on a stakeout with Frank. . . . What? What the hell are you talking about? . . . No, of course I didn't. . . . Doreen, slow down. I can barely understand you. . . . Of course I haven't. . . . What? . . . No, of course I didn't, Honey. It must be some kind of prank call . . . What? No, I don't think it's funny at all."

Malone looked over at Dolan, his eyes full of questions.

"Is her number saved on the phone? Please check. Okay, it's there. I'm going to get to the bottom of this. Of course it's not true, Honey. This must be some kind of sick joke. Of course, I don't know who this person is. Don't worry; I'm going to get to the bottom of this. Yes, I'll see you later. Okay, okay, I love you. Alright, I will see you when I get home."

Dolan hung up his cellphone. He looked at Malone in a state of confusion.

"What's going on, Eddie?"

"Some sick bitch called my house. She told my wife that I have been banging her ass off for the last six months. She said her period is late, and she is demanding money to pay for an abortion."

"What? Do you have any idea who this person is?"

"Hell no, but she's got Doreen mad as hell at me. The caller said I have the sexual appetite of an undersexed, rabid mountain goat."

Malone glared at Dolan suspiciously. "Are you sure you don't know who this woman is, Eddie? It sounds like she knows who you are," Malone said jokingly.

Dolan frowned. "Who would do such a thing, Frank?"

Malone stared out the windshield of the Explorer at the Rousseau residence. "I'm not sure, but I might have a hunch."

Later that night, at the Last Stop Saloon, Sarah looked stunning as she mixed drinks and chitchatted with the regulars. The front door swung open; a howling wind-driven downpour was roaring outside. In walked two men Sarah had never seen before. They removed their trench coats. They were wearing dark suits, white shirts, and ties. They headed over to the bar and sat down. Sarah made her way over to them.

"Good evening, gentlemen. Some night outside, eh? You picked the right place to seek shelter. What can I get for you?"

Special Agent Hogan ordered a scotch and water while Morris requested a draft beer.

Sarah flipped two coasters on the bar and said over her shoulder, "Coming right up."

The agents knew from tapping Malone's cellphone that he was in a struggling romantic relationship with the attractive bartender. They had decided to approach Sarah with a similar story line to the one they had used with Victoria Hamilton.

Malone and Dolan had no intention of backing off the Kerry Hamilton murder case. The powers at the highest level of the Justice Department had decided to give them no choice. Their approach was similar to when the Justice Department files a frivolous lawsuit on someone. They weren't necessarily seeking a conviction. Many times, their mission was to make the legal process the punishment. The federal government was always in the driver seat when it came to prosecuting a case because they had unlimited resources.

Hogan was leading a team of FBI operatives. Their current mission was to make the lives of the detectives as miserable as possible. Their plan included incrementally turning the screws on them until they finally relented. The Bobby and Annette Rousseau "predicament" was a big deal. The United States government was not about to let two headstrong detectives in Midtown cause a disaster in Washington.

Sarah returned with their drinks and placed them on

the coasters. Hogan momentarily stared at Sarah. It was easy to see why Malone was attracted to her. Her vibrant gray eyes were highlighted by her black silk shirt and her unruly mane of dark hair. Her tight jeans drew attention to her lithe figure as she moved about effortlessly. *Malone* was *a lucky man*, Hogan thought, emphasizing the past tense.

Back at the stakeout, Malone and Dolan were discussing the phone call Dolan's wife had received, when Annette Rousseau's Land Rover pulled into the home's driveway. The garage door opened, and she parked her vehicle inside. She got out and looked across the street at the two men inside the Ford Explorer. The detectives watched her every move. Their purpose was to make sure the Rousseaus didn't pursue another victim while they were trying to gather enough evidence for an arrest warrant.

The silence in the Explorer was interrupted by Malone's cellphone ringing. He saw it was Victoria Hamilton. "Hello, Victoria. What can I do for you?"

"Hello, Frank. I wanted to make you aware that two FBI agents paid me a visit earlier today. They said they were conducting an internal affairs–like investigation on you. Do you know anything about this?"

"No, I don't. What did they say?" he asked curiously.

"They said some terrible things about you, Frank. They said you are using your position to persuade vulnerable family members of victims to sleep with you. They painted an awful picture of you."

Malone swallowed hard. "It's difficult for me to comprehend how inappropriate that was, Victoria. I can assure you that none of it is true."

"I suspected as much. Why do you think they would do something like that?"

"I am trying to figure it out as we speak. We have identified two very viable suspects in Kerry's case. Apparently, the federal government feels a need to interfere with our investigation. However, at this point, I am not sure why."

"I buried my daughter earlier today, Frank," she said sadly. "I am heartbroken. My life will never be the same. I don't care about a squabble between two law enforcement agencies. My concern is about the person who killed my daughter. I want that person to be held accountable."

"I can assure you, Victoria, that is my entire focus. There's nothing anyone can do that will keep me from pursuing an arrest and a conviction in this case. You have a number of emotional mountains to climb. You don't need any of this. I am disgusted that there are people in law enforcement who are not making your concerns their number-one priority. Rest assured; I am not guilty of anything so reprehensible. They are trying to intimidate me by destroying my character, but there is nothing anyone can do to me that will scare me off your daughter's case."

"I didn't think you were guilty, Frank. I trust my instincts. My instincts tell me that you are an honorable man."

"Thank you, Victoria, your confidence in me is all I need to keep me going." Malone hung up the phone. He looked over at Dolan. "My sense on this turns out to be right. I know exactly who was behind that phone call to your wife."

Meanwhile, back at the Last Stop Saloon, Sarah was delivering a second round of drinks to the two men in dark suits.

"Your name is Sarah Summers, isn't it?" Hogan asked.

"It is," Sarah replied hesitantly.

"I am Special Agent Hogan with the FBI. This is Special Agent Morris. We are conducting an internal affairs investigation on a homicide detective named Frank Malone."

Sarah's gray eyes grew wider.

"Are you familiar with Frank Malone, Ms. Summers?"

"How do you know my name?" Sarah asked.

"It's part of what we do. Frank Malone is likely guilty of some very disgraceful behavior. If our investigation confirms that, we are prepared to make sure that he is terminated and never works in law enforcement again."

"What kind of behavior?" Sarah asked curiously.

"He has used his position of authority to pressure female relatives of murder victims into having sex with him."

Sarah laughed spontaneously.

"That's ridiculous. Frank Malone would never do something like that. He's a very honorable man. He would never take advantage of anyone who was grieving over the loss of a loved one. It is not in his DNA to do something like that."

"Are you familiar with a stripper by the name of Alexandra Martin?"

"Yes, I haven't met her, but Frank has mentioned her to me. He met her during the Monster of Midtown case. Her roommate was murdered by the killer. Frank did everything he could do to protect her after her roommate was killed."

"Well, Ms. Summers, according to Ms. Martin, Malone has been bopping her ever since. Ms. Martin feels like she was coerced into having sex with him. She was afraid after her roommate was murdered that, if she didn't, the police would not protect her. Since that time, he has threatened to arrest her for drug possession and prostitution if she didn't continue to have sex with him."

"There is no way any of this is true," Sarah said confidently. "I know Frank Malone. He would never do something like that. I have never met Alex Martin, but I assure you, she is lying."

"I hope you're right, Ms. Summers, but I tend to doubt it. I find it particularly shameful when a lawenforcement officer abuses his authority."

"You apparently have no idea who Frank is. If you did, you would know none of this true," Sarah insisted.

"To be honest with you, Ms. Summers, I think he is guilty as hell and I'm going to nail his ass to the wall because of it."

"That doesn't sound very fair or open-minded, Agent Hogan. You seemed to have convicted him already. I hope for your sake you give Frank the benefit of the doubt."

"Giving people the benefit of the doubt is not what we do, Ms. Summers."

"Then carry on at your own risk, Special Agent Hogan. Frank isn't going to like you coming in here and trying to use me to ruin his life. And he especially is not going to like what you are saying about him. You better check your facts. If you don't, you're going to be dealing with a very angry Frank Malone. I don't think you're prepared for that."

"Have it your way, Ms. Summers, but he's probably bopping that little stripper with the world-class ass as we speak. You can get us our tab now," Hogan said as both agents smiled.

Sarah went to the computer register and printed their tab. When she returned, she handed the bill to Hogan. She made it a point to examine the FBI agents very closely.

"Are looking at something in particular, Ms. Summers?" Hogan asked.

"I am making a mental picture in my mind of what you look like now. Because after I tell Frank what you have been saying about him, I'm sure you're not going to look that way for long." Sarah turned abruptly and walked away.

CHAPTER 15

Dolan parked his Explorer in his garage. He had no idea how his wife was processing the unknown female caller's claims. He pushed the button to close the garage door. He opened the door that led to the mudroom. He hung his trench coat on a coat peg. He opened the door that led to the kitchen.

Doreen was sitting at the kitchen table. She stood up when he entered. She stared at him. He could tell she had been crying. Her eyes were puffy and teary. "What is going on, Ed?"

"It's related to work, Honey." Dolan tried to explain. "There's something about the Kerry Hamilton case that has the federal government's attention for all the wrong reasons. The FBI put that woman up to it."

"What, why?" she asked impatiently. "That doesn't make any sense. Why would the FBI do that to a police officer?"

"We don't know why yet, but we do know they're trying to force Frank and me to back off the Kerry Hamilton murder investigation. That's the reason why that woman called you. They are doing the same thing to Frank. They are trying to assassinate our characters and drive a wedge between us and the people we care about. It is the nastiest, most underhanded thing I have ever seen. Please don't believe anything that woman said. If you do, some really bad people are going to accomplish exactly what they set out to do. Please don't let them do it."

"Ed, you're telling me something that is really difficult to believe."

Meanwhile, Malone was headed to the Last Stop Saloon when his cellphone rang. He looked at his caller ID and answered. "Hello, Alex. How is the new job working out?

"Really good, but that's not why I called you," she said with a serious tone.

"What's up?"

"Two FBI agents came into Tommy D's today."

"What did they want?"

"They had some pretty awful lies to say about you."

"Like what?" Malone asked.

"They said you're screwing half the women in Midtown."

"You've got to be kidding?"

"No, I'm not. Apparently, the only woman in Midtown you're not screwing is me," Alex said facetiously. "I have been practically throwing myself at you for almost a year, and I get nothing from you. Honestly, I'm a little insulted, Frank. What does practically every other woman in Midtown have that I don't have? I mean, I'm in a position now where I can even serve you a nice Italian meal afterward," she said, giggling. "What is going on, Frank?"

Malone chuckled mirthlessly. "I can appreciate your sense of humor, Alex; however, forgive me if I don't find it as amusing as you do."

"What are these clowns up to, Frank?"

"It's a long story. I'll tell you all about it the next time I see you. Right now, I need to put a stop to this."

"Wait, don't hang up, Frank. Now that we have established that you're more open to having sex, I want you to know that all my previous offers still stand," Alex said, giggling with amusement.

"I'll make a note of it," Malone deadpanned. "Good night, Alex."

Malone disconnected the call. This was starting to get on his nerves. Whatever was going on, the FBI was on a mission to destroy everything in its path to protect the Rousseaus, but why?

The rain outside was quickly becoming sleet as Malone drove down the waterlogged streets of Midtown toward the Last Stop Saloon. Once inside, he removed his saturated trench coat. He looked for Sarah as he strode toward his usual stool at the far end of the bar. Instead of her familiar smile, her face conveyed a look Malone had never seen from her before. Instantly, he concluded that the FBI agents must have also confronted Sarah with the same unsettling lies that they had told Victoria Hamilton and Alex.

Due to her relationship with Malone, Sarah had been drawn into the Monster of Midtown case. The killer had actually come into the saloon and threatened her. Now she was being pulled into the Kerry Hamilton investigation. Malone fumed quietly. He was incensed that she was being tugged into another one of his "work-related issues." He walked up to the bar. Sarah walked over to him. He laid his trench coat over the stool next to the one he sat on. He examined her lovely face. He could see an underlying turmoil was churning inside her.

"Let me guess, two FBI agents came in here. They told you I was abusing my position of power to seduce female family members of murder victims."

Sarah's face softened. Her countenance conveyed a sense of incredulity. Malone was very close to knowing exactly what had occurred. *How did he know that?* she wondered.

"Did they tell you I coerced Kerry Hamilton's mother into bed? Or did they tell you that I have been regularly having sex with Alex? Which one was it?" Malone asked, obviously annoyed.

"Just the latter; they said you have been having sex with Alex since the day you met her," she responded, unable to hide her distress.

"It's not true, Sarah. Alex is just a friend," he tried to explain.

"What is this all about, Frank?"

"For some reason the FBI has made it their mission to run Eddie and me off the Kerry Hamilton murder case. Evidently, character assassination is going to be their primary weapon. I have been warned by a retired FBI agent that they might try to do something like this. They must have tapped my phone. I knew they were capable of influencing people and world events with lies, sabotage, and distortions, but I never thought they would get around to Eddie and me."

"But why, Frank?"

"I don't have an answer to that yet. We have identified two suspects in Kerry Hamilton's murder. For some reason the Justice Department is moving heaven and earth to protect them. They even stopped by Kerry Hamilton's house to feed her mother the same lies they apparently told you. She just buried her daughter earlier today. She doesn't need any of this. In addition, they had a woman call Eddie's wife. She told Doreen that Eddie's been regularly having sex with her and that she is pregnant. She demanded money for an abortion."

"Dear G-d. How did Doreen take that?"

"I'm not entirely sure. As far as I can tell, not well. I know Eddie was not looking forward to going home."

"They were so convincing, Frank. I am ashamed of myself for letting any semblance of doubt creep into my mind. I'm so sorry."

"It's quite understandable. All this came out of left field. I am the one person who should be sorry. It is so unfair that you have once again been drawn into a case I am working on."

Sarah examined Malone's face. At a glance it conveyed a hard-bitten, unrelenting toughness with all its deep lines and sharp features. Few knew what lay underneath. It was a wonderful natural disguise to conceal the compassion that resided within him. That face had served him well for over thirty years as a homicide detective.

"That's the way it is when you are on a team, Frank."

Malone genuinely smiled, only the way Frank Malone could. "Come here," he said.

Sarah rounded the end of the bar. The lovers embraced. She looked up into his eyes. "I love you, Frank Malone."

"I love too."

The rest of the men in the bar watched with envy. The women they were with released a grateful sigh of relief.

CHAPTER 16

The next morning Malone summoned Tommy Jackson, Matt Dillon, Trace MacDonald, Kinsey Phillips, and Eddie Dolan to conference room one.

Once everyone was seated, Malone took a place in the front of the room and began, "Eddie and I have become aware that the FBI is adamant about taking over the Kerry Hamilton murder investigation. We believe they have tapped our cellphones. As a result, they have contacted people in our personal lives. They are engaging in a campaign of personal destruction to protect the two suspects we have identified in Kerry Hamilton's murder. I don't have a reasonable explanation for any of this. However, I do know this: We are not going to stand by and let the people responsible for Kerry Hamilton's murder get away with it.

"I have called you here, because from here on out, you should not communicate with Eddie or me on our cellphone or our office telephone. Do not text us or email us anything related to the Kerry Hamilton case.

You should only communicate with us face-to-face until further notice.

"Also, I am pulling everyone off all their previous assignments. I want to set up a twenty-four-a-day stake-out on the Rousseaus for the foreseeable future. Trace and Kinsey, you two cover Annette Rousseau's dance studio during working hours. Eddie and I will stake out their residence from 8:00 a.m. to 8:00 p.m. Tommy and Matt will take the overnight shift. Henry Gonzalez and Robyn Butler will cover for Eddie and me when we have to divert our attention elsewhere. I want the Rousseaus to feel our presence. I especially want to eliminate any chance of another murder occurring while we gather evidence to make an arrest."

Malone then directed his attention to Kinsey. "Were you able to find anything on the Web or social media related to the Rousseaus that might be helpful?"

"It's the strangest thing, Frank. Outside of Annette's website for the dance studio, I can't find anything on those two. I have gone back over three years, and I have come up with nothing. It's extremely odd. It's like they didn't exist before they got to Midtown. However, I can tell you what else I am seeing."

"What is that?"

"There's been a significant uptick in negative chatter on social about the Midtown Police Department.

Suddenly, out of nowhere, people are talking about how incompetent we are; especially with regard to the Kerry Hamilton case. I found that really odd because the case is only nine days old. I don't understand how people could have gotten so upset in such a short period of time. It's very strange."

Malone looked over at Dolan. They both realized Kinsey's findings might be connected to the issues they were having with the FBI.

"One other thing, Frank. There is a lot of chatter on social media about you the last few days, and it's not good. Several comments came from people claiming to be females. They are making some awful remarks."

"I can only imagine," Malone said, obviously irritated. "Unfortunately, it doesn't surprise me. It appears the Feds have been working overtime."

Just then Lucy stuck her head inside the conference room door. "I am sorry to interrupt you. I just received a call from your Uncle Jack, Frank. He said he wants to meet with you at 4:00 p.m., at your old stomping ground. I asked him to be more specific, but he said you would understand."

Malone looked over at Dolan, who nodded to confirm the significance of Lucy's message. After the meeting, Malone made arrangements for Henry Gonzalez and Robyn Butler to relieve Dolan and him at 2:00 p.m.

on the Rousseau stakeout so they could attend the meeting with Jack Mizell.

Later, on the way to Midtown's VFW pub, Malone peered at the passenger side-view mirror of Dolan's Explorer to make sure they weren't being followed. "How did it go when you got home last night, Eddie?" Malone asked.

"Whoever that woman was who called my wife, she really did a number on her," he responded with frustration. "She must have been convincing as hell. Doreen was not happy when I got home. And things weren't much better this morning when I was getting ready for work. I'm going to try to run down where the call came from later. However, I get the feeling it's going to lead to a dead end."

"It wouldn't surprise me. You weren't able to convince Doreen it wasn't true?"

"I don't think so. This is probably going to be an issue that lingers between us for a while. I am pretty certain she has her doubts."

"If it's any comfort to you, Hogan and Morris made a visit to the Last Stop Saloon last night. They spoke to Sarah."

"What?! That doesn't comfort me at all, Frank. All it does is piss me off. What did they say?"

"They basically told her I have been screwing half the women in Midtown . . . including Alex."

"You know, Frank, I get the distinct feeling these two so-called FBI agents are really enjoying this personal destruction business. I never anticipated anything like this."

"It conveys desperation on their part. People make mistakes when they're desperate. We have hope at some point, they do."

Dolan pulled his Explorer into the VFW parking lot. The detectives made sure they hadn't been followed before getting out. Then they braced themselves for the misty rain and dipping temperatures outside. Once inside the pub, they quickly located Jack Mizell sitting on his customary barstool.

"Hey, Jack."

Mizell turned and saw their familiar faces. "Hey, Frank, Eddie," he said cautiously. Mizell looked around the bar suspiciously, got off his stool, and waved for the detectives to follow him. He had a manila folder in his hand. The three men sat at a table in a secluded corner of the room.

Mizell inhaled deeply. "You two really stumbled onto a doozy. I'll start from the beginning. Bobby Rousseau's real name is Harry Niles. Twenty years ago, he was a flailing actor in Hollywood. He decided to venture into the pornographic film industry where he began to make a name for himself as a director and producer.

"Somewhere along the line Harry meets an ex–ballet dancer named Tina Russell, aka Annette Rousseau. Harry recruits her into the pornographic film industry. Tina begins using the stage name Nadine Skin. She quickly becomes one of the hottest things going in the porn business."

Malone and Dolan nodded to confirm that they could certainly understand how Annette could make a meteoric rise in the pornographic film industry.

"Anyway, can you think of a better place than the porn business to find your soulmate, and your wife to be?" Mizell asked sarcastically. "Eventually, the happily married couple produces over a hundred well-received pornographic films together. The money is rolling in. At some point, Tina opens a dance studio, apparently so she can remain connected to her ballet dancing roots and maintain her hellacious figure."

Malone and Dolan nodded again.

"Somewhere along the way Harry meets several 'investors' who are launching a human-trafficking operation on the Texas border. The investors needed additional 'start-up' cash so they recruit Harry Niles and the popular Nadine Skin to invest in their operation. Eventually, big dough starts rolling in. I mean really big dough.

"Well, back in Washington, D.C., several noisy congressmen and senators are calling for better security at the border. Simultaneously, the investors are sensing that their lucrative 'business activities' on the border may be coming to an end. They immediately hatch a plan to dispatch Harry and his bride to D.C. Their mission: Get Tina to seduce several influential political figures who are calling for a more secure border.

"Harry and Tina immediately begin hanging out in popular restaurants and bars in the D.C. area, where the political class is known to frequent. In due course, Tina ends up seducing a half dozen or more senators, congressmen, and a couple of presidential cabinet members. Unbeknownst to them, Harry secretly videos it all.

"Meanwhile, out west in Brantley, California, local police are starting to put together a connection between Tina's dance studio and two teenage girls who were raped and murdered. Back in Washington, Harry, being the 'creative entrepreneur' that he is, emails the sex videos of Tina and her influential lovers to the attorney general. Take a guess what party they are affiliated with?"

Malone shrugs his shoulders. Dolan shakes his head.

"They all belong to the same political party and it's the one currently in power. Along with the videos, Harry sends a blackmail message to our newest tax-paid stars in the pornographic film business. He promises to expose them all if they continue to stick their collective noses into immigration policies that would negatively impact their human-trafficking operation on the border. In addition, he demands that our upstanding officials in Washington persuade the local police department in Brantley, California, to back off their murder investigation involving the two porn-star lovebirds. Ultimately, Harry ends up with all the leverage and demands a 'get out of jail free card.' As a result, our politicians in Washington do what they always do—something really stupid. They play along with Harry and Tina.

"The attorney general, in his ultimate wisdom, hatches a plan. With the assistance of the U.S. marshals, he essentially puts Harry and Tina into a witness protection program. Their identities are changed to Bobby and Annette Rousseau, and anything related to their past is completely erased. Harry and Tina are provided with a whole new makeover, courtesy of the federal government, including new Social Security numbers, passports, driver's licenses, etcetera. The attorney general convinces authorities in Brantley to let the FBI take over their two murder investigations. Then they relocate the happy couple to a destination outside Brantley's jurisdiction. Guess where that is?"

"Midtown," Malone replied rhetorically.

"Exactly."

"The place where they then proceed to commit another rape and murder," Dolan added.

"And now the Rousseaus are pulling the same card again to get out from underneath their murder in Midtown," Malone said. "The United States government is essentially harboring two serial killers, all to protect the reputations of our 'upstanding' political class. That's enough to make someone with an ironclad stomach puke." He shook his head in disgust.

"That's politics, Frank," Mizell replied. "At least you know our tax dollars are being well spent." Mizell handed Malone the manila envelope. "Inside are hard copies of a number of internet news articles from three-years ago, suggesting that Harry and Tina Niles are suspects in the murder and rape of two teenage girls in Brantley, California. Both victims are linked to the same dance studio owned by Tina. There is a picture of a very fit dance instructor included named Tina Niles. I also included pictures of her husband, who has links to the pornographic film industry, one Harry Niles.

"You'll never find any of this on the Web now," Mizell pointed out. "I got these from a former colleague of mine in the Bureau. Everything related to Harry and Tina Niles has been erased. It's all lost in cyber space. The only thing you will find on the Web now regarding either one of them is related to Annette Rousseau and her dance studio in Midtown. The U.S. Marshals are very effective at the witness protection business.

Unfortunately, they're now using their resources to protect serial killers."

Malone looked at Dolan, silently conveying how grim the situation appeared.

"One more thing, Frank," Mizell added. "The people in Washington are desperate to hide their sex scandal. Desperate people are predisposed to do some really stupid things. If you keep pushing this thing, there's no telling what the Feds will do to stop you. Whatever they end up doing, you can be sure no one will ever be able to trace Hogan and Morris back to the FBI, but rest assured, the link is there. There are big reputations and political ramifications at stake. My former colleague tells me the Feds have reached out to international operatives used previously by the CIA. I don't have to tell you what that could mean. There is no doubt your lives could be in danger."

"I appreciate what you're saying, Jack," Malone replied. "But if they would consider that, why don't they just take out the Rousseaus and be done with it?"

"Harry has the ultimate insurance policy, Frank. He made sure he conveyed, to all the affected parties, that he has distributed copies of the videos to several unknown persons. They have been instructed to release the videos publicly if Harry and/or Tina should suffer an unfortunate accident that leads to their demise."

"Harry holds the final trump card," Dolan concluded. "It's all very clean and neat."

"The United States government is being held hostage by two serial killers," Malone further realized. "The Feds are spending all this capital to protect a two-bit porn star and her director husband. On top of it, they think it makes more sense to destroy the personal lives of two detectives than to put a stop to all this. I never thought something like this could ever happen. Washington has a lot more problems than I thought."

"Do you want some good advice, Frank?"

"Sure, Jack."

"This thing is way bigger than you and Eddie. They have an endless supply of resources to get what they want on this. Just let the Feds relocate them and be done with it. The Rousseaus will be out of your jurisdiction and out of your hair."

"Basically, do what our colleagues out west did?"

"Yes, exactly! It would be a lot easier, Frank, and probably a lot healthier too."

"Yeah, but wherever they decide to relocate the Rousseaus, it will happen again. Somewhere, some innocent girl will have an interest in taking ballet dancing lessons, and it will cost her everything. Eddie and I will essentially be serving that girl's life up on a silver platter. I can't live with that, Jack."

"Frank, you can't solve the world's problems. Stick to Midtown; at least you can solve one here."

"Would you do it, Jack?"

"Yes, I would if I was outgunned like you guys are. It's a matter of mathematics, Frank."

"You're forgetting about Kerry Hamilton and her mother. What about them?"

"I'm not sure you fully comprehend what the Feds are capable of, Frank. They can destroy lives, reputations, careers . . . or even worse. You two are about to piss off a lot of people who have considerable power." Mizell recognized he wasn't convincing Malone to back off. "Frank, you're one hell of a cop, but you're also one bullheaded son of a bitch. That bullheadedness just might get you and Eddie killed."

Malone smiled. "It's Eddie, he brings the worst out in me," Malone joked. "Thanks for your concern, Jack, and your advice. You have answered a lot of questions for us."

"You're making me wish I hadn't, Frank."

Malone and Dolan stood up. They shook hands with Mizell.

Mizell offered a final warning. "Remember, they'll stop at nothing, Frank, to get their way. They'll destroy your reputations, your marriages, your bank accounts, your credit, and they'll even take your freedom away to stop you. Don't think for one minute that they don't have the inclination and the will to do it. But more importantly, they have the power to do it . . . and to cover it up."

Malone smiled again. "I'll see you around, Jack."

"I hope so, Frank."

CHAPTER 17

Malone and Dolan stepped outside the VFW pub into a wispy snow flurry. They instinctively surveyed their surroundings on their way to the Explorer. Was someone watching them? They saw no one.

When they got in the Explorer, Dolan looked at Malone. "Ten days ago, you could have never convinced me that something like this was even possible."

"Unfortunately, it has all become too real, Eddie."

"What next, Frank?"

"We can't go it alone, Eddie. I've got to get the police chief and the mayor on board."

The dipping temperatures of Midtown's dreaded winter were beginning to roll in. Malone looked out the passenger side window of the Explorer. He wanted justice for Kerry and Victoria, but he also didn't want the Rousseaus to become someone else's problem. He had other things to consider too.

"Eddie, you have a wife and two daughters to think about. These bastards may have already irreparably harmed your marriage. That's way too big a price to pay. I better go it alone the rest of the way."

Dolan stared out the windshield as the weather conditions worsened. He knew what the risks were, and he knew what needed to be done. "No way in hell anyone is running me off this case, Frank," he finally uttered without looking at Malone.

"Have it your way, partner," Malone responded.

When he got back to the precinct, Malone called the police chief's cellphone from a line in conference room one. When the chief answered, Malone told him to call the number back on a secure line.

"What's going on, Frank?"

"I'll explain when you call me back."

Malone waited in the conference room until the chief called him back. He shared the information he had received from his unnamed source.

The chief was incredulous. "This sounds like it was ripped right out of a damn spy novel."

"Unfortunately, it's not fiction, Chief. When you peel away the layers of the onion, we are left with allowing two serial killers to get away with murder in order to conceal sexual misconduct in Washington. It's appalling to think that these two reprobates have all the leverage over our federal government."

"I don't want the same thing to happen to us here in Midtown," said the police chief. "If we let them walk, then we will have something to hide too. We can't let that happen here. I'll set up a meeting with the mayor tomorrow. We need to convince him to see it our way. I don't know which way he'll ultimately go, but I know he will wobble his way there for sure. It's crucial that you move fast, Frank. We need an arrest as soon as possible. If you don't have enough evidence to get an arrest warrant now, find a way to get it. Pull out all the stops. Kick down some doors if you have to. I'll run cover for you on my end."

"Okay, Chief," Malone said to confirm his understanding. "Remember; don't communicate with me on your cellphone, your office phone, or your computer."

"I understand, Frank."

Later that day, Malone and Dolan relieved Henry Gonzalez and Robyn Butler to finish out their stakeout shift at the Rousseaus' residence. Bobby Rousseau remained inside while Annette was still at the dance studio. Trace and Kinsey had her covered.

"Eddie, we need to somehow jump-start our investigation. The Rousseaus know we're watching them. It's unlikely they'll try anything now. The answers are probably inside that house. We need a search warrant, but we don't have the evidence right now for a judge to give us one."

"What do you think we'll find in the house?"

"Videos perhaps, possibly something belonging to Kerry, restraining paraphernalia, DNA evidence, finger-prints, etcetera."

"Do you actually think all that could still be in the house?"

"I do—they think they're untouchable. In their minds, there's no reason for them to destroy evidence or discard anything that is important to them. I'm sure they think the Feds can keep us from getting a search warrant. Right now, I want them thinking that way."

Dolan kept his eyes on the rearview mirror while Malone spoke. He thought he saw something peculiar. He looked in the driver side mirror for a better view of what was going on behind them.

"Frank, there are two guys sitting in a dark-colored SUV behind us."

Malone looked in the passenger side-view mirror. "I see them."

"I think it's Hogan and Morris. I wonder what they are up to?"

"I'm not sure, but let's put a stop to it."

Dolan put the Explorer in drive. The headlights on

the SUV flicked on when they drove away. Malone kept his eyes on the passenger side-view mirror as the SUV followed them.

Dolan intermittently watched the road and the SUV in his rearview mirror.

"What the hell do they think they are going to gain by following us, Frank?"

"I have no idea. Maybe they just want to annoy the hell out of us because that's exactly what they're doing. Virtually none of this is making any sense."

Dolan drove through a green light at an approaching intersection. The SUV had to stop when the traffic light turned red.

"They caught the light, Frank."

Malone pointed ahead of him. "Make a quick right into this alley, Eddie,"

Dolan turned into the alley and shut the headlights off. Moments later, the SUV drove by. Dolan backed out of the alley, turned his headlights back on, and followed the SUV.

"Get right up behind them, Eddie. Let them know we're here."

Dolan drove within a couple car lengths of the SUV and turned his high beam lights on.

Morris looked in his rearview mirror. "They're behind us."

Hogan looked in his side-view mirror. "What the hell does Malone think he is doing? Pull over at the entrance to that abandoned drive-in theater up ahead on the right. If Malone wants trouble, that's exactly what he is going to get. I've had it with this guy."

Morris pulled over, and Dolan followed suit. Hogan jumped out of the SUV and marched quickly toward the Explorer. Malone and Dolan jumped out of their vehicle. Hogan approached them with obvious malicious intent. Already incensed because the two "agents" had made it a point to approach Sarah, Malone picked up his pace toward Hogan. Hogan quickly determined that Malone welcomed a physical confrontation. He was more than willing to accommodate him.

Hogan made another quick determination. This had already gone too far. Nothing was going to turn down the temperature between the two men. Both knew a physical confrontation was inevitable. Hogan decided he would get the jump on Malone. As he approached him, he quickly drew back his right hand and threw a punch at Malone.

Malone adeptly blocked it and converted it into an arm bar. Malone had Hogan's arm pinned between his left bicep and chest. He grabbed Hogan's right wrist with his right hand, quickly drew back his left arm and cracked Hogan in the face with his left elbow. Blood immediately splattered everywhere. Hogan dropped to his knees in a daze. Morris moved to aid Hogan.

Dolan stood in front of him and pressed a straight arm with an open palm into his chest. "Don't try it," he commanded.

Morris backed down.

Hogan was on his knees, his back straight. Malone could see, although he was vertical, he was virtually unconscious. Malone gently pushed him, and he fell backward.

Morris called out, "You're done, Malone! You just assaulted an FBI agent. It's all over for you."

Malone advanced on Morris. "The dashboard camera on our vehicle captured this entire ridiculous episode, Morris. He threw the first punch. He wanted a fight, and that's exactly what he got." Malone pulled out his cellphone from his coat pocket. He grabbed Morris by his tie knot and snapped a picture of him.

"We'll see if you two really are FBI agents, Morris."

Malone moved back to the dazed Hogan, grabbed a handful of his hair, pulled his head up, and snapped a picture of him too. Morris watched Malone with disdain. Malone let go of Hogan's hair, and Hogan's head dropped back down onto the ground.

Malone strode back over to Morris. "What's the crime for impersonating an FBI agent, Morris? I have a good idea about who you are and who sent you here. And we know everything about the Rousseaus."

"You don't know squat, Malone!"

"I know this, if you ever contact anyone close to Eddie or me again, the Rousseaus won't have to release the sordid details of your Washington sex scandal, I'll do it! I will make sure everyone knows that the FBI hired you to run interference for two serial killers. We have the documents to back it up. Tell whoever sent you here to back off. They picked a fight with the wrong cop."

"The public will never side with you, Malone, once we get done with your reputation," Morris yelled angrily.

"We'll see which version sells the best. Yours is about two cops. One who cheats on his wife and the other who coerces sex from female family members of murder victims? All of those supposed victims will readily line up to dispute your claims. Our version is about two cops trying to arrest a couple of serial killers. By the way, those killers have the entire federal government mobilized to conceal their crimes. Why are they doing this? Because they want to hide a Washington, D.C. sex scandal and protect a human-trafficking ring on the Texas border. Whose version sounds better, Morris?"

"You don't know they are serial killers. If you did, you would have arrested them already."

"Rest assured, Morris, I will, and you can tell that to whoever sent you here. You see things have changed. We know everything. Ultimately, that means the Rousseaus have a trump card, we have a trump card, and the federal government has a big fat nothing." Malone smirked at Morris. "Come on, Eddie; let's get out of here before I do something I really regret." Malone turned and then paused for a moment. "You better call fire/rescue, Morris. Your friend might have a concussion."

Malone and Dolan turned and walked briskly back to the Explorer.

Dolan put his vehicle in drive and stepped on the accelerator. As he drove off, he started shaking his head and laughing. "I've got to give it to you, Frank. You sure know how to shake things up."

Eddie dropped Malone off in the 9th Precinct parking lot and headed home. Malone got in his vehicle and paused to contemplate the entire situation. *You'd think everyone in law enforcement would be on the same page when it comes to stopping two serial killers.* Malone had seen a lot of disgusting things in his thirty-plus-year career, but this situation was right at the top. He was sickened by the behavior of officials at the highest level of government. The whole thing was wearing on him. He wasn't naive; he knew the federal government engaged in unseemly activity from time to time.

However, mobilizing their awesome power to personally destroy the lives of two innocent detectives was shameful at best. In doing so, they were indirectly supporting a human-trafficking ring on the Texas border and protecting two serial killers.

Malone's cellphone rang. It was Dan Kaufman, his lawyer friend in Naples, Florida. Malone had become friends with Kaufman when he previously served as a prosecuting attorney in Midtown. They had worked together on a number of cases that resulted in the convictions of some really bad characters.

"Hi, Danny. What's going on?"

"I trust you are well, Frank," Danny said warmly. "My firm still has that private investigator's position available. The position needs to be filled in the next few weeks. I have told everyone here about you. They're very anxious to meet you and bring you on board. Are you still interested?"

"I'm still thinking it over, Danny. It's going to require a major step on my part."

"I know, I know. You still have some time to make your decision, buddy. This is an easy gig for someone like you. It's mostly tracking down witnesses, vetting new hires, doing background checks, and stuff like that. The best thing, Frank—it's warm here. You can throw away your long underwear."

"I appreciate you giving me the opportunity. It's a very kind gesture. I'm still trying to visualize myself not being a Midtown homicide detective."

"I know it seems like a big move, Frank, but once you make it, you'll wonder why you ever hesitated. The best career move I have ever made was getting out of Midtown. You'll enjoy working with everyone at the firm. Most times, you'll be working about thirty hours a week. You'll have a lot more time to concentrate on your health—and your love life."

"Let me give it some more thought, Danny. I'll get back to you in the next few days."

"Okay, Frank, I look forward to hearing from you."

Malone hung up. Naples could be just the right move for him and Sarah. He reached in his coat pocket for the box that contained Sarah's engagement ring. He had an overwhelming urge to give it to her right away. He knew today was her day off. Now was the perfect time to present her with the ring.

He wanted to tell Sarah immediately what he was considering. He knew, based on their previous conversations, she was open to moving to Naples. Besides, he wanted to talk to someone about anything other than all the wretched details going on in his world. He longed to touch her and be touched. He ached for her comforting way. He wanted to kiss her full lips and hold her close. Sarah was the only person who could make all the ugliness in his world go away . . . at least temporarily. Tonight was the night. He initially wanted to make a big fuss and give her the ring on Christmas, to make it a memorable moment, but he couldn't resist the urge to do it now. He wanted to see her reaction. He wanted to make her happy.

The rain was turning into a horizontal snow flurry. He drove carefully on the slick streets of Midtown to Sarah's apartment building. Only a few people in Midtown had ventured out on such a dismal night.

Once he closed the Hamilton case, he would retire. He would take Sarah to Naples, Florida, where a far less stressful job awaited. They would get a place together. The weather would be much more inviting. He envisioned Sarah wearing a bikini, with glistening tanned skin. He saw the two of them drinking margaritas on a white sandy beach under a canopy composed of palm fronds. He imagined a tropical red flower tucked behind her ear.

He took the elevator to the fifth floor. His heart raced in anticipation. Despite his age, he felt like a high school kid in love for the first time. Actually, he likely was in love for the first time.

He knocked on Sarah's apartment door. She opened it. Her beautiful gray eyes were teary. Her face was contorted with anguish.

"What's the matter, Sarah?"

The tears started flowing freely. He stepped in the doorway and hugged her. Her arms remained limp. He looked over her shoulder. A portly man in a brown coat was sitting in a chair in her living room. He watched the two lovers with a strange expression on his face.

Malone gently pushed Sarah to arm's length, holding her by the shoulders. "Who is that guy, Sarah?"

The portly man stood.

Sarah's tears continued flowing. "His name is Les Matheson. He's a private detective."

Sarah had several eight-and-a-half-by-eleven-inch sheets of paper in her right hand. Malone gently grabbed her right wrist and raised it. They were pictures. He gently took them from her and examined them. They were of someone who looked like Malone and a woman, both nude and engaging in a variety of sex acts. They looked like they had been taken through an open window. The likeness to Malone was uncanny.

Malone was initially mesmerized by the pictures. He saw himself participating in something he had never partaken in. Finally, his mind began to process the images. He knew organizations like the FBI and CIA had access to unlimited resources, technology, and sabotage networks. He knew the federal government was very adept at destroying political regimes and adversaries overseas. He looked back at Sarah. He saw a look that he had never seen before on her face, a look of excruciating pain. She was beginning to emotionally unravel.

"Sarah, listen to me. Those pictures are not real. Please believe me, this is some kind of artificial intelligence deception," he quietly said. "Trust me, I am telling you the truth. They are trying to destroy me; they are trying to destroy us."

Malone could see he wasn't convincing Sarah. He left her and approached the portly private investigator.

Matheson raised his hands in a motion of surrender. "Now, now, control yourself, Detective. Don't do anything you'll regret," he said with a distinct European accent.

"Tell her it's all bullshit, or you won't believe what happens next!"

"The pictures speak for themselves, Detective," he said defiantly.

Malone dropped the pictures and snatched the lapels on Matheson's coat with both hands. "Tell her it's fake, it's all fake, or I swear I am going to beat the hell out of you right here where you stand."

Sarah called out from behind Malone. "Don't hurt him, Frank! I know they're not real," Sarah said, attempting to quell the situation.

Malone looked back at her. He was uncertain whether Sarah was being honest. Nevertheless, he attempted to compose himself. He dragged Matheson over to the apartment door and slammed him against it. "Who put you up to this? I want a name, dammit!"

"My client is the husband of the woman in those pictures. I can't divulge his identity; it would be unethical. He hired me to follow you. I took the pictures two nights ago."

Malone shook Matheson. "You lying son of a bitch! Don't give me your 'unethical' crap! Give me a name!"

Silence ensued. Malone reared back with his right hand.

Sarah grabbed his clenched fist. "Don't, Frank, you'll ruin your career. You've already destroyed our relationship. You'll lose everything else. You will be arrested by officers from your own department!"

Malone paused; he looked back at Sarah and let Matheson go. "No one is going to arrest me. This guy is some kind of federal government agent, operative, or contractor. The Feds are trying real hard to scare Eddie and me off the Kerry Hamilton case. They may not know it yet, but I can blow the lid off this whole charade. They are going to find out real soon that they only have two options left—either back off their personal destruction campaign or kill me."

Sarah's gray eyes opened wide. "But the pictures, Frank?"

"They're not real, Sarah, you have to believe me. They're trying to intimidate me. They want to demonstrate that they can destroy everything I have. I'll prove it to you." He looked at Matheson. "Why are you here?"

"I told you the woman in the picture is my client's wife."

"But that doesn't explain why you would come here to show the pictures to Sarah. What does that accomplish—aside from destroying my life? What is your so-called client's motivation . . . revenge?"

"No, my client wants to salvage his marriage. He and I thought Sarah might be able to persuade you to end your relationship with my client's wife."

Malone seethed. "That doesn't explain how you learned about Sarah or our relationship for that matter. How did you learn about Sarah, Mr. Matheson?"

"My job is to find things out, Mr. Malone."

Malone turned to Sarah. "It's all a lie, Sarah. The federal government knows about our relationship because they have been illegally tapping my cellphone."

"Why in the world would the federal government want to do such a thing, Frank?" she asked, unconvinced. "None of this makes any sense."

"Leverage, Sarah, that's why. They want to use it to

run me off the Kerry Hamilton case." Malone could see the disbelief in Sarah's expression. After all, there was "Malone" in all his naked glory with a naked woman. Persuading her otherwise seemed like an exercise in futility.

Malone opened Sarah's apartment door. He looked over at Matheson. "Get the hell out of here you son of a bitch," he said softly.

Matheson quickly complied. Malone closed the door after him and turned to Sarah. She turned away and cupped her face in her hands. She began sobbing uncontrollably. Malone gathered himself. "Sarah, don't let them take away the one thing I want more than anything else. If you let them, they'll win. Those pictures are not real, I promise you."

She turned toward him. "Frank, you should have just been honest with me. We're not married. I don't own you. You can do whatever you want. I should have known that a fifty-two-year-old man who has never been married before might have a problem with commitment."

"I don't have a commitment problem at all," he said, exasperated. "I'm all in on us. The pictures are a fake, Sarah. Besides, you're a forty-year-old woman who has never been married before either. I have never had those 'commitment' thoughts about you." Malone paused a moment; that was the exact wrong thing to say. He tried again to demonstrate that the pictures were a fake. "Do you see what they're doing, Sarah? They have us discussing something I never thought we would ever have to think about."

Sarah examined his chiseled face. She always thought the deep lines were an indicator of wisdom, conveying a compassionate worldliness. "Frank, I think you should go. I need some time alone to sort through all this."

"Sarah, please don't push me away," Malone pleaded. If you push me away, those bastards are going to win."

"You pushed me away, Frank. I love you with all my heart, but how can I ever get those images out of my mind?"

It was all sinking in. Sarah was right. It was unreasonable to think that any sensible person could look at those pictures and conclude otherwise. Malone was in a hole he couldn't dig himself out of. There was no way to erase those images from Sarah's mind . . . ever.

"Okay, Sarah, I'll leave you alone to sort through this. I understand why you don't believe me. Those pictures look real to me too. They would convince anyone. The only reason I know they're not real is because I know that's not me, but how could you possibly know? Just realize one thing. I would never cheat on you. And it's not because that is what is expected in a relationship. It's not because monogamy is some accepted social norm. I wouldn't do it because I love you and I have no desire to be with anyone else. You're the only one for me, Sarah."

The once passionate lovers stared at each other. The passion that had existed between them was replaced by incalculable pain and perceived broken trust. A new wave of tears flowed from Sarah's eyes.

Malone turned, walked to the door, and opened it. He looked back at her. A single tear rolled down his hardened face. "I love you, Sarah." He meekly turned and left.

Sarah collapsed on her sofa. Mozart, her cat, attempted to comfort her, but she was inconsolable.

Malone climbed into his Explorer. In the blink of an eye, all that was good in his life had been wiped away. There was nothing he could ever do to erase those horrible images from Sarah's mind. It was one thing to become aware of infidelity; it was entirely different matter to actually see it . . . even if it wasn't real. In a sense the saboteurs had won. They had successfully destroyed Malone's relationship with Sarah. However, he wasn't going to let them run him off the Kerry Hamilton case. The price of justice would be expensive, but Malone was determined to pay it.

When Malone got home, he took a bottle of Irish whiskey from his kitchen cabinet. He unscrewed the cap and drank directly from the bottle. He retrieved the box from his coat pocket with Sarah's ring in it. He opened it. It was all for naught. There was no turning back. There was nothing he could do to make it all go away. He couldn't apologize his way out of it, even though he had done nothing wrong. Sarah would never trust him again. He wasn't angry at her. How could he be? He understood her feelings. She had been thoroughly deceived. Everything he had ever wanted was now out of reach.

Malone continued to drink. He thought about the Rousseaus' brazen extortion scheme against the U.S. government and the resultant trail of carnage that ensued. At least three teenage girls had been murdered. A number of political figures were being blackmailed, a widely successful human-trafficking ring was still operating on the Texas border, and Malone's relationship with Sarah was in shambles. Only the Rousseaus remained unscathed. That had to change, and Malone was hell-bent on doing it.

A text alert sounded from Malone's cellphone. It was from the police chief. Malone was expected to attend a 10:00 a.m. meeting the next morning in the mayor's office. He immediately texted Dolan to advise him of his meeting. Dolan would have to relieve Tommy and Matt alone the next morning on the Rousseau stakeout.

CHAPTER 18

The first really bitter-cold day of the winter season greeted Malone as he ascended the steps to City Hall. Once inside, he took the elevator to the ninth floor. He waited a few minutes before the mayor's professional receptionist informed him that the mayor was ready to see him. The police chief was already sitting in one of the two chairs in front of the mayor's desk. He stood and greeted Malone. They both sat down.

The mayor exhibited his familiar disagreeable disposition. "Good morning, Lieutenant Malone."

"Good morning, Mayor."

"I'll get right to the point. I received a call from the attorney general's office yesterday. His office informed me that you are not cooperating with them. He said you handed over an investigation file that was ridiculously void of information. Is that true, Lieutenant?"

"Mayor, the Rousseaus are serial killers. They are linked to at least two other murders in addition to Kerry Hamilton. They are heavily involved in a human-trafficking ring on the Texas border. These are two dangerous, reprehensible people."

"Lieutenant, forgive me for being so blunt. Right now, I don't give a shit about that. I can't run Midtown without federal grant dollars. That's the bottom line. The Feds are going to move the Rousseaus out of Midtown before the end of the month. Then they will be someone else's problem."

"Mayor, the Rousseaus feel empowered because they have leverage over several members of Congress and presidential cabinet members."

"Didn't you hear me, Malone? I don't give a damn about that. The voters elected me to run Midtown. I can't do it without federal grant money. It's as simple as that. The Rousseau problem in Midtown will be resolved by the end of the month. You need to stand down."

"That's what I am concerned about, Mayor. They will become someone else's problem. The Rousseaus will open another dance studio. Somewhere, some innocent teenager has an interest in ballet dancing. Ultimately, she will be lured to her demise by Annette Rousseau."

"You don't know that, Malone!" the mayor said while raising his voice.

"Mayor, these people are killers," Malone said while maintaining his composure. "They have a compulsion you and I can't understand."

"Let me interject something here," said the police chief. "Malone has a point, Mayor. We are law enforcement officers. We can't knowingly let these serial killers leave Midtown to kill somewhere else. At some point somebody has to inject a little sense of honor into this awful mess. I don't want the blood from a high school girl three states over on my hands. I can't live with that."

"JD, I didn't say this is an easy decision. Quite frankly, it makes me sick to my stomach to do it, but somebody has to. Without federal dollars, our police and fire departments will be gutted, many of our parks and recreation programs will go away, and the resources in our public works department will dry up. The quality of life in Midtown will sink through the floor. The reality is we just have no choice. And I haven't even mentioned the personal havoc they can wreak on all of us."

"I am well aware of their personal destruction capabilities, Mayor," Malone said. "They have already started them. They are trying to wreck my partner's marriage, and they have destroyed a personal relationship in my life that was very important to me."

"I'm sorry about your love life, Malone, but I have nine hundred thousand residents in Midtown that I am concerned about. I was elected to represent them."

"Mayor, perhaps there's a win-win solution that can get the Rousseaus off the street and, at the same time, not have a negative impact on our federal funding," said the police chief.

"Forget it, JD. We are past that point. I have already promised the attorney general's office our cooperation."

Malone tried one last approach. "Mayor, I hold the biggest trump card in all of this. I can practically change the political landscape in Washington with what I know. We have leverage. Let me speak to the people you are talking to."

"Forget it, Malone. I have already given the attorney general's office my word. In less than a few weeks we can put this whole sordid mess behind us."

"But how do we live with it, Mayor?" Malone asked. He got up from his chair, nodded at the police chief, and left the mayor's office.

The mayor looked sternly at the police chief. "Malone is a loose cannon, JD. Keep him in check."

"I know when I have a winning hand, Mayor. Malone has enough information to blow the lid off this whole thing. He essentially holds all the cards. You need to respect that. You and I are not vulnerable, yet. However, we will be if we let the Rousseaus out of Midtown. The federal government has made a lot of mistakes. The worst mistake they made is pissing off the wrong cop. I am advising you not to get in bed with the Feds on this, Mayor. It won't end well."

"If you can't keep Malone in check, JD, you'll have to fire him."

"I can't fire an employee without just cause. You signed a contract with the police union ensuring that would never happen."

"Then find 'just cause' somewhere, JD. I can't let a police lieutenant dictate public policy in Midtown."

"Think about what you're doing, Mayor. You are asking me to fire a thirty-year veteran employee without any justification, who is trying his best to arrest a pair of serial killers. Those maniacs killed the daughter of a Midtown taxpayer, for heaven's sake. What can go wrong if we protect serial killers?" the chief asked rhetorically. "I'll tell you what can go wrong, Mayor . . . everything. We'll open ourselves up to one hell of a lawsuit. Can you imagine when the public finds out that we knowingly let two serial killers leave Midtown? We'll both be run out of public service, forever. I don't want that on my tombstone."

The police chief paused momentarily and then began again with a more measured tone. "Mayor, we are still in a good position on this. What can the Feds do after we make an arrest? They sure as hell won't want the public to know what they have been up to in this case. They'll just have to sit it out. They'll have no choice."

"That might be true, JD. They probably will sit it

out for now. But then every administrator and bureaucrat in Washington will climb all over our ass for the next thousand years. They'll ram every regulation they can think of down our throats. They will be on a never-ending mission to punish us and, by extension, the good people of Midtown. It won't happen overtly, but they'll find every excuse in the world to withhold grant money from our city for the rest of time. The IRS will scour through our personal taxes every year with a fine-tooth comb. They'll never forget what we did. They'll drag us into court every chance they get. They'll find a million ways to hurt us. They could even indirectly de-bank us.

"Do you know what that means, JD? It means we won't be able to get loans to fund capital projects. We won't be able to put our money in bonds or other investment vehicles or transfer money from one financial institution to another. Hell, we won't even be able to do payroll. How can I run a city if we don't have a way to compensate our employees? It's not like they've never done this kind of stuff before. That's the way they do business, JD. Let's face it; the Feds got us by the short hairs. I can't let a rank-and-file cop call the shots on this. That's flat-out irresponsible. I was elected by the people. I should be the person who makes the final decision on this, JD, not Malone."

After his meeting with the mayor, Malone headed over to join Dolan on the Rousseau stakeout. As he was driving, his cellphone rang. It was the police chief.

"Hi, Chief, before you say anything, remember my phone has been tapped."

The chief hesitated for a moment. "Understood, Frank. I'm calling you in regard to your recommendation to transfer Detective Dolan out of Homicide to the Robbery Division. Go ahead and proceed with the transfer as we previously discussed."

Malone hesitated.

"Do you understand me, Frank? Go ahead and process Dolan's transfer paperwork, like we discussed."

"Yes, Chief, I will put it together and submit it to your office by the end of the week."

"Make sure you keep his transfer quiet, until I have had a chance to process everything. Do we understand each other, Frank?"

"Yes, Chief, I understand."

The police chief had just given Malone a cryptic message to go ahead with the Kerry Hamilton murder investigation regardless of the political ramifications. Malone pulled up behind Dolan's Explorer. The temperature outside had dipped into the low twenties. Malone tapped on Dolan's passenger side window. Dolan unlocked the door, and Malone entered.

"How did your meeting go?"

"I couldn't convince the mayor to keep us on the Kerry Hamilton case. However, the police chief just gave me the green light to continue on . . . at least for now. What's Bobby Rousseau been up to?"

"Everything has been quiet here. Annette left the house about 8:30 a.m., presumably for the dance studio. I checked with Kinsey and Trace. They confirmed she arrived there at 9:00. Bobby got the mail around noon, and that's been about it."

An hour later, there was still nothing stirring at the Rousseau house. Malone had been unusually quiet.

"Frank, is something bothering you?"

"It's this confounding case and all its potential implications. The mayor is not completely off the rails on this. The Feds have his ass in a vise. His position makes sense. I'm not sure what the Feds will do if we keep moving toward making an arrest. They are going to great lengths to protect the Rousseaus. The Feds are way out on a limb. They're not going to like being embarrassed. Voters will be incensed if they hear what their federal government has been up to. It's hard to predict what they may do or the retribution they may consider."

"That's their problem, Frank. I sure as hell don't care what happens to them after what they have done to us."

"They'll certainly try to make it our problem," Malone countered.

Another fifteen minutes of silence ensued until Dolan broke it.

"It's hard to believe the Feds are doing this, Frank. Doreen is barely speaking to me. That woman who called really did a number on her. I don't think I will ever be able to convince her one hundred percent that none of what that woman said is true."

"I'm in a similar boat. Some guy made a visit to Sarah's place last night. He said he was a private investigator. He showed her some kind of artificial intelligence–generated nude pictures of me with another woman."

Dolan was aghast. "You've got to be kidding me!"

"Sarah is convinced that what she saw is real. How could she not be? They looked real to me too. There appears to be no going back. Our relationship is most likely over. She'll never be able to get those images out of her head. It will always remain something between us."

"Jack Mizell was right, Frank. They are playing for keeps."

"Yeah, well I'm going to make them pay for it," Malone replied.

Malone reached into his coat pocket and retrieved

the box that contained Sarah's engagement ring. He opened it and showed it to Dolan. "To make matters worse, when I went over to Sarah's apartment last night, my plan was to give her this."

Dolan examined the ring and then Malone's face. Malone's pain was visible. All Dolan could do was shake his head.

Malone struggled to crack a smile. He reached inside his coat pocket and pulled out two cigars. "I even bought us some high-rent cigars to celebrate the occasion." Malone returned them to his inside coat pocket.

"This is absolutely nuts, Frank. This thing has gotten way out of control. Sarah is perfect for you. You two are great together. We can't let them get away with this."

"All we can do now is our job. Sometimes doing what is right can be painful as hell."

Just then Annette Rousseau pulled her Land Rover into her garage. Malone and Dolan watched her actions closely, but the garage door lowered moments later, and they lost sight of her.

Annette went inside and saw Bobby peering through the shutters of their bedroom window. He looked at his wife as she entered the room.

"They're still watching us," she stated.

"Yeah, I know. It's no big deal. They can't touch us. I called our lawyer. We're going to turn the heat up on the Feds."

"They were very intimidating when they came by the dance studio. They seem especially determined. I am worried; that Malone scares me."

Bobby tried to calm his wife's fears. "They are trying to unnerve you. Let's show them we couldn't care less."

As night fell, the temperature outside dropped. Dolan poured a cup of hot coffee from his thermos and handed it to Malone. Then he poured a cup for himself. They saw Annette Rousseau open the shutters in her bedroom. She was completely nude. Her husband joined her. He was also nude. They fondled each other roughly and then their behavior grew more explicit. They faced the window, clearly letting the detectives know they were in full view.

Dolan looked over at Malone. "These two are sick, Frank."

"I know. I shudder to think about Kerry Hamilton spending her final moments with them. We have to get inside that house, Eddie. We need a search warrant in the worst way."

Later, after their sexual escapade, the garage door opened again. The Rousseaus got in Annette's Land Rover. Bobby took the driver's seat. He backed the vehicle out of the garage and headed in an easterly direction. Malone and Dolan followed. Bobby drove to Midtown's finest steak and seafood restaurant. He gave the Land Rover's keys to a valet parking attendant, and the couple went inside.

The detectives watched the Rousseaus enter the restaurant. While sitting in the Explorer, they discussed the merits of obtaining a search warrant with the evidence they currently had.

Malone stared ahead, contemplating the situation. He looked at Dolan. "Let's go inside and shake things up."

They buttoned their heavy trench coats, crossed the parking lot, and entered the restaurant. Dolan approached the maître de, who was wearing a black suit, white shirt, and black tie. He showed him his identification. A piano player was playing soft dinner music in the background.

"We are not here for dinner. We just want to have a conversation with two of your customers," Dolan informed the maître de.

Malone spotted the Rousseaus. He walked toward them; Dolan followed him. There was an open table next to the couple. It was covered with a white table-cloth, and a candle was burning inside a glass globe. The detectives sat down. Bobby Rousseau had a curious look on his face. Annette's face indicated concern, bordering on fear.

"Hello, Bobby. What's for dinner? We haven't been formally introduced yet. I'm Frank Malone, and this is my partner, Eddie Dolan. We're Midtown Police Department homicide detectives. We're looking into the rape and murder of a local high school girl named Kerry Hamilton."

Bobby was indignant. "So, what does that have to do with us?"

"It has an awful lot to do with you. You two raped and killed her," Malone responded.

Bobby dismissed Malone's accusation. "You're crazy, Malone. You have nothing. You would make an arrest if you had evidence to prove that."

The waitress delivered two appetizers to the Rousseau table—grilled calamari for Bobby and broiled scallops for Annette. Malone unraveled a linen napkin on his table and retrieved a fork that was inside. He reached over, plucked a scallop from Annette's plate, and ate it. "You made an excellent choice, Annette. You're really going to enjoy that."

Annette conveyed a look of disdain and fear.

"I'm sorry, Annette. How rude of me. I didn't consider the appetite you likely worked up after that little sex show you put on for us back at your house," Malone said derisively. "You must be starving."

Bobby Rousseau remained calm. A waitress approached the table. She attempted to hand Malone and Dolan menus, and asked them what they'd wanted to drink.

"We won't be dining or drinking tonight," Dolan said. "We are here to briefly visit with our friends."

The waitress eyed the two tables, her gaze skeptical. She sensed the Rousseaus were uncomfortable with the situation. After a brief moment of silence, she turned and walked away.

"Why are you here disturbing our dinner, Malone?" Bobby asked.

"I just wanted you to know that I don't care if you have the federal government by the balls. We are not going to back off . . . ever. I could care less who your little wife has humped in Washington. The Feds have made a lot of bad decisions involving you two monsters, but the biggest one they made was dumping your ass here, in Midtown."

"I don't know what you're talking about, Malone," Bobby said unconvincingly. "And I don't like the way you're talking about my wife in such disparaging terms."

"Bobby, the English language doesn't have the words available for me to accurately express the contempt I have for your wife."

"You know, Malone, I'm starting to take offense at your crude behavior. That's why I'm blowing this town. Local cops like you, with your toy guns and elementary school badges are beginning to annoy me."

"You're not going anywhere, Bobby. I'm going to permanently nail your ass to a wall in our luxurious state prison."

Malone looked at Annette Rousseau. "That goes for you too, sweetie. You won't be able to hump your way out of this when I get done with you."

Malone stood up, and Dolan followed his lead. The detectives towered over the Rousseaus. Patrons and staff watched them leave. Everyone in the restaurant knew that the conversation between the parties had not been a cordial one.

Once outside, Dolan could barely contain himself. He slapped Malone on the back. "You sure have a way with words, Frank. How do you come up with this stuff?" he asked approvingly.

"Actually, I'm just making it up as I go, Eddie."

CHAPTER 19

The next morning, Associate Attorney General Howard D. Waltrip entered into a conference phone call with Bobby Rousseau and his lawyer, William Pollack. Associate Executive Assistant FBI Director Trevor Masters was also on the call.

Pollack started the conversation.

"Howard, my client and his wife were out having dinner last night in a very nice restaurant. While they were dining, they had a very disturbing confrontation in the restaurant with two Midtown Police Department detectives. I thought your department was addressing our situation with local authorities. What occurred last night was not only unfortunate but also unacceptable. My clients were embarrassed by the actions of these two Neanderthals."

"I can assure you, Bill, we have been addressing your client's situation with the Midtown mayor," Waltrip replied. "However, there is a police lieutenant in Midtown who has been very uncooperative. This is a particularly delicate situation. We have to tread lightly. We don't want any of this to get before the eyes of the public. I'm asking you and Mr. Rousseau to exercise some patience while we deal with this matter. We are making arrangements to relocate your clients and change their identities again, but it takes time. There are real estate documents, bank accounts, Social Security numbers, passports, driver's licenses, and a whole host of other documents that have to be addressed. We can't get it all done overnight. We should be able to move your clients out of Midtown in the next seven to ten days."

"That may be too long, Howard," Pollack replied. This Lieutenant Malone is becoming a real pain in the ass. He's making all kinds of inappropriate threats."

"Yeah, and I don't like the way he speaks to my wife," Rousseau added.

"We are aware of Lieutenant Malone and Detective Dolan. We have had operatives working diligently day and night to persuade them to back off. Unfortunately, they've proven to be very stubborn," Waltrip explained.

"Well, get it done, Howard. Whatever you're doing isn't working. Talk to the mayor again. There has to be some way to convince Malone and Dolan to see it our way. My clients are upset. They have had about enough of these two."

"Like I said, we have addressed the situation with the mayor," Waltrip attempted to explain again. "However, please understand he is in a very precarious position. We are essentially asking him to break the law. He has to move cautiously on this. The police chief and this Lieutenant Malone have dug their heels in. They are very recalcitrant. Everyone is concerned about their exposure on this . . . and rightfully so."

"Don't give me that crap, Howard," Pollack countered. "And I especially, don't give a damn about their exposure. The federal government has the ability to convince anyone to see it their way. All they have to do is focus their collective minds on getting it done."

"Listen to me, Bill. The behavior of your clients has put the Justice Department in a very untenable position. Their last indiscretion was completely unacceptable, to say the least. We went to great lengths and a great deal of expense to change their identities and set them up in Midtown. All they had to do was keep their noses clean. They brought this problem on themselves. Now all of us are vulnerable on this, except the two Midtown detectives. We're essentially asking everyone else to jump into a pile of shit with us, and they're understandably reluctant to do it."

Bobby Rousseau interrupted everyone. "Listen to me, Howard—I don't want any of your condescending bullshit. If you don't do something about Malone now, you'll be seeing your friends in my home movies on the evening news every night. In an instant, your party will lose its congressional majority and eventually the presidency if you don't get this Malone character off my back. Why is the FBI sitting on their collective asses? Those two cops have insulted me and my wife. Either you get Malone off my back or go buy some popcorn, because it's going to be showtime."

Trevor Masters responded, "We have done a hell of a lot to get Malone and Dolan off your back, short of having them assassinated on Main Street. Malone is proving to be a very difficult person to convince. Two nights ago, he kicked the shit out of one of our most reliable operatives. He did it because he doesn't appreciate how we have been treating him and his partner. We wouldn't have this problem if your clients could just resist their deviant impulses."

"Shut your pie hole, Masters, or I'll drop this whole thing right in your lap now!" Rousseau hollered.

"Alright everyone, please calm down," Waltrip urged. "None of what we are doing right now will convince Midtown law enforcement officials to stand down. Bill, we'll just have to keep massaging this thing until we can finish the process of relocating your clients. Please bear with us. Everyone needs to dial down the tone and exercise some patience. Meanwhile, Bobby and Annette need to behave themselves."

"We can exercise all the patience you want, Howard, but whatever you're doing on your end is having no effect on Malone and Dolan," Pollack countered.

"Let me see what I can do, Bill. In the meantime, bear with us," Waltrip urged.

"You need to pick up the pace. We are losing our patience. Goodbye, Howard."

Pollack abruptly hung up the phone.

"Trevor, are you still on the line?"

"Yes, go ahead, Howard."

"See what you can do to buy us more time in Midtown. Meanwhile, I need to take a shower and scrub the filth off me with a wire brush. Every time I speak to those two bottom feeders, I feel like I need a hot shower and a good dose of disinfectant. How did we ever let ourselves get in bed with these idiots?"

"I'm with you, Howard. I have no idea how we got here, but our current position stinks to high heavens," Masters acknowledged.

"This is what happens when you throw a bunch of influential stiff dicks and two degenerate porn star serial killers into a blender. We deserve everything we're getting," Masters admitted.

"The only two people doing the right thing in this

whole mess are Malone and Dolan, and we're trying our best to destroy their lives. How's that for irony? I'll speak to you later, Trevor."

Back at the 9th Precinct, Malone was sitting in his office drinking his morning cup of coffee. He had assigned Gonzalez and Butler to morning stakeout duty at the Rousseaus' residence. He was concerned that the Rousseaus might remove evidence from their home after the little dustup they had in the restaurant the previous night. He directed everyone on stakeout duty to keep a watchful eye out.

He had started going through the hard copies of news articles and social media excerpts Jack Mizell had provided when Dolan entered his office. Malone knew he needed to get a search warrant fast before the Feds relocated the Rousseaus.

"Good morning, Frank."

"I'm glad you're here, Eddie. I have an idea. I have been going through all the paperwork that Jack Mizell gave us. We know there is a connection between the two girls murdered in California and Tina Russell's dance studio. The girls lived in a town called Brantley. Brantley is about an hour outside Los Angeles. The girls' names were Catalina Valdez and Karen Stewart. Their houses are relatively close together. As much as I can tell, it looks like they went to the same high school. They might have even known each other. We need to talk to their parents and the Brantley detectives who worked the two murder cases. You call the Stewarts, and I'll call the Valdezes."

Malone handed Dolan duplicate copies of the documents he had.

"I'll set up an interview with the Valdezes at 9:00 a.m., the day after tomorrow. You put together a noon meeting with the Stewarts. Remember; don't use your cellphone or your desktop phone in case the lines are still being tapped. I'm going to use the phone in the conference room. We'll visit the Brantley Police Department after we meet with the parents of the two girls. I'll have Lucy reserve us plane tickets and make hotel reservations."

"I'll get on it, Frank."

After Dolan left, Malone went down to conference room one. He accessed the California Department of Transportation database from one of the computers. He quickly located the address and phone number of Carlos and Corina Valdez. He dialed the number. A female voice answered.

"May I please speak to Corina Valdez."

"This is Corina."

"Corina, my name is Lieutenant Frank Malone, from

the Midtown Police Department's Homicide Division. I'd like to speak to you and your husband about your daughter, Catalina."

A moment of silence ensued.

"You are a police detective?"

"Yes, I am."

"From where?"

"A place called Midtown."

"Have you arrested my daughter's killer?"

"No, ma'am, I haven't, but I am closing in on them."

"Them?"

"Yes, I think two people may have been involved in your daughter's murder. It is my opinion that the same two people raped and murdered a female high school student here in Midtown."

"What do you need from me, Lieutenant?"

"Please call me, Frank. I'd like to meet with you at your residence on Thursday morning, at 9:00 a.m. Does that work for you?"

"We'll make it work, Frank. It's been over three years since my daughter's murder. We still don't have any answers."

"Was the case investigated by the Brantley Police Department?"

"Yes, Detective Stephen Barrett was the primary investigator who originally worked my daughter's case.

We initially thought he was making great progress, but then suddenly, all the momentum seemed to drain out of the case. We called him regularly. Eventually, he told us he was at a point where he needed someone from the public to come forward with additional information to reenergize his investigation. Apparently, no one has come forward. My husband and I are very frustrated.

"Several months later, another girl my daughter's age was murdered. The circumstances appeared very similar. Detective Barrett worked both cases. We have met with that girl's parents. Essentially, they have had the same frustrating experience that we have had. Eventually, we were told the FBI was taking over the investigation."

"I want to speak to you about all that," Malone assured her. "I also want to show you pictures we have gleaned from a convenience store security video here in Midtown. I would like to see if you recognize the person in the video."

"This seems very promising, Frank. My curiosity meter is going crazy. Why can't you just email me the pictures? My husband and I will look at them and respond immediately. It would expedite things."

"I want to show them to you personally. If you recognize this person, I will need you to sign an affidavit attesting to that fact. I'm trying to gather enough evidence to acquire a search warrant here in Midtown. Your signature on the affidavit will be used as evidence in an effort to convince a judge to issue a search warrant. It works better when I go before the judge if I have personally presented the pictures to you and witness your signature on the affidavit."

"I will cooperate with you in any way I can, Frank. We have waited a long time for justice . . . way too long."

"I will see you at 9:00 a.m. on Thursday morning."

Malone hung up and went back to his office. He looked at his cellphone to see if Sarah had tried to contact him. She hadn't. Perhaps it was best. It would only confirm to those who had tapped his phone that their efforts to disrupt his life had been successful.

Eddie's presence interrupted Malone's thoughts. "I have confirmed a noon meeting with the Stewarts," he said. "Also, I just got a text message from my wife. That woman called again demanding we pay for her abortion. My wife is beside herself with anger. I knew being a cop could be hard on a marriage, but I never envisioned something like this. This last message could be the final blow to our marriage. This woman really has Doreen upset."

"I'll go to LA myself. You should stay back and tend to your family matters."

"No way, Frank. Besides me being at home right now will only make matters worse. Above and beyond all that,

I want to be in on the arrest of the Rousseaus more than ever." Dolan paused and then continued, "However, I think I will go home early so I can prepare for tomorrow. Maybe I can smooth things over with Doreen. Send me a text on the flight times, and I'll pick you up in the morning."

"Okay."

After Dolan left, Malone went over to Lucy's office and asked her to book two flights to Los Angeles and reserve a hotel room for the next day. Later, he decided to get a bite to eat. Once outside, he was confronted by plunging frigid temperatures. Old Man Winter was settling in for his long annual stay in Midtown. Malone's heavy coat rippled vigorously in the gusting wind. Thanksgiving was a week way. There wasn't much for Dolan and him to be thankful for this year. Their lives were being tossed into disarray over the federal government's efforts to protect the husband and wife serial killers.

Malone couldn't stop thinking about Sarah. The notion of losing her was agonizingly painful. The most frustrating part was that neither one of them wanted the relationship to end. Nevertheless, it was ending. Sure, they were having their difficulties, but it wasn't like they were insurmountable. Just a few days earlier, their biggest problem was not seeing enough of each other. Now, they were on a course to never see each other again. The thought was inconceivable. He had bought Sarah the ring because he wanted to begin a new chapter in his life, but that was all gone now.

Malone decided to dine at Tommy D's. As he drove the lifeless winter streets of Midtown, his thoughts returned to Sarah. Articles of trash whipped up into the frigid air. The homeless population had already retreated back into the dark crevices of Midtown to avoid the blustery, cold winds. Malone had driven these same streets for over thirty years. His mind always immersed in the facts of a case he was working on. Most of his adult life had been spent alone. Of course there had been other women along the way, but none of those relationships required a deep emotional commitment. He certainly never gave them one. But his relationship with Sarah changed all that. She never formally asked him for a commitment; it just happened. There was no specific line of demarcation that he could point to that said, "This is it. This is going to be the only woman I will ever want and the only woman I will ever need." It just effortlessly happened. That's what made their relationship so special.

Yes, they were going through a rough patch when all this started. They both had needs that weren't being met, but it was because of their conflicting schedules. It wasn't because their love had waned. *If you have to have problems, that's the best reason,* Malone concluded.

He thought of all the special moments they had shared. The trust they had between them was shattered in an instant without a single violation ever being committed. He couldn't believe he was heading back to the life he had prior to Sarah. It had been so easy to be alone back then, but now the thought of it seemed so daunting.

He pulled into a parking space at Tommy D's. The temperature outside had dipped even further since he had left the 9th Precinct. He opened the entrance door and was immediately welcomed by the boisterous voice of Tommy D.

"Yo, Frankie, welcome to my fine establishment!"

Rita came over to greet Malone. She took his heavy coat and hung it on a nearby rack. "Would you like to sit in Alex's section, Frank?"

"Of course," he said.

Rita led Malone over to a table in the far corner of the dining room. Rita leaned in and whispered in Malone's ear, "Alex is working out great, Frank. She's been nothing less than a complete joy to work with. Thank you for bringing her to us. We are very grateful."

"I'm so glad to hear that."

Rita handed Malone a menu, not that he needed it. He had all the entrées committed to memory. She patted Malone on the shoulder. "It's good to see you, Frank."

As Rita walked away, Alex, wearing a sheepish grin,

approached Malone. "So, what do you think of my work outfit, Frank?"

She twirled around. She wore a conservative white oxford shirt that was stretched to the limit across her ample bosom, but she couldn't help that. She had on blue jeans with no holes, and a white apron was wrapped around her thin waist. There were straws and an order pad sticking out one of the pockets.

"You look sensational as usual . . . and well rested I might add."

"I am happy here, Frank. Thank you for getting me this job. Tommy and Rita are wonderful people. I'm glad to be out of the stripping business. You saved me from myself, once again."

"I'm glad it's working out."

Alex sat down across from Malone. A look of concern was on her face. "Frank, you don't look so good. You look like something is weighing heavy on your mind."

"I always have something on my mind. It's the case I have been working on. It has been challenging."

"I've seen you in the middle of that Monster of Midtown investigation. That case had to be stressful too, but this is different. You don't look yourself. I have never seen you this way before. What's going on, Frank?"

"Nothing too much . . . what looks good tonight?"

"Come on, as you like to say, Frank, spill it!"

"It's a long story. I don't want to bore you with it."

"You're my only customer right now. It's dead in here tonight. I have nothing, but time. Let's have it, Malone, cough it up. What is going on?"

Malone hesitated and then gave in. "It's the Kerry Hamilton case."

"The one involving those stupid FBI agents who came in here with that made-up story about you?"

"Yeah, that's the one. They paid a visit to the Last Stop Saloon and spewed that crap to Sarah."

"For real, what did she think?"

"It was unsettling for her at first, but she got over it, and we got past it."

"That's good, so what's the problem?"

"Well, I went over to her place the other night, and this strange dude was there. I asked her what was going on. She tells me he's a private investigator hired by the husband of a woman he has naked pictures of."

"So, what does that have to do with you?"

"I was in the pictures too . . . naked."

"What? You with another woman! I don't believe it!"

"It wasn't real. It was some kind of artificial intelligence/computer-generated image, but it looked real. It was an image of me having sex with this other woman. It nearly knocked Sarah off her feet."

"I bet it did," Alex said, expressing concern.

"There were several pictures, and they all looked real as hell."

"And Sarah fell for it?"

"How could she not? They looked real to me too. I was almost convinced that it was me, even though I knew it wasn't. Anyway, there is nothing I can do about it now. I'll never be able to erase those images from her mind. Those pictures have driven a permanent wedge between us; even if she took me back, those images would always stay with her forever. Eventually, the subject would come up again. I guess it is better that it ends now than at some point in the future when we have invested a lot more time and energy."

Alex reached across the table and grabbed Malone's hand. She laid her other hand on top. "That is so terrible, Frank. I see your point. How do you convince someone to un-see something they have already seen? You're right; it's an impossible situation. You don't deserve this, Frank. I should have slugged those two FBI agents when I had the chance."

There was a pause in their conversation as the two friends gathered their thoughts. Alex stood up and dutifully pulled out her order pad. "Do you know what you want to eat, Frank?"

"I'll have chicken parmesan and a glass of chianti."

"Good choice, I'll be right back."

Alex was upset by Malone's predicament. She walked over to the serving window and handed the order through the window to the chef, Tommy D. She looked over at Malone in the corner of the dining room. He was scrolling through something on his phone. She thought about how he had saved her life when she was threatened by the Monster of Midtown. After her roommate was murdered, he had paid for her to stay in a hotel room where she would have security. Then he went out of his way to get her a job at Tommy D's, and he even took care of her "Miguel" problem. He called her regularly to check in on her and see how she was doing. He did all that because he honestly cared about her. Few others, if anyone, had ever cared for her like that.

There were plenty of times when Malone could have sought "compensation" for all his good deeds, but he never did. He did all those things because he was genuinely interested in her well-being. Nobody gave a damn about a down-on-her-luck stripper who had few, if any, prospects, but Frank Malone did. None of this was fair.

CHAPTER 20

Dolan picked up Malone the next morning, and they drove to Midtown's International Airport. Eddie parked his Explorer in the long-term parking lot. They took a shuttle to the departure level and went inside. The line to get through security was long and slow. Everyone shuffled along. The negative comments about air travel were familiar. Eventually, they were seated together in row seventeen of a 747 jet. A short time later, they were in the air and headed for Los Angeles by way of Dallas, Texas.

"How was Doreen when you got home last night?"

"Not good, this thing is really taking a toll on us. I'm not sure our marriage will survive it. Have you been able to resolve anything with Sarah?"

"No."

"Have you called her?"

"No, it all seems so pointless. Everything is up to her now. I don't see how she'll ever be able to get beyond those pictures. Making contact with her will only make the inevitable more painful. I have to let her go so she can find someone else. She deserves to be happy."

Dolan shook his head. "You deserve to be happy too, Frank. Your approach to love is too pragmatic. You're applying logic to love. There is nothing more illogical, more irrational, or more unreasonable than love. Relationships are complicated, Frank. There's no set of rules that you can follow. However, giving up shouldn't be an option. I doubt you'll ever find someone comparable to Sarah again."

Malone looked at Dolan curiously. "Who the hell are you . . . Dear Abby?"

"Who is that?"

"Some woman back in the day who thought she knew everything."

As they soared through the skies, Dolan explained an epiphany he had from the previous night. "I was thinking about our situations last night, Frank. One way or another, the phone calls, the visits from strangers, and the pictures are going to end once we make an arrest. Once the arrest process begins, the Justice Department will have no choice but to back off. Things will only get worse for them if they don't. I explained that to Doreen last night. It made sense to her. It seemed to give her a reason to pause. She agreed that it would be ironic if that occurred. Of course, my theory is contingent upon us making an arrest. You should run it by Sarah, Frank. It might get her to thinking. It could help."

"I'll think about it, Eddie, but first things first. If we're ever going to make an arrest, we need a search warrant for the Rousseaus' home first. Hopefully, our meetings in California will go a long way toward that end, but time is of the essence. For all we know, the Rousseaus will relocate by the time we get back to Midtown. Then we will never find them."

"You know, Frank, your sense of optimism needs some work."

They had time to kill during their layover in Dallas. Malone decided to call Victoria Hamilton. "Hi, Victoria. It's Frank Malone. I just wanted to give you an update on Kerry's case. I am in Dallas, Texas. Detective Dolan and I are on our way to Los Angeles to speak to the parents of two other murder victims. Their cases and the circumstances surrounding them are nearly identical to Kerry's case."

"That sounds like progress, Frank. How will you use that information to affect the investigation into Kerry's case?"

"Making an arrest in a murder case requires a solid foundation of building blocks. What we don't see in Midtown, we might see in the California cases. Demonstrating a pattern can often be a compelling factor when a prosecutor makes his or her case. In addition, making a connection between multiple crimes can give prosecutors in different jurisdictions more than one bite at the apple to get a conviction. For example, even if we lost our case in Midtown, it could provide a prosecutor in another jurisdiction a path forward to get a conviction in their case. Essentially, it would give us multiple opportunities to get the perpetrator off the streets."

"I can appreciate all that, Frank, but I want a conviction in Kerry's case. My daughter deserves that."

"That's our ultimate goal, Victoria. I'll speak to you again when I get back to Midtown."

Later that day, the two Midtown detectives landed in California. They paid for a rental car, and Dolan drove to their hotel in Brantley. On the way, they observed the awful conditions in Downtown Los Angeles. The signs of urban blight were everywhere. The widespread homeless situation and the omnipresent squiggly lines of gang graffiti were evident on virtually every corner. Abandoned buildings had become places of refuge.

"It looks a lot like Midtown, only with palm trees and sunshine, Frank."

Malone nodded in agreement.

"I guess to some extent, Midtown's problems are universal," Malone commented.

They checked into their hotel room, which was

designed to look like a Spanish hacienda. They ate a late dinner in a nearby Mexican café and went to bed early. They were up the next morning just after daybreak. The time zone change had disrupted their internal clocks. They had coffee in the hotel lobby and chatted with other guests in the hotel. Later, they had a banquet-style breakfast that included scrambled eggs, bacon, and bagels. Then Dolan drove the rental car out to the Valdez home in the Brantley suburbs. They both took note of the warm, dry air and the parched, windburned landscape on the way. They observed the densely populated area and the endless number of magnificent homes. Everything appeared so dry. It was easy to see why the area was so susceptible to the notorious wildfires that seasonally threatened the area.

The Valdez home was nestled in a typical California upper middle-class neighborhood. The home was a fine example of Spanish architecture with its stucco walls and clay barrel roof tiles. Palm trees, a variety of cacti, and colorful bougainvillea flowers were dispersed throughout the property. The detectives stopped for a moment to enjoy the warm, dry breeze—something they rarely felt, if ever, in Midtown.

Corina and her husband, Jose, opened the front door before Dolan could knock. Everyone introduced themselves. They invited the detectives inside and then out back to their veranda. There was a pitcher of cold iced tea in the center of a wrought iron and glass table. Colorful Mexican tiles and tan wicker furniture were the staple motif of the home's décor. Everyone sat down.

Corina poured a glass of iced tea for everyone. She spoke first. "My husband and I were very encouraged by your phone call. We are anxious to hear if you have made progress in our daughter's case."

"To be specific, we haven't been working on your daughter's case," Malone said. "Midtown is located in the Midwest, several states over. However, we are working on a case that appears to have many similarities to your daughter's case. We are hoping, with your help, that we can make a connection that will eventually lead to an arrest in our case. We think the culprits in our case are the same perpetrators in the Brantley cases."

Malone's comment immediately got Jose Valdez's attention. "You said perpetrators, Lieutenant Malone, like in more than one?" he asked.

"Yes, I did. We believe there are two people responsible for the murder of a high school girl in Midtown. We also think they may have a connection to your daughter's case."

"What can we do to help you?" Corina asked.

"How old was your daughter, Mrs. Valdez?"

"Please call me Corina. She was sixteen at the time of her murder."

"I'd like to show you several pictures. We got them from a convenience store security video in Midtown." Malone removed the pictures of Annette Rousseau from a manila envelope and handed them to Corina. Her husband leaned in to examine the pictures along with her. "That's Tina Russell," Corina said immediately. "She was Catalina's ballet instructor. Tina killed my daughter?"

"There is a distinct possibility that she participated in the rape and murder of a high school girl in Midtown. She was also that girl's ballet dance instructor."

Corina moved forward in her chair. "That makes sense, Lieutenant Malone. Detective Barrett of the Brantley Police Department was the original lead investigator on my daughter's case. He asked us questions about Tina and her husband many times. I asked him if they were suspects. He said 'no,' it was just part of his process of eliminating people who were in my daughter's orbit. He seemed very motivated at the outset to find our daughter's killer. Then we heard rumors that the FBI was becoming involved in the case. Initially, we thought that might be a good thing. Then it appeared to us that Detective Barrett's role in the case was becoming greatly diminished. That was very frustrating for us, to say the least, because he was our primary contact person.

Ultimately, he said the case had gone cold. He needed someone to come forward with more information to reinvigorate the investigation. Eventually, he informed us that the FBI had completely taken over the case, and he was no longer involved."

"Did he say why?"

"He said the FBI had more resources than the Brantley Police Department. Therefore, they were better equipped to get results. To me, I got the sense that Barrett was not happy about the FBI taking over the case. I think he got pushed out against his will, but I don't know why."

Jose concurred with Corina's assessment.

"Were you given a name and number for the FBI's lead investigator who was taking over your daughter's case?" Dolan asked.

"Yes, I called him," Corina responded. "At first, he seemed very enthused, but then he stopped taking our calls. In time, the case was turned over to another agent, and then another, until all lines of communication had broken off. We have no idea what the status of the investigation is right now. We are very frustrated."

"I see. Let me ask you another question. Did you ever meet Ms. Russell's husband?" Malone asked.

"No," both parents said simultaneously with a shake of their heads.

"What did you think of Ms. Russell at the time?"

"I thought she was a very good instructor, as well as a good role model for Catalina. My daughter liked her very much. She seemed knowledgeable and very interested in my daughter's ballet dancing progress."

"Do you know if your daughter was ever alone with her?"

"I guess it's possible. But if it happened, it was only for a brief period and in the context of individual attention and dance instruction. I didn't think anything of it. I just thought she was taking an interest in developing Catalina's dancing skills. I can't believe this. I enrolled my daughter in that class. I drove her there and picked her up every day. I paid for those classes. I'll never forgive myself."

"To be clear, you don't think Tina was ever alone with your daughter for an extended period? There were no private, individual lessons or anything like that?" Dolan asked to confirm clarity.

"No, not that I recall; I can't believe that bitch killed my daughter."

"First things first, Corina. It's very important that we proceed with our investigation one step at a time," Malone said. "We have to be very systematic in our approach if we are going to get a conviction in Midtown. Are you willing to sign an affidavit attesting to the fact that your daughter was murdered, and that Ms. Tina Russell was her ballet dance instructor?"

"I sure as hell will," Corina assured the detectives.

"How about you, Mr. Valdez, can you attest to the fact that Ms. Russell was Catalina's dance instructor?"

"I'm afraid I can't, Lieutenant. I never met this Tina Russell in person. My wife handled everything regarding Catalina's dance lessons. She drove her to and from her classes."

Corina Valdez signed the affidavit that Lucy had typed up for Malone.

As Malone and Dolan were leaving, Corina urged the detectives to continue their pursuit for justice. "My daughter meant everything in the world to me. I will do whatever it takes to help you. I will fly to Midtown in a New York minute to testify if you need me to. I appreciate the effort you are making. This is the first time we have had hope in a long time."

Malone reached out and grabbed each of Corina's hands. He held them and looked into her eyes. "I can assure you that we will do everything in our power to get justice for you and your daughter. You can count on it."

"You're not concerned about the FBI, Lieutenant? I think they may have bullied Detective Barrett off my daughter's case."

"No, I'm not concerned," Malone said defiantly.

Corina Valdez reached out and embraced Malone. She looked into his eyes. "Thank you, Lieutenant. Finally, someone is standing up for Catalina."

The Stewarts' home was about a thirty-minute drive from the Valdezes's home. Their house was very similar in style and design. The Stewarts greeted the detectives warmly. Mr. and Mrs. Stewart quickly identified Tina Russell, aka Annette Rousseau, as their daughter's ballet dance instructor. Like Catalina's parents, they both thought Tina was an effective role model and dance instructor. Unlike Catalina Valdez, their daughter often stayed after class for individual instruction from Tina. She also attended a field trip that Tina chaperoned with several other students to see a professional ballet performance in Downtown Los Angeles.

The Stewarts signed the affidavit attesting to the fact that Tina Russell, their daughter's dance instructor, was the woman in the pictures from the Midtown convenience store security video. They also had the same experiences as the Valdezes when it came to Detective Barrett. At first, they both thought he was making significant progress with his investigation. He asked them dozens of questions about Tina Russell and her husband on several occasions. Neither of the Stewarts had met Tina's husband. The Stewarts agreed with the Valdezes' assertion that Barrett's investigation into their daughter's murder had lost momentum. Similarly, they were also informed at some point that the FBI was taking over the investigation. They too experienced the same shuffle of investigators until eventually there was a breakdown in all communications.

Once they completed their interview with the Stewarts, Malone and Dolan headed to the Police Administration Building in Brantley. It was a four-story structure exhibiting the familiar Mediterranean-architectural design that was so common in the area. They went in the front entrance and through the lobby's metal detector. They took the elevator to the second floor, where the Detective Bureau was located. They identified themselves to the receptionist and asked if Detective Stephen Barrett was available.

The receptionist dialed a three-digit extension, and someone answered on the other end. She explained that there were two out-of-town visitors asking to see Detective Barrett. "Okay, I will tell them."

The receptionist informed Malone and Dolan that Detective Barrett would be out in a few minutes to take them back to his office. Right on cue, Detective Barrett appeared. He was a tall, slender man who looked to be in his early forties. The two Midtown detectives followed Barrett back to his office. Malone and Dolan formally introduced themselves and sat in the chairs in front of Barrett's desk.

"What can I do for you?" Barrett asked.

"We are interested in your investigation into the deaths of Catalina Valdez and Karen Stewart," Malone informed Barrett.

"The Brantley Police Department is no longer involved in either of those investigations. The FBI has taken over the cases. I haven't had a role in either case for almost two years. I know you have come a long way, Lieutenant, but I'm afraid there is not much I can do to help you. May I ask why you're so interested in these Brantley cases?"

"There has been a murder in our jurisdiction that has striking similarities to the Valdez and Stewart murders," Malone said. "We think there is a connection."

"May I ask what the similarities are?"

"Of course, first and foremost, our victim was a high school senior. Her age was similar to your victims. She was taking ballet lessons at the time of her murder. The victims in your jurisdiction were also taking ballet lessons."

"I can see why you came to your conclusion, Lieutenant. However, those are pretty broad similarities."

"The connection is even more striking when you consider that the Midtown victim had the same ballet instructor as the Brantley victims even though the dance studio in Midtown is over fifteen hundred miles away. The dance instructor in Midtown is known as Annette Rousseau, but she was known as Tina Russell in Brantley."

"I formally interviewed Tina and spoke to her on a number of occasions," said Barrett. "I was unable to make a tangible connection between Tina and the victims in Brantley, other than that she was their dance instructor."

"Did you speak to her husband?"

"Harry Niles—yes, I did."

"Did you see any connection between him and the two murder victims?"

"I did not," Barrett quickly replied.

"Detective Barrett, before I ask the next question, I want you to understand that you can trust us. Anything we discuss here will not leave this room. Why did the Brantley Police Department decide to let the FBI take over the investigation of these two cases? The local jurisdiction has the obligation and all the legal authority."

Barrett hesitated and diverted his eyes. Malone and Dolan could see the question had made him uncomfortable. "The FBI has a lot more resources than we do. It was a better fit for them to investigate the cases."

Malone approached the question from a different direction. "Detective Barrett, the FBI has insisted on inserting themselves into our investigation in Midtown.

In fact, they want to take over the entire case. I'm sure you are aware of how unusual that is. Did you have the same experience here in Brantley?"

Barrett opened his mouth to speak but then clenched his teeth. Malone and Dolan could see Barrett struggling with the question. The Midtown detectives were convinced that Barrett had indeed had the same experience.

"Lieutenant Malone, I'd rather not comment on the FBI's role in the Brantley murders. You should direct any questions you have to them."

"I understand, Detective Barrett. Without going into detail, it sounds like you might be familiar with the dance instructor, her husband, and possibly their Washington, D.C. connection."

"I have no comment, Lieutenant Malone."

"Detective Barrett, you are aware that we are likely dealing with two serial killers," Malone reminded him. "It looks like these two animals were able to muster up enough leverage in Washington to get them a 'get out of jail card free' here in Brantley. Time is running out in Midtown. These two killers are going to be relocated, much like they were in Brantley. Then we will lose them, and they'll likely kill again somewhere else. Is there anything you can give us that will help our investigation?"

Barrett pondered the question.

"Please, Detective Barrett, we need your help. I know

it wasn't your decision to turn your cases over to the FBI. Nevertheless, that decision cost a seventeen-year-old girl her life in Midtown."

"Lieutenant Malone, it's likely your presence here is already known outside the confines of these walls. That's a problem for me. I want to help you, but I have a wife and two small children to think about. I assure you that any help I give you will likely cost me my job. I can't afford that. I've got fifteen years in. I'm five years away from being fully vested. I want to help you, but I have a family to consider. This is not what I signed up for when I became a cop. But the price for me to help you would personally cost me way too much. I have two young daughters, for G-d sakes, to think about."

Malone silently pleaded with Barrett with his eyes and body language.

Finally, Dolan broke the uneasy silence. "Please, Detective Barrett. I also have two daughters. We need your help. Somewhere out there someone else's innocent daughter is going to unwittingly cross paths with these monsters. You have a chance to save that girl's life."

Barrett hesitated and then stood up. He opened the second drawer from the top of a gray filing cabinet located behind his desk. He pulled out a file and plucked out two pieces of paper. He looked at the two Midtown detectives.

"Stay here. I'll be right back."

Barrett went to the office copy machine and made a copy of both sheets of paper. He returned to his office and handed the copies to Malone.

Barrett lowered his voice. "The bodies of the Brantley murder victims were discovered in different remote locations. The elements had taken their toll on their remains. However, we were still able to collect trace DNA evidence. What I have given you is the results from testing that DNA evidence. They confirm a match with DNA samples we collected from Tina Russell and Harry Niles, before the FBI took over the cases. I'm asking you not to tell anyone where you got this information. Also, I trust you not to formally introduce this information as evidence in any court proceeding that you may bring against Niles and Russell. I'm giving it to you only to confirm that you are on the right track . . . and that's all I am going to do. You have to promise me that you'll keep my name and this information out of your investigation. Do not call me as a witness in any case in Midtown related to Russell and Niles. Do not call me on my cellphone, or my office phone, do not email me, or text me about anything related to your case in Midtown or the cases in Brantley. This is the last time we will ever communicate with each other, for the sake of my family, Lieutenant."

Malone and Dolan quickly understood what Barrett was up against.

"I understand, Detective Barrett," Malone said.

Malone and Dolan stood up and shook hands with the Brantley detective. The two detectives turned to leave. Malone looked back at Barrett with admiration. "Thank you, Detective. I commend you for your bravery."

"I don't feel so brave," Barrett said sadly. "I feel more like a coward, but that's the price I have to pay to support my family."

Back in their rental car, Malone received a text message from the police chief. It read: "Please call me ASAP on the most secure line possible."

Malone looked at Dolan. "Something is cooking in Midtown."

Dolan drove to a big-box store in Brantley, where Malone purchased a burner phone. He called the police chief's clerical assistant with his new phone. Lilly Richards answered.

"Hi, Lilly. It's Frank Malone. Is the chief in?"

"Yes, he is."

"Tell him it's me. I need to speak to him on the extension in the conference room down the hall, not from his desktop phone or his cellphone."

"Okay, Frank. I'll transfer you into the conference room, and he'll pick up there."

Malone waited several minutes before the police chief picked up.

"Chief, I got your text message."

"Brace yourself, Frank; I have heard from a good source that the Feds will likely move the Rousseaus this Thursday on Thanksgiving. They must be figuring everyone will be preoccupied with the holiday and take their eye off the ball. You have three days to make an arrest."

"Understood."

"One more thing, Frank; the mayor called me less than an hour ago. The FBI contacted him. They told him they have information that indicates you have been coercing sexual favors from family members of murder victims. The FBI said this activity has been going on for years. The mayor directed me to remove you from the Hamilton case, effective immediately."

"Chief, I can assure you that none of this is true."

"I know, I know, Frank. I asked the mayor why we are hearing this from the FBI and not the so-called victims. I told him that doesn't make any sense."

"What did the mayor say?"

"Nothing, dead silence. I couldn't see him, but I imagine he had that same stupid look on his face he always gets when he receives confirmation he is dead wrong about something. Nevertheless, Frank, despite the mayor's stupidity, the fact that they're moving the Rousseaus on Thursday underlines the need to make an arrest as soon as possible."

"I'm all over it, Chief."

Malone hung up. He looked over at Dolan. "They're moving the Rousseaus this Thursday."

"That doesn't give us much time," Dolan responded.

On the way to the Los Angeles airport, Dolan was reminded by Malone's mention of Thanksgiving. It was a holiday ritual that Malone would have dinner with Eddie and his family on Thanksgiving.

"Frank, about Thanksgiving, I don't think Doreen is up to having guests this year."

"Don't worry about it, partner; I understand. I wouldn't be good company either," Malone said wryly. "I have a lot on my mind too."

Two hours later, Malone and Dolan were in the air on their way back to Midtown.

CHAPTER 21

Sarah turned the heat up in her cranberry-red Mustang on her way to the Last Stop Saloon. The temperature outside had dipped into the single digits. Her mood was as glum as the current atmosphere that had draped Midtown.

It was unlike her, but Sarah had been depressed for days over her situation with Malone. She still loved him, but how could the relationship continue long-term? Those startling images of Malone with another woman shocked her to say the least. They weren't married. Yes, Malone was free to do whatever he wanted. She had no desire to persuade him to do otherwise. If that's what he wanted, then he had every right to pursue it. But he had never given her any indication that was something he wanted. They had shared so much together, so many intimate moments, it all seemed so real to her. How could everything go in such a different direction so quickly? It was out of character for Malone to cheat on her. He had never given her any indication that was something he wanted. He was a grown man. Surely, he had other lovers before he met her, but he seemed so invested in her. She just couldn't make any sense of it.

She wondered where their relationship would have gone if she hadn't seen those disturbing pictures. In most cases, people only heard about their spouses' or significant others' indiscretions. They didn't actually see them in all their naked glory. It would likely have been easier for her to forgive Malone if she hadn't seen the pictures, but it wouldn't change what had happened. The transgression still occurred.

On one hand, she wanted to forgive him because she wanted to continue their relationship. On the other hand, she didn't think she could live with those images bouncing around in her head. Perhaps she should give him opportunity to explain. She was aware that he had said the pictures were not real, but how could that be possible? Malone was not a liar. But on this occasion, he must have lied because he was desperate to conceal his behavior.

What if the pictures weren't real? What if Malone was telling her the truth? He would have all the reason in the world to be frustrated and hurt. This whole thing could be for naught if he was telling the truth—or if she just forgave him. They could still be together, perhaps even making plans to move to Naples, Florida. The last ten months had clearly been the best time of her life.

Just a few days earlier, their biggest problem was not seeing each other enough. Now she was on the precipice of never seeing him again. Tears dripped from Sarah's vibrant gray eyes as she pulled into the parking lot at the Last Stop Saloon.

At the Dolan residence, Doreen sat alone at her kitchen table, sipping a hot cup of coffee. She was thinking about the upcoming Thanksgiving holiday and how her life had changed so dramatically so quickly. The phone calls from that woman had come out of nowhere and changed everything. She could not forget that horrible screeching voice yelling that her husband had impregnated her and that she wanted money to terminate the pregnancy. Doreen's first inclination was to give her the money to make her go away. However, that wouldn't change the damage to her marriage. It wouldn't change anything regarding her husband's infidelity.

Or perhaps it would. It seemingly would make it easier to reconcile with Eddie if the constant reminder of a child wasn't present and needing to be cared for. But she wasn't sure that was something she wanted. The child would be biologically a part of Eddie. What would he think about aborting his child, even if he was having it with a woman other than his wife? It wouldn't change the fact that he had slept with her. Should she even care if their marriage was over? This was Eddie's problem, not hers.

For Doreen, abortion had always been a political issue discussed by pundits on television. It was a subject used to drive a wedge between people. It was not something she would ever personally face. She had always been pro-choice, yet she also believed in some limitations to abortion. She certainly thought that abortion had its place when the life of the mother was on the line or in cases of rape or incest. But those incidences were extremely rare. What if the sole reason for an abortion was based on inconvenience or to avert embarrassment? Should this woman's pregnancy be terminated solely because the pregnancy was the result of an extramarital affair? Was that an acceptable reason? She never dreamed she would be asking herself such questions.

She continued to ponder her current situation. Two consenting adults engage in sex. One of those adults has the financial wherewithal to properly care for the child. Should a pregnancy be terminated under those conditions? Should she, Doreen, demand an abortion as part of a reconciliation plan with her husband? Is that requirement fair to Eddie? Is it fair to the fetus? What about her family? After all, she had two teenage daughters to consider. What would they think about a half-sibling suddenly being introduced into their family? What if she required Eddie to pay for an abortion to save their marriage, then later determined that she didn't want their marriage to continue even though there was no child? Then what? It would be too late for the fetus. Certainly, the other woman was going to have a say in all this. The woman was so adamant about having an abortion. She certainly was not in the mindset to care for an unwanted child.

Again, these were all questions that she never thought she would have to consider. There was also Eddie's claim that the woman was part of a federal government scam to coerce her husband to remove himself from the Kerry Hamilton case. She had never heard of such a thing. It didn't make sense that the federal government, the FBI, or whoever would try to purposely destroy a police officer's marriage to protect serial killers? That seemed preposterous to her. But what if Eddie was telling her the truth? What if she stopped receiving the calls once an arrest was made in the Hamilton case? Wouldn't that prove Eddie had been telling her the truth? She had never known him to lie about anything. He had always been a good husband and father. Nevertheless, the whole premise of the federal government and the FBI sabotaging their marriage for such an abhorrent reason was too incredible to believe.

Back at the Last Stop Saloon, Sarah was mixing drinks for regulars, newcomers, the sober, and the marginally intoxicated. The front entrance door swung open, and a rush of frigid air followed behind the new customer. In walked a confident, curvaceous woman with pronounced cheekbones and crystal-clear blue eyes. She removed her heavy wool coat. She was wearing painted-on skintight jeans, thigh-high black boots, a gray sweater, and a black fleece vest. She moved to an open barstool, folded her coat over the back, and sat on the adjacent stool.

Sarah was grateful that the top three buttons on the woman's sweater were unbuttoned. They would never have been able to contain her ample bosom. Sarah was certain that a wayward button torn from the woman's sweater could become a dangerous projectile.

Sarah flipped a coaster on the bar in front of the young woman and asked, "What would you like to drink?"

"I'll have a gin and tonic."

The woman admired how pretty Sarah was.

Sarah walked away, mixed the requested drink, and returned. She placed the drink on the coaster.

"Is your name Sarah?" the young woman asked.

Sarah stared at her momentarily with her striking gray eyes. She was taken aback by the question from a person she had never met before. "Do I know you?" Sarah asked curiously.

"No, we have never met. I'm a friend of your boyfriend, Frank. I guess he's your ex-boyfriend now."

"Are you here to tell me that you have slept with Frank?" Sarah shook her head. "This is getting out of control. I can't believe this."

"Heavens no, I'm not here to tell you that, Sarah. Sadly, I have never slept with Frank, but it's not because I haven't offered . . . actually many times. I'm here to tell you something entirely different."

Sarah was perplexed. She stared at the stranger. Her curiosity meter was running on overdrive. "Who are you?" she eventually asked. "What is this all about? Why are you here?"

"My name is Alexandra Martin. My friends call me Alex. Frank calls me Alex."

Alex reached over the bar to shake hands. Sarah hesitantly accommodated her. Sarah recognized the name. Frank had mentioned her several times.

"The reason I'm here, Sarah, is because Frank is my friend. He actually saved my life once . . . well, maybe more than once. I met him after the Monster of Midtown murdered my roommate. My roommate and I were nude dancers at a club called Silver Stiletto's. Actually, I was still a dancer there up until a couple weeks ago. For some reason, Frank took a liking to me, and it wasn't for the reason you may be thinking. He likes me as a person and a friend. I have never had a friend like Frank before. He has stayed in touch with me for the past year. He has constantly urged me to get out of the dancing business. He thought dancing nude for a living would make for an unhappy and unfulfilling life for me. You see, I had a pretty rough childhood. My stepfather sexually abused me from the time I was twelve until I left home at age sixteen. I have been out on my own ever since, but that's a story for another day."

"Why are you telling me all this, Alex?" Sarah asked curiously.

"I told you, Sarah, because Frank is my friend. A few weeks ago, I ran into Frank by happenstance in a sandwich shop. I was sporting a black eye that my ex-boyfriend, Miguel, had given me. So, Frank tells me, 'that's it, Alex, you're coming with me.' He drags me over to an Italian restaurant named Tommy D's. Frank knows the owners. Anyway, he talks them into hiring me. I've been there ever since, waiting on tables. I'm out of the dancing business for good because Frank cares about me. No one has ever done anything like that for me."

"That's all very heartwarming, Alex," Sarah said with a sense of sarcasm, "but what does any of this have to do with me?"

"You're a funny girl, Sarah," Alex said, returning the sarcasm. "You're very pretty too. Now I see why Frank is so crazy about you. Anyway, enough of that, I'm not finished yet. After I got hired, I leave Tommy D's with Frank. He asks me where he can find Miguel. He says he wants to have a word with him. I tell him where he works, and we wait for him in the parking lot until he got off. I was really concerned at the time because Miguel is a street fighter; he's very strong, and a lot younger than Frank. Nevertheless, Frank confronts him and tells him to stay away from me . . . for good. Do you want to know what happened next?"

Sarah shrugged her shoulders and shook her head. "No, not particularly, but I'm sure you're going to tell me anyway."

"I like you, Sarah, you're really funny. Anyway, Miguel takes a swing at Frank."

Sarah's eyes widened.

"You know, Sarah, you have some really wild pretty eyes. They're actually gray, aren't they?"

Sarah didn't respond.

"Anyway, back to my story. So, Frank proceeds to kick the living shit out of Miguel. After he almost knocks him completely unconscious, he tells him that if he ever hears he's within ten miles of me, he's going to come back and kick his pathetic ass all over Midtown. I haven't seen Miguel since."

Alex sat back on her barstool appearing obviously proud of herself.

Sarah pondered for a moment everything that Alex said. "I'll ask you again, why did you come here, and why are you telling me all this?"

"I told you because Frank is my friend, Sarah. I know you have been overwhelmed with a bunch of lies lately. It must be very confusing for you. I also know for sure Frank really likes you . . . a lot. He could have had me anytime he wanted. I can assure you of that. Believe me I don't get rejected, but Frank turned me down. You probably don't know any of this because Frank doesn't need any accolades or someone patting him on the back. The dude is a first-class boy scout, probably an eagle scout. He's not like other dudes. He just goes about his business. Frank Malone is old-school. He would never do anything stupid like you think he did. I know about the pictures. Frank told me. That's all a bunch of crap. That's not the way Frank Malone rolls. Can't you see that?"

Sarah's eyes were starting to tear up. "Did Frank send you here to tell me all this?"

"Oh hell no! He'd probably kill me if he knew I was here. Frank cares about other people's feelings, Sarah. He would never do anything to hurt anyone, especially someone he really cares about . . . like you. The Feds came to the restaurant where I work. They tried to lay the same bullshit story on me that they laid on you. They were spewing all this crap about Frank trying to strong-arm sex from family members of murder victims. I saw right through that lie. I told them to take a hike. I practically threw them out of the restaurant."

"You did that?" Sarah asked.

"Hell yeah, nobody says that about a friend of mine, especially a friend like Frank."

Sarah paused for moment. "Maybe I can learn something from you, Alex."

"You probably can. I have been around the block a few times . . . well, truthfully, I have been around the block so many times it makes me dizzy thinking about it," she said with a giggle. "However, I must warn you, most of the stuff I can teach you would be a bunch of useless bullshit you can't use anywhere," she said giggling again.

Sarah laughed with her. "Do you want another drink, Alex? It's on me."

"Why not? I have been nothing but a Goody Two Shoes ever since Frank got me my waitress job. It's starting to ruin my image."

"Now we can't have any of that, can we?" Sarah replied, laughing.

CHAPTER 22

After their flight back, Malone and Dolan found themselves sheltered inside the 9th Precinct. Ten inches of snow had dropped on Midtown in the last twelve hours. Snowdrifts had caused a two-foot buildup of snow against buildings and parked cars. Heavy-duty, four-wheel-drive trucks were plowing the streets to pave the wave for emergency personnel to respond, if needed. For the moment, most of Midtown was paralyzed by the quickly amassing snow.

Malone had decided to make an unannounced visit to the home of the Honorable Judge Carson Whitlock. The two detectives had assembled various pictures from the video tapes they had collected. Malone put the signed affidavits; DNA reports; the information from Jack Mizell; and a summary of the federal government's smear tactics into a manila envelope. His plan was to present everything he had to the judge in hopes of persuading him to issue a search warrant.

Malone knew a visit to the judge's private home was highly irregular. However, time was running out, and he didn't want to disclose the federal government's tactics in open court. Malone had appeared before Judge Whitlock many times. He had submitted hundreds of search warrant requests over the last fifteen years. He knew Judge Whitlock was very deliberative when he evaluated evidence before making his decisions. It was Malone's intention to disclose as much evidence as possible without compromising his promise to Detective Barrett.

Malone wanted to stay clear of the political blowback in Washington when he finally arrested the Rousseaus. He didn't want Midtown to become the subject of political retribution. He recognized that the mayor's concerns were legitimate. However, his primary concern was justice for the victims and their families. If all the sordid details in the case eventually came out, the political figures in Washington would have to deal with it. Malone was not about to let the Rousseaus get away with murder again.

Dolan carefully navigated the icy streets of Midtown. Judge Whitlock lived out in the suburbs in a splendid all-white Colonial Revival–style home. The sidewalk to the front door had been cleared of snow. A three-foot-high mound was piled along the perimeter of the pavement. Dolan rang the doorbell. Moments later, Judge Whitlock himself opened the door. The judge was a distinguished-looking man with premature white hair and powder-blue eyes. He had on a robe and slippers.

"Lieutenant Malone, Detective Dolan, this is certainly a surprise! What can I do for you?"

"Judge, we need to expedite your approval on a search warrant. We are running out of time, and we are up against significant forces that are trying to derail our investigation."

Judge Whitlock looked puzzled. "This is highly irregular, Lieutenant Malone."

"I am aware, Judge. I am asking for a few minutes of your time to explain."

The judge invited the detectives inside. The home was grand and meticulously decorated with fine antique furnishings, wonderful works of art, and wide, expansive black walnut floors. Malone and Dolan followed the judge into his den. Magnificent, finely finished black walnut paneling covered the walls. Hundreds of leather-bound books filled the wood shelving behind the judge's desk.

"Have a seat, gentlemen."

Malone and Dolan removed their heavy coats and sat down.

"Okay, gentlemen, why is time running out? What makes this search warrant request so urgent that you felt the need to come to my home?"

Malone leaned forward on his chair. "This search warrant request pertains to the Kerry Hamilton murder case. I'm sure you have probably read the papers. Her body was recently discovered on Old Highway 9."

"Yes, I have read about the case."

"It hasn't been released to the media, but she was murdered and her body was posed in a manner similar to the Monster of Midtown victims."

The judge involuntarily raised his eyebrows. "Oh dear, that is disturbing."

"We have gathered CCTV videos from a number of traffic lights and businesses along Old Highway 9. We came across a woman in one of those videos."

Dolan reached into the manila envelope he had prepared and retrieved a still picture from one of the videos. It was a picture of Annette Rousseau. He handed it to the judge.

"That picture was gleaned from a security video in a convenience store located on Old Highway 9," Malone said. "The woman's image was captured around the time Kerry's body was dumped. She happened to be the victim's ballet dance instructor. We have tried to learn more about this woman ever since we discovered the video. She has virtually no paper trail, internet presence, or social media history. However, we have obtained information about this woman and her husband from a confidential source formerly employed at the FBI."

Dolan handed the judge copies of the documents that Jack Mizell had provided.

Malone spoke while the judge examined them. "This woman and her husband previously lived in Brantley, California. They were known there as Tina Russell and Harry Niles. He was a producer/director in the pornographic film industry, and she was an actress in the same industry. She also owned a ballet dance studio in Brantley. Two female high school students were separately enrolled in her classes. They were murdered approximately two months apart. Their bodies were both disposed of in desolate areas. A detective in Brantley made a connection between those murders and the dance studio.

"Meanwhile, Niles joined a team of investors engaging in a human-trafficking operation along the Texas border. It was apparently a very profitable endeavor. It got the attention of several Washington, D.C. big shots.

"Simultaneously, the pressure in D.C. was reaching a boiling point to crack down on the number of illegal migrants crossing the border. This compelled Niles and Tina Russell, who had become his wife, to head to Washington, where she promptly seduced a number of key political figures. Niles secretly videotaped all of the encounters.

"Meanwhile, back in California, Brantley detectives are beginning to close in on Niles and Russell for the two murders out there. That's when Niles pulls out his extortion card. He threatened to show the sex videos to the world if the Feds didn't bail them out of their California problem. Out of desperation, the Feds decide to go down a very dark road. They compel the Brantley Police Department to turn their two murder investigations over to the FBI. The FBI then lets the investigations die a slow death. While this is going on, the Feds place Niles and Russell into a witness protection–type program. They relocate them out of Brantley, provide them with new identities, and give them a whole new fresh start. You can probably guess where they were relocated to."

"Midtown," the judge concluded.

"That's correct. Niles and Russell are now known as Bobby and Annette Rousseau. They immediately rewarded the federal government for their kindness by raping and murdering Kerry Hamilton. They made it look like a Monster of Midtown copycat murder. Presumably, for their own sexually depraved benefit. Eddie and I went out to California over the weekend. We obtained signed affidavits from the parents of the two Brantley victims. The affidavits confirm that the woman in the picture you are holding in your hand was their daughters' ballet dance instructor in Brantley.

"In addition, we have DNA testing proof that the Rousseaus are connected to the murders in California. However, we cannot formally submit that material to you in our search warrant request. We have given our word that we would not use Brantley's DNA testing information in any official capacity. I'm showing it to you so that you have a complete picture. I want you to be confident that we are targeting the right people. It is my opinion, even without the DNA results, we have presented you with enough evidence to meet the threshold to grant us a search warrant."

"But why the sense of urgency, Lieutenant?" the judge asked. "Why couldn't this wait until tomorrow?"

"Tomorrow will be too late. We have good information that the Feds are planning to relocate the Rousseaus on Thursday . . . Thanksgiving. In addition, the FBI and the attorney general's office have engaged in a very personal smear campaign to get Detective Dolan and me to back off the Hamilton investigation. They may have irrevocably destroyed Detective Dolan's marriage and my relationship with my soon-to-be fiancée."

"But you're not going to back off?" the judge surmised.

"No, sir, we're not. They have murdered and raped at least three high school girls that we know of. There is no way in hell we're going to let them get out of Midtown.

However, we need a search warrant to have any chance at stopping them."

"What do you specifically expect to find?" the judge asked curiously.

"It's all in the search warrant request. We think we may find items belonging to Kerry Hamilton, possibly DNA evidence, fingerprints, and potentially videos of her being raped and murdered."

The judge was incredulous. "Do you actually think that you'll find video evidence of her murder in the house?"

"It is very possible, certainly the rape. They are voyeurs, filming their sex acts is part of their makeup. It's important to them. On top of it, they were in the pornography business. I believe there is a good chance they videoed Kerry's rape and possibly her murder. We need to find that video. Serial killers often collect personal items or mementos from their victims. It will be compelling evidence if we can find something belonging to Kerry that proves she was in that house."

Dolan handed the search warrant request form to the judge. The judge examined it, signed it, and handed it back to Dolan.

"I must tell you both," the judge said. "You have always acted like consummate professionals when you have been in my courtroom. I have always admired and appreciated that. However, I would be remiss if I didn't tell you how proud I am to serve with you in our mission to protect the good citizens of Midtown. You two have gone to great lengths to get justice for Kerry Hamilton. I'm sure the people of Midtown will never really know the full extent of your sacrifice. Thank you for your unwavering service."

Malone and Dolan stood up, shook hands with Judge Whitlock, and then left.

The judge watched them through his front window as they trudged off toward Dolan's Explorer. A swirling haze of zigzagging snowflakes whipped around them. Judge Whitlock was well aware that the rapidly deteriorating weather conditions were dangerous for anyone who ventured out on such a night. The foul weather had already forced virtually everyone in Midtown to retreat to a place where it was safe and warm—everyone except Eddie Dolan and Frank Malone.

CHAPTER 23

Malone had anticipated that his drive to work the next morning would be treacherous because of the overnight snowstorm. Thankfully, Midtown's public works department had already plowed and salted the streets by the time he was on the road. He arrived at the 9th Precinct a few minutes before 5:30 a.m. and made the day's first pot of coffee. Lucy wouldn't be in for another hour.

He had used his burner phone the night before to schedule a morning meeting with his investigation team. He wanted everyone on the same page before they arrived at the Rousseaus' home to execute the search warrant. At 6:00 a.m., the group assembled in conference room one. The chatter between the detectives ceased when Malone made his way to the front of the room.

"Good morning, everyone. As you know, last night Eddie and I obtained a search warrant for the home of Bobby and Annette Rousseau. We will head over there after our meeting and arrive unannounced. All occupants inside the home will be removed before we begin the search. Eddie has reserved TAC channel four for our use."

TAC channels were used for tactical and special operations activity and during multiple incidents occurring simultaneously. A TAC channel would minimize confusion by preventing users on different scenes from talking over one another.

"Eddie, please direct the on-duty traffic sergeant to assign a uniformed officer to our scene. We will need the officer to manage the occupants once we get them outside. I don't want anyone inside other than official personnel while we are conducting our search."

Dolan gave Malone a thumbs-up, confirming he would get it done.

"Primarily, we are going to seize all electronic devices like laptops, hard drives, cellphones, CDs, thumb drives, etcetera that might contain pictures, videos, audio recordings, and the like. We are also looking for fingerprints, blood evidence, and other trace DNA evidence. CSI will join us in our search. They will collect and process any physical evidence we may find. Finally, we are also looking for any clothing, jewelry, or mementos that may have belonged to Kerry Hamilton or possibly other victims."

Ten minutes later, an entourage of police vehicles left the 9th Precinct and headed to the Rousseaus' residence.

Dolan informed dispatch when Malone and he had arrived on scene: "Detective 119 to Dispatch."

"Go ahead, Detective 119."

"Detective 119 and Lieutenant 21 have arrived at 17 North Columbus Drive, reference the execution of a search warrant."

"Acknowledge, Lieutenant 21 and Detective 119, I show your arrival at 17 North Columbus Drive, reference exercising a search warrant . . . 0700 hours."

All the other arriving police units made similar announcements upon arrival.

Malone led a parade of detectives up the icy walkway toward the Rousseaus' front door. Malone knocked on the door with the search warrant in his hand. The door opened moments later.

Annette Rousseau, aka Tina Russell, stood in the doorway, wearing only a pair of skimpy panties and a devilish smile. "May I help you?"

Malone neither hesitated nor flinched. He handed her the search warrant. "Ms. Rousseau, I'll remind you that my name is Lieutenant Frank Malone. I am handing you a court-ordered search warrant. We are here to conduct a search of the premises."

"I wish I would have known you were coming, Lieutenant," Annette responded, feigning a false sense of bravado. "I would have dressed for the occasion."

"Please step aside, ma'am."

Annette spread her arms. "Take me, Lieutenant. I have nothing to hide," she said, giggling. "Search away!"

"Ms. Rousseau, I suggest that you put on something warm. You will not be permitted in the house while we conduct our search. Is your husband in the house?"

"No, he went out for bagels and coffee."

"How long ago was that?"

"About thirty minutes."

"When do you expect him back?"

"I'm not sure. There's a cute little chick working behind the counter at the coffee shop. He has had his eye on her. He may be gone for hours, Lieutenant," she said with a cackle.

Malone turned around and asked Kinsey Phillips to come forward. "Kinsey, please accompany Ms. Rousseau to her bedroom while she dresses. I'm sure she'll appreciate having warm clothes on while she is standing outside."

Kinsey passed Malone, entered the Rousseaus' home, and followed Annette to the primary bedroom in the house. Malone wanted Kinsey to accompany Annette to ensure that she didn't conceal any incriminating evidence along the way or retrieve a weapon.

As Annette glided away in only her panties, Dolan admired her slender, sleek figure. Then he muttered to

Malone, his voice dripping with sarcasm, "This search is starting out much better than I anticipated, Frank. She does have a certain amount of charm about her."

"I can see a lot, Eddie, but I wouldn't describe it as charm."

Once Annette was dressed and outside, the detectives and CSI technicians entered the home and began their search. A uniformed patrol officer stayed with Annette outside. The detectives immediately began collecting items like the Rousseaus' laptop, hard drive, iPad, cellphones, a Kindle, an audio-recording device, and hundreds of DVDs and thumb drives that were readily visible. They searched for a home CCTV security system, but there was none. They combed through the desk in the den, dresser drawers in the bedrooms, closets, kitchen cabinets, the basement, the attic, and anywhere else they could think of.

Of particular interest was a safe they discovered in the den next to the desk. It was approximately three feet in height and about eighteen inches wide. It was secured by a dial combination lock. They searched for the safe's owner manual but couldn't find it. However, they were able to determine the manufacturer.

Malone went outside. Annette was standing on the sidewalk, wearing a heavy, long wool coat, and shivering. It was extremely cold.

"Ms. Rousseau, we found a safe in your den. Please provide me the combination so we can open it."

"I forgot the combination," she said immediately.

"I'm very disappointed in you, Ms. Rousseau," Malone said sarcastically. "I am asking for your cooperation. This process will go much smoother and faster if you cooperate with us. The sooner you cooperate, the sooner this process will be over."

"Do the letters F.O. mean anything to you, Malone? I don't like you."

"Have it your way, Ms. Rousseau."

Malone detected a slightly higher pitch in Annette's voice. Her attractive green eyes quickly averted from Malone's glaring stare. Malone sensed that the contents inside the safe were important. He went back into the house.

Once inside, Malone instructed Matt Dillon to call the safe's manufacturer. Perhaps there was a way to reset the combination to enable them to open it. If not, they would have to rely on a very competent professional locksmith they had used in the past who had safecracking capabilities.

Malone became increasingly concerned about Bobby Rousseau's whereabouts. Too much time had passed for a simple trip to pick up breakfast. Malone called Sergeant Skip Anderson on his cellphone.

"Hey, Frank. What's up?"

"Skip, we're over here at 17 North Columbus Drive executing a search warrant. One of the owners went out for a breakfast run prior to arrival. I'm getting concerned that he might be making a run for it. Please send a couple of officers to the local bagel and doughnut shops in our area to look for him. I'll email you his DL picture and his vehicle information. Also, set up checkpoints at the entrances to all highways that lead out of Midtown. Be aware, this guy could be dangerous."

"Okay, Frank. We'll find him if he's still anywhere in Midtown."

Malone called dispatch on his cellphone.

"Midtown Dispatch."

"This is Lieutenant 21. I am going to email you I.D. and vehicle information on a suspect named Bobby Rousseau. Please put out a BOLO on him."

"Acknowledge, Lieutenant 21."

Malone then got Kinsey Phillips's attention. "Ask Annette if she'll voluntarily go back to the 9th Precinct with you. We don't have enough to make an arrest as of yet. Hopefully she wants to get out of the cold. I get the distinct feeling there is something important in that safe. Start an informal conversation with her. Use your irresistible charm to try to get her talking," he jested. "It may take us hours before we can actually open that safe.

Make her feel like it's inevitable. Maybe she'll come clean and give us the combination. Also, try to go back to the beginning with her. We need to establish an information trail on her and her husband. Eventually, put the squeeze on her if the nice approach doesn't work. Hopefully, she is the weak link between her and her husband."

"Understood, Frank. I'll do my best to get her talking."

Meanwhile, CSI technicians were engaged in the laborious task of collecting fingerprints, hair samples, and possible DNA evidence from everywhere in the house. They hoped to find evidence that would place Kerry Hamilton in the Rousseaus' home. Certainly, indisputable biological DNA evidence would be the ultimate find.

Tommy Jackson went outside for a breather. Malone followed him out.

"We're collecting a lot of items that indicate a very kinky sexual relationship between those two," said Jackson. "Sadomasochism was a big part of their sex life, Frank."

"That doesn't surprise me. My hope is we can connect some of that stuff to Kerry Hamilton and possibly the girls in California."

Meanwhile, Bobby Rousseau was parked at a shopping mall, contemplating his escape out of Midtown. Over an hour ago he saw several black Ford Explorers and a marked police unit parked in front of his house. He immediately fled the area. He quickly determined that Malone couldn't care less about his videos and whatever leverage he had in Washington. Malone was forging ahead with his investigation anyway. The Feds previously had success persuading law enforcement officials in other jurisdictions to allow the FBI to take over their investigations. However, Malone was proving to be a whole different animal. He wasn't backing off despite the Feds' considerable powers of persuasion.

Bobby knew his wife was vulnerable. She could only hold out for so long. It was only a matter of time before they would break her. He loved her, but she was weak. Malone had successfully rattled her. Bobby knew he had to leave her behind. He didn't want to go to prison. He knew their home was filled with tangible evidence of their crimes. He never dreamed the authorities would get access to it. He thought his federal protection plan was impenetrable. What happened? Why was everything breaking down? After all, he had Washington right where he wanted them. He came to the same conclusion as he had before; it had to be because of Malone.

Back at the 9th Precinct, Kinsey tried to make Annette feel comfortable in interrogation room two. "Can I get you a cup of hot coffee, Annette?" Kinsey asked.

"Yes, please. I take cream and sugar."

"Do you need to use the restroom?"

"No, I am fine."

Annette removed her heavy coat, revealing her sleek dancer's physique, just not to the extent she had earlier. Kinsey returned with Annette's coffee made to her specifications. She had also poured herself a cup. Kinsey had recruited Hector Gonzalez and Robyn Butler to observe her conversation with Annette via a closed-circuit television screen in an adjacent room. That was standard police operating procedure.

"Are you comfortable, Annette?" Kinsey asked.

"No, not really. I don't like a lot of strangers rummaging through my house."

"I can empathize with you. That's why I invited you here. I thought you would be more comfortable where it's warmer. You are free to leave whenever you want. You're not under arrest or anything like that. However, things will go smoother if you cooperate."

Kinsey made a quick determination to proceed without Annette actually stating that she would cooperate.

"Should I call you Annette or Tina?"

"You can call me Tina. That is my birth name."

"Why did you change your name from Tina to Annette?"

"Harry wanted me to. Harry is my husband's real name."

"Was Harry involved in an immigration scheme on the Texas border?"

"I wouldn't call it a scheme. He was involved in a business venture in Texas to help immigrants cross the border."

"Was it illegal?"

"Some people made that accusation."

"Why?"

"Because it involves immigration; it is a real hot-button, political issue. It has everyone's dander up in Washington. Harry was working with people who were trying to help migrants get across the border. He was trying to help poor people get a better life."

"That seems like a noble cause, but there are laws. Was Harry breaking any laws?"

"I don't think so, but Harry can answer that better than I can. He handled all that. I believe his primary involvement was from an investment perspective. Harry is an investor, people needed help, and they were willing to pay for it. It's basic capitalism. It was a win-win business proposition. People were helped, and investors made a profit.”

“But someone apparently made a determination that Harry was involved in illegal activity . . . right?” Kinsey asked in a probing manner.

“It’s complicated. There are a lot of complex laws and rules related to immigration. It wasn’t Harry’s intention to break the law. If he did something wrong, it was a paperwork thing. Like I said, he was only an investor. He wasn’t involved in any day-to-day operations.”

“We have information that part of the business included drug and sex trafficking. Is that true?”

“It’s pretty lawless down there on the border. People get involved in all sorts of things. That wasn’t Harry’s intent, but maybe some of the other investors engaged in some things like that. Harry was in it because he wanted to help people.”

“I see. Was Harry ever arrested for sex trafficking on the border?”

“Yes, but erroneously.”

“Were you ever involved in sex trafficking?”

“No, not from a legal perspective. However, I enjoy sex and engage in it often.”

“Where did you meet your husband, Tina?”

“In California.”

“I mean more specifically.”

"'We met at an exotic dance club. I was a dancer. Harry liked what he saw. He thought I had a future as an actress in the film industry."

"The pornographic film industry?"

"Yes, Harry was a director and producer. He was looking for new talent," she said, smiling. "Like I said, he liked what he saw. He thought I had a bright future."

"When did you two get married?"

"About two years after we met."

"Did having sex with other people in the film industry affect your marriage in any way?"

"Hell, yes, it did! It sent our sexual enjoyment to new heights. We enjoy watching each other have sex with multiple partners. We're not into limiting ourselves. We don't get tied down by a bunch of hang-ups; we're not into putting up stupid barriers around us. They're too confining."

"Did you both eventually leave the pornographic film industry?"

"Yes."

"Why?"

"The immigration opportunity on the border came our way. Harry saw a good business opportunity, so we moved to Texas."

"I see. Back to Harry's arrest for sex trafficking—was his case ever adjudicated?"

"No."

"Why is that?"

"Because we made a deal with the Feds."

"What kind of deal? What was your leverage?"

"I'm not sure what you are asking."

"You both moved to Washington, D.C. for a time . . . correct?"

"Yes, for a short period of time."

"Why."

"For business and to have some fun."

"What kind of fun?"

"Sex. You see, Kinsey, the stuffy shirts in Washington appear to be so high and mighty when you see them on television. However, they have kinky sexual appetites, just like everyone else. It took me about a month to seduce six senators, several presidential cabinet members, and an attorney from the attorney general's office. Harry secretly filmed it all. The next thing I know, the United States government wants to be our best friend. They were bending over backward to change our identities and relocate us. It is funny how that works," she said, chuckling.

"So, you blackmailed them?"

"No, not at all, it's more like we became business partners. We were in the business of getting people over the border. They are in the business of allowing and concealing it."

Kinsey realized that Tina liked chatting about her promiscuous sex life. She saw it as a way to keep her talking. She kept referring back to it when there was a lull in their conversation. She had already made at least one direct admonition to several serious crimes.

"Let's go back to when you and Harry were in California. You were a ballet dance instructor back then . . . correct?"

"That's correct. I have always had an interest in dancing."

"During that time, two of your students were raped and murdered. Then you left California and opened a studio in Midtown. Now, another one of your students has been found raped and murdered. How do you explain that?"

"Coincidence, I guess."

"Coincidence?"

"Yes, coincidence."

"Tina, let's quit dancing around the subject and cut to the chase. Frank Malone is never going to rest until he gets an arrest and conviction for Kerry Hamilton's murder. This is a death penalty state. This is going to be a death penalty case. You have an opportunity to make things right. You can save yourself and save us a lot of time. Right now, you are in a position to negotiate with us. You can help us and yourself simultaneously. Malone will eventually get access to the safe in your house. We know the contents inside are important. You know it too." Kinsey saw a momentary look of concern in Tina's facial expression. "Come on Tina; tell me how to get in the safe before Malone gains access without your help. I need the combination now. If you wait, and there is something incriminating in there, there will be no reason for Malone to negotiate with you later."

"I know Malone's type, Kinsey. Authoritative, sexually deprived, makes up for his sexual inadequacies by threatening women. I can read him like a book."

Kinsey laughed to herself. She knew Frank would get a kick out of that characterization of him. "You see, Tina, it's like this: It seems every time you open a dance studio somewhere, some of your students end up raped and murdered. How do you explain that? That's way beyond a coincidence. I'm trying to help you help yourself before it's too late. It's time to cooperate."

Meanwhile, back at 17 North Columbus Drive, Malone was now convinced that Bobby Rousseau was not going to return from his breakfast errand. Malone sent Rousseau's DL picture and the description of his vehicle to all media outlets. Malone included text that indicated he was a person of interest in the murder of Kerry Hamilton. Malone wasn't officially calling Bobby Rousseau a fugitive from justice yet, but he did believe he would eventually get there.

Simultaneously, Rodney Armstrong, owner of Midtown's twenty-four-hour locksmith service was arriving on scene at 17 North Columbus Drive. He met up with Malone.

After they greeted each other, Malone said, "The safe is in the den. Matt Dillon got a phone number for the safe manufacturer's primary technician. He called several times, but his calls went directly to voicemail. He left a message, but we haven't heard back from him yet. Here's the technician's name and phone number."

Armstrong examined the information on the paper Malone handed him. "Pete Harrison, I know him. This is his office number. I'll call him on his cellphone."

"Great, time is of the essence, Rodney."

"It always is with you, Frank," he said, smiling.

Malone's cellphone rang. It was Kinsey. "What's up, Kinsey? How is your conversation with Annette going?"

"She likely has admitted to several crimes, but she hasn't cracked on Kerry's rape and murder, yet. I think there's a chance I can get her there. Right now, we're just rehashing her sexual perversions, and there are many. She is one sick chick, Frank. I think it's time we take a break. I'm going to leave her by herself in interrogation room two for a while. It'll give her time to think about her situation. I think she is starting to get concerned about facing all this without Bobby."

"That makes sense. Meanwhile, we've put out an APB on Bobby. It looks like he's on the run. Let Annette know Bobby has made a decision to move on without her. It might loosen her."

"Okay, Frank, but I must tell you that this chick is pretty loose already."

Dolan approached Malone after he hung up with Kinsey. Malone filled him in on their conversation.

Malone and Dolan went back inside the Rousseau residence. Rodney Armstrong was on a call with Pete Harrison.

"Are you making any progress?" Malone asked quietly.

"Hold on a minute, Pete. Not really, it looks like I will have to crack this thing myself."

"Can you do it?"

"Of course, Frank," he said with a grin.

Malone gave Rodney a thumbs-up.

CSI technicians continued to gather trace evidence and place what they collected into airtight, nonporous, ziplock bags. Meanwhile, the detectives had collectively stopped their search to watch the locksmith attempt to open the safe. They were fascinated by his skills. Sure enough, he got the safe open in just over thirty minutes. He immediately backed away to allow Malone access to the contents.

Malone approached the open safe, bent down, and looked inside. He glanced back at Dolan. "Bingo."

There were three thumb drives, three pairs of panties placed individually inside their own plastic bag, and nearly $50,000 dollars in cash, all in twenty-dollar bills.

Elizabeth, a CSI technician, removed all the articles from the safe and placed them into individual evidence containers.

Once she was finished, Malone approached her. "Elizabeth, I need to know yesterday if one of those undergarments belonged to Kerry Hamilton."

"Understood, Frank. Give me about two hours after I return to the lab, and I'll have the results."

DNA testing capabilities had improved dramatically over the years. Previously, it would have taken twenty-four to seventy-two hours to confirm a DNA match. In the past, many times a suspect would be released prior to confirmation. Of course, that was problematic, but now it was no longer a concern.

"Also, please process those thumb drives for DNA material immediately. I need to view them as soon as possible," Malone said with a sense of urgency.

"Yes, sir. It will be handled with all due haste."

"I know I can count on you."

Malone and Dolan left the CSI technicians and other detectives on scene. They drove back to the 9th Precinct. They ran into Kinsey on the way to Malone's office.

"Is our girlfriend still in the interrogation room?" Malone asked.

"Yes, do you want to speak to her?"

"Not yet. I'm waiting for DNA results on three undergarments and three thumb drives we found in the Rousseaus' safe. Keep Annette in the interrogation room until I see what's on those thumb drives. I assume they're important, because they were in the safe. Hopefully, the next time we talk to Annette, we will be able to put her skinny ass in a vise."

"She just might enjoy it, Frank," Kinsey responded dryly.

CHAPTER 24

Malone looked up from his desk when the CSI technician knocked on his open office door. "Come in, Elizabeth. Sit down."

Elizabeth took a seat across from Malone and handed him a small bag that contained the three thumb drives from the Rousseaus' safe. "I have good news, Frank, if you want to call it that. One of the panties in the safe belonged to Kerry Hamilton. The other two pairs contain DNA from two different unknown female donors."

Malone frowned solemnly. "They'll likely match the two murder victims in California."

"The Hamilton DNA confirmation locks down your case, Frank."

"Yeah, but one of our suspects is still on the loose," Malone said, expressing concern.

After Elizabeth left, Malone uploaded the content of the three thumb drives onto his computer. He emailed the material to Dolan so he could also review it. Malone then began going through the content on the first thumb drive. It was shocking, to say the least. He saw Kerry

Hamilton staked out on a bed. Her wrists and ankles were secured to four bedposts. She was nude. The scene was apparently videoed by a cellphone secured on a tripod, because both Annette and Bobby Rousseau were present in full view. They were also nude. The camera remained stationary throughout. Malone could barely watch it. The sadistic cruelty was unimaginable. He was disgusted and appalled by what he saw. The Rousseaus zealously did unspeakable things to Kerry. First, they drugged her against her will. Then they proceeded to torture her in a horrifying, depraved manner. There were periods when Kerry whimpered, cried, and eventually screamed because of what she was forced to endure. She pleaded for the Rousseaus to stop their assault, but they zealously continued on. Malone couldn't imagine how two adults could do such things to anyone, let alone an innocent teenager.

Malone then viewed the content on the other two thumb drives. The scenes and activity were similar, except the victims were two different teenage girls. Malone assumed that the two girls were Catalina Valdez and Karen Stewart. He never thought he would ever see something like that. The victims were writhing in pain, and the Rousseaus appeared to be enjoying every minute of it.

Malone's thoughts were interrupted by a knock on his open office door. It was Dolan. Malone waved him in.

The color had drained from Dolan's face. He sat down and momentarily stared at his partner, searching for the right words to express his thoughts. Finally, he said, "My G-d, Frank, I have never seen anything like that in my life. If there was any doubt that we are doing the right thing, that's over now. The Rousseaus are depraved beyond words; they're monsters. Kerry and the other girls are barely older than my daughters."

"I know," Malone said, shaking his head in disgust.

Malone dialed Kinsey's extension. "Kinsey, I want to have a word with Annette."

Kinsey sensed something different in Malone's voice. She had never heard that tone from him before. "Okay, Frank."

Twenty minutes later, Kinsey and Annette were sitting in interrogation room two. Malone joined them while Dolan watch on closed-circuit TV in the adjacent room.

"Annette, you are going to be arrested for the rape and murder of Kerry Hamilton."

She stared ahead, not making eye contact with him, while Malone read her the Miranda rights.

"I am going to do everything in my power to make sure you get the death penalty. I have never met anyone who deserves it more. You're a very unique woman, Annette, or Tina, or whatever your name is. I hope I never cross paths with someone like you ever again."

"Go somewhere else with your indignation and death penalty scare tactics, Malone. Juries don't execute women; that's a known fact. Besides, prison life doesn't scare me. I'll have access to all the sex I want there. It'll be a virtual playground for me."

"Generally, your opinion on the death penalty might be true. However, I am sure there isn't a jury in jurisprudence history that has ever seen anything like what I am going to show them. You see, Annette, we got into your safe. I have seen your home movies, and they are disgusting. I am sure they'll make quite an impression on a jury—one that the jurors will likely never forget for the rest of their lives. I know I will never forget what I saw. The cruel acts that you and your husband inflicted on those girls were on a level beyond anyone's comprehension. You and your husband are pure evil, Annette, and I can assure you, I know what evil looks like."

"I don't need any high and mighty speeches from you, Malone," Annette said defiantly.

"Your husband is on the run. He's left you here to fend for yourself. You're all alone, and the death penalty is looming. Your day of reckoning is here."

Tears started dripping down Annette's face. Genuine fear had swept away her facade of bravado.

"Take her downstairs and book her Kinsey," Malone said.

"I want to speak to my lawyer," Annette insisted while sobbing.

Malone abruptly left the interrogation room, leaving a female monster to ponder her fate and Kinsey wondering what Malone had seen on the videos.

Meanwhile, Bobby Rousseau hadn't eaten since early that morning. He had several face masks in the glove compartment of his Land Rover. They were leftovers from the days of the COVID pandemic. He also had a black baseball cap and sunglasses. He donned all three, along with his black wool coat, and went inside a fast-food restaurant to order a couple of hamburgers and something to drink.

While waiting in line to order, he contemplated his situation. Two hours earlier, he had attempted to enter the interstate and make his way out of Midtown. However, there was a roadblock set up on the entrance ramp. He went on social media. Hundreds of comments were being made referencing dozens of checkpoints police had set up to keep Kerry Hamilton's murder suspect from leaving Midtown. A full-scale manhunt was underway.

Rousseau finally made it to the counter, where a young woman was entering food orders into a computer.

The young woman behind the counter thought she recognized the man, even though he wore a mask, a hat, and sunglasses. She also thought his behavior seemed suspicious. Sure, there were still a few people wearing masks despite the fact that the pandemic was over. However, there was something different about this particular man that drew her attention.

She took the man's order. Then she left the counter to ask a coworker to cover for her. She went into the back room and perused various social media sites on her cellphone. She saw the images of Bobby Rousseau that Malone had sent out to the media. Despite the man's attempt to disguise himself, she was certain he was the fugitive that everyone was looking for. She called 911. She informed the operator that the suspect in the Kerry Hamilton murder case was in the restaurant where she worked. When she went back to the counter, the man was gone. He didn't wait around long enough to receive his order.

Dolan's portable radio hummed with activity as he sat in his cubicle. He heard units being dispatched to that same fast-food restaurant in Midtown's Van Buran District. He raised dispatch on his radio, requested, and received approval to operate on TAC channel three. He quickly walked over to Malone's office. "Frank, do you have your radio on?"

"No, why?"

"Rousseau was spotted in a fast-food restaurant on the corner of Main and Van Buren Streets. Several units have been dispatched to the location."

Malone quickly got up from his desk chair. "Let's take a ride out there."

Rousseau heard the wailing sirens of several responding police units coming from multiple directions. He was uncertain that he had enough time to get in his vehicle, back out of his parking space, and leave the area before police arrived. As a result, he took off on foot. He ran out of the restaurant parking lot, down the block, and into an alley. Sirens howled from every direction.

Malone and Dolan were in Eddie's Explorer driving code one (without warning lights and siren) to the Van Buren District. The Van Buren District was a known blighted area in Midtown. It was filled with distressed high-rise buildings used for public housing. A wind-driven snow flurry began to sweep through Midtown. The first arriving police officer at the restaurant informed responding units that the suspect had fled in an unknown direction. Night was beginning to fall. Several streetlights were out in the sadly neglected area, adding to the overall darkness.

Dolan slowly drove up and down the streets in the dilapidated area. Malone seized a battery-operated spotlight from the back seat of Eddie's Explorer. He used it to illuminate dark crevices and alleys that were hidden from the fading illumination of the straining streetlights. As Dolan drove, Malone shined the spotlight into several partially hidden areas where Rousseau might have sought refuge, but he wasn't there.

A police officer announced over the radio that he saw a man on foot running north on Parkland Boulevard. He met the description of the suspect. Dolan made a left turn and headed toward the area where the suspect was last spotted. On a street corner ahead, several homeless people were gathered around a trash can seeking warmth from its burning contents. The orange flames provided minimal relief from the artic, wind-driven conditions. Malone briefly shined the spotlight on the group to see if Rousseau was among them. He was not. Dolan continued to drive up one street and then down another, looking for the fleeing fugitive.

Both detectives were listening intently to the radio when another police officer came on the air. He said he had spoken to a delivery truck driver who had seen a white male, meeting the suspect description, "frantically running east" on Third Avenue.

Dolan made a quick right turn and headed that way. A feral cat scampered out of the darkness and crossed in front of the Explorer's path. Dolan quickly stepped on the brakes to avoid hitting it. Malone shined the spotlight on two junkies preparing for a fix. They quickly attempted to conceal their temporary salvation.

Another police officer announced on the radio that he saw a white male running north on Seventh Street. Dolan spotted a sign up ahead that indicated Seventh Street. He turned right and headed north. Malone saw the blurry image of a man up ahead, running, and then disappearing into the darkness. He directed the spotlight on him. It was Rousseau.

Rousseau immediately veered left into a condemned high-rise building. A five-alarm fire had severely damaged the building several months prior. Dolan sped up to where Rousseau had entered the building.

"Stop here, Eddie. I am getting out. Go around back in case he comes out the other side."

Malone grabbed Eddie's handheld flashlight and disappeared into the dark, burned-out structure. Malone turned the flashlight on. The darkness was so black that the flashlight's beam of light was barely able to illuminate the path forward. Black soot-stained walls, streaked with water veins. The building reeked with the obnoxious smell of smoke. Malone heard the scampering ascending steps of Bobby Rousseau. He was heading up a stairway somewhere to Malone's right. He found the stairwell and followed the fugitive's uneven steps.

Meanwhile, Dolan had driven around to the back side of the building. He saw no one. He wondered if Rousseau had already exited the building and headed in another direction—or was he still inside? He concluded that he must be inside because he didn't see Malone either. He called Malone on his portable radio. "Frank, are you still inside the building?"

"Yes, Rousseau is heading up a stairway toward the roof. The stairwell is located just inside the front entrance, on the right. I'm in pursuit."

"Understood, I'm headed your way."

Malone could hear Rousseau's frantic steps and his heavy, uneven breathing echoing in the stairwell. He continued his methodical ascent. Breathing was difficult for him as well due to exertion and the noxious black soot suspended in the air. Nevertheless, he continued his pursuit.

Dolan was now on the first floor searching in the darkness for the stairwell Malone had referenced.

Rousseau made it to the top of the stairs. He kicked

open the bulkhead door that led to the snow-covered flat roof. He heard Malone relentlessly climbing the stairs after him. He ran to the four-foot-tall parapet wall that outlined the roof's perimeter. He looked over the edge. He saw the street twelve floors below. He was cornered. *Why did I flee to the roof?* He asked himself. There was no place for him to go now.

Malone's steps grew louder. Rousseau frantically looked for a means to escape, but there was none.

Malone exited through the open bulkhead door and stepped onto the roof. He had his 9mm service weapon in his right hand and Dolan's flashlight in the other.

Rousseau turned and leaned against the parapet wall. Malone approached. Rousseau turned again and looked over the edge of the parapet wall. He made a quick ill-thought-out calculation. He climbed up on top of the parapet wall.

Meanwhile, Dolan had finally started his ascent to the roof.

Rousseau faced the approaching Malone. "Stop right where you are, Malone, or I'll jump. I mean it. I'm not going to prison. Leave the roof immediately, or I am going to jump. If you don't leave, you will have essentially murdered me."

Malone stopped and smirked. He inserted his weapon back into his shoulder holster. "Get off the wall, Bobby.

It's all over. You and I both know you're not going to jump."

"Yes, I will. I mean it, Malone!"

Malone retrieved a cigar from the chest pocket inside his coat. It was one of the cigars he had purchased to celebrate his engagement to Sarah. He placed the cigar in the corner of his mouth. He reached deeper inside the pocket and pulled out a book of matches.

Rousseau watched the curious macabre actions of Frank Malone. He recognized the indifference Malone was exhibiting regarding his threat to jump. Malone struck the match, cupped his hands, and puffed on the cigar until it was burning on its own.

Meanwhile, Dolan could be heard still climbing the stairs.

A wind-driven snow flurry began whipping around the rooftop of the twelve-story structure.

A desperate Rousseau called out to Malone to threaten him once again. "I mean it, Malone—back off, or I will jump."

Malone took a long drag on his cigar and blew the smoke out through his nostrils. He cavalierly waved his hand. "Be my guest, Bobby. Go ahead and jump. I don't give a damn."

Rousseau paused for a moment. He realized his threat to jump wasn't going to convince Malone to back off.

He smirked. "Some public servant you turned out to be, Malone. You'll have to live with killing me for the rest of your life." He snickered. "I'll see you in hell someday."

Rousseau spread his arms, leaned back, and dropped off the parapet wall, silently plunging to his death. Malone nonchalantly walked over to the parapet wall and looked over the edge. He saw Rousseau's shattered body below, half on the sidewalk, and half on the asphalt street pavement.

"I'll live with it just fine, Bobby," Malone muttered to himself.

Dolan emerged from the open bulkhead door, out of breath. Malone was leaning against the parapet wall, smoking his cigar. Dolan looked around curiously. "Where's Rousseau? Is he up here?"

"Not anymore."

Malone extended his right arm and pointed his thumb down. Dolan was incredulous. He hurried to Malone, looked over the edge, and saw Rousseau's mangled remains. He looked back at Malone. "That's going to be one hell of a messy cleanup, Frank."

Malone reached into his coat pocket and retrieved another cigar. He offered it to Dolan along with the matches. Dolan accepted them both. He put the cigar in his mouth, struck a match, and puffed on the cigar until his too was burning on its own. He turned and leaned back against the parapet wall beside Malone. He looked out over the urban landscape of Midtown. Police sirens wailed in the distance.

"You know, Frank, it's not a bad view up here."

"No, it's not, Eddie. No, it's not."

CHAPTER 25

Sarah braved the cold conditions on Thanksgiving morning to go to her favorite coffee shop. She was in a melancholy mood over the state of her relationship with Malone. Following Alex's visit, Sarah started questioning her doubt in Malone's infidelity. She had looked at the pictures the PI left more closely. She thought she could detect subtle differences in the shape of the man's body in the pictures. She decided to seek refuge in a place where people were in a festive holiday mood. She was about to enter through the front door when a man with a familiar face was exiting. It was the man she knew as Special Agent Hogan from the FBI. Hogan's left eye was purple and puffy. A wad of cotton protruded from the left nostril of his bent, swollen nose. Sarah and Hogan made eye contact.

Amused, Sarah smiled. "I told you Frank Malone wasn't going to like what you were saying about him."

Hogan momentarily stared at her, then spun on his heels and abruptly walked away.

The coffee shop hummed with activity. Sarah's senses

were soothed by the aroma of hot coffee and fresh pastries. She got her order, a small-medium-blend coffee with cream, and found a table to sit at. The warm beverage was a source of comfort on such a windy, bitterly cold day. The air inside the coffee shop was filled with conversation. People were discussing politics, upcoming holiday football games, and a variety of other topics. Sarah was scrolling through several social media sites when everyone's attention became focused on the television screen mounted on the wall.

The mayor of Midtown was speaking from a podium in the first-floor lobby at City Hall. The police chief, Frank Malone, Eddie Dolan, and a woman Sarah recognized from media reports as Kerry Hamilton's mother stood behind the mayor. Closed caption text scrolled across the bottom of the screen to transcribe what the mayor was saying.

Meanwhile, Doreen was in her kitchen, glumly chopping vegetables in preparation for Thanksgiving dinner at the Dolan house. Her daughters were out somewhere with their friends. She was alone with her thoughts. She wasn't looking forward to her favorite holiday.

She turned on the TV in anticipation of the Thanksgiving Day Parade. She hoped the parade would provide a distraction from all her unhappy thoughts. She felt clinically depressed over the situation with her husband. This was not going to be the Thanksgiving Day celebration she had envisioned several weeks earlier. Coverage leading up to the parade was suddenly interrupted to broadcast the press conference at City Hall. She saw Eddie and Frank standing behind the mayor. That immediately got her attention. She stopped what she was doing, sat down, and listened to the mayor.

"Good morning, everyone. I know the Kerry Hamilton tragedy has captured everyone's attention. I am here to provide an update on the case. Late yesterday, the Midtown Police Department arrested Tina Russell, also known as Annette Rousseau, in connection with the murder of Kerry Hamilton. Ms. Rousseau had been Kerry's ballet dance instructor. Ms. Rousseau's husband was also a suspect in Kerry's rape and murder. He committed suicide last night following a police chase. He jumped off the roof of an abandoned twelve-story building in the Van Buren District of Midtown.

"I'd like to recognize Chief Parker and all the members of Midtown's Police Department, for their professionalism, dedication, and bravery. Midtown will certainly be safer now that these two alleged depraved killers are no longer on the loose. I want the citizens of Midtown to know that my administration will always be an ardent supporter of law enforcement in this town. However, this is not a day for me to speak about that. It's a day for Kerry's mother to speak for herself and her daughter. With that, I turn this microphone over to Victoria Hamilton."

At the same time Doreen Dolan turned up the volume up on her television, across town, Sarah got up and moved closer to the TV screen mounted on the wall.

On-screen, the woman standing behind the mayor approached the podium. Her eyes were puffy and bloodshot, and she looked exhausted. Her slumped posture and slouched body language suggested defeat. However, as she began to speak, her shoulders appeared to expand, and her posture suggested defiance.

"Good morning, everyone, my name is Victoria Hamilton. I am Kerry's mother. My daughter was raped and murdered several weeks ago. Kerry's former ballet dance instructor has been arrested in connection with those crimes. Apparently, her husband, who is now deceased, was also involved. I drove Kerry to all her dance lessons." Victoria's voice cracked as she was being overcome with emotion. "Unbeknownst to me, I unwittingly handed my daughter over to two monsters. I will have to live with that mistake for the rest of my life. I assure you it won't be easy."

Sarah's eyes welled up, and Doreen wiped away tears.

"I owe a debt of gratitude to Chief Parker and all the members of the Midtown Police Department. I want to thank them for their hard work and dedication to get justice for Kerry. However, I would be remiss if I didn't specifically mention Lieutenant Frank Malone and Detective Edward Dolan. They confronted obstacles in this case that no police officer should ever have to face. The investigation involving these two sick individuals cost them a lot personally . . . in fact, far too much. What they have endured was beyond the call of duty. That's the other tragedy in this horrible case. Despite significant personal hardship, these two men persevered to get justice for my precious Kerry. For that, I will be forever grateful to them." Victoria turned to acknowledge Malone and Dolan.

From their respective places miles from City Hall, tears streamed down the faces of both Doreen and Sarah.

"These two men have asked me not to elaborate on what they faced during their investigation. I strongly disagree with them on this point, but I will respect their wishes. I owe them at least that. However, someday, I hope the full story will come out." Overcome with emotion, Victoria choked back tears. "I apologize, but I will not be able to continue."

Not one onlooker had a dry eye.

Malone and Dolan immediately approached Victoria to comfort her. A voice from the media crowd called out. It was Will Sutton. "Lieutenant Malone, perhaps you can tell us now what you and Detective Dolan faced during your investigation. Ms. Hamilton's statements have piqued everyone's interest."

Malone looked at the throngs of reporters. "I have no comment," he said.

"Can you tell us anything about this case, Frank, that the public should know?" Sutton asked.

Malone looked back at Sutton. He pondered the question for a moment before he answered. "Sometimes the price of justice costs a lot more than we could ever imagine."

With that, Malone and Dolan ushered Victoria away from the podium and out of City Hall's lobby.

Tears streamed down Sarah's face. Two men standing beside her were drinking coffee and having a discussion. She overheard their conversation. One said to other, "Malone . . . isn't he the cop who shot it out with that serial killer last February?"

The other man nodded. "Yeah, that's him. You know, Midtown might be the armpit of the entire country, but it would be a lot worse without Frank Malone around."

Sarah attempted unsuccessfully to choke back her tears.

Meanwhile, Doreen wiped away her tears with a dish towel. She got up from her chair and returned to preparing Thanksgiving dinner with much more vigor and enthusiasm. Although her nose was running and her tears were still flowing, she now had a sober sense of optimism that her favorite holiday could be salvaged.

Later, Dolan dropped Malone off at the 9th Precinct. "What next, Frank?"

"I'm going to start filling out some of the paperwork on the case."

"I'll come up and help you."

"No, you go home to your family. I'm just trying to keep busy. I can handle most of what has to be done by myself. What I can't get done today, we can do on Monday. I have no place to go anyway."

"Are you sure, Frank?"

"Yes, I'm sure. I'll see you on Monday."

"I'm not looking forward to going home. I'll stay and help you. I don't think it's going to be a good day at the Dolan house."

"No, you have to go home. It's Thanksgiving. You should at least be there for your daughters. Again, I'm just trying to keep busy. You have more important things to do. I'll see you Monday."

With that, Malone got out of the Explorer and headed up the steps to the 9th Precinct. Dolan somberly watched him for a moment as the cold winds rippled his heavy trench coat. Malone was right; the cost of justice could be very expensive.

Dolan pulled away from the curb. Midtown was nearly deserted because of the holiday. Families gathered inside as bitter-cold winds blew up and down the vacant streets of Midtown. Dolan dreaded facing all the tension and mistrust awaiting him at home. Nevertheless, he knew he had to put on a good face for his daughters. It wouldn't be easy. His stomach churned as he pulled into his driveway. He exited the Explorer, took a deep breath, and walked over to check the mailbox. Why? There was no mail delivery on Thanksgiving. Was it force of habit, or was he just delaying the inevitable anguish that lay ahead?

He turned and headed up the sidewalk toward the front door. The door opened. Doreen stepped out onto the front porch. She had her familiar warm smile back. Dolan immediately noticed the change. Victoria Hamilton had convinced Doreen that her husband was telling her the truth.

Doreen stepped down the porch steps and over to her

husband. She wrapped her arms around him and placed a warm kiss on his lips. "I'm sorry, Ed. I'm so sorry I didn't believe you. Please forgive me."

In Washington, D.C., the deputy attorney general walked into his boss's office.

Deep in thought, the attorney general was looking out the window at the epicenter of governmental power in the United States.

"Sir, I wanted to let you know that they just finished a press conference in Midtown. Tina Russell has been arrested for the kidnapping, rape, and murder of that high school girl. Her husband, Harry Niles, committed suicide last night to avoid being arrested. He jumped off a twelve-story building."

The attorney general smirked.

"Sir, how do you want to handle Midtown moving forward?"

The attorney general turned and looked at his deputy. "Don't do anything. I can't control what the Washington bureaucrats in other departments will do to them, but I can control what we do . . . don't do anything. I'm just glad this whole sordid mess is over, at least for us . . . at least for now. However, I certainly can't speak for our members in Congress who will be starring in the Harry and Tina home movies. I am appalled at what we have done. Everyone knows politics is a dirty game. I'm not sure they could ever imagine how dirty until now. At least it worked out right in some ways. Harry and Tina got exactly what they deserved."

"They sure did, sir."

"I'll say one other thing about this whole sleazy affair. It would have been so easy for all of us to do the right thing, but none of us did, except for that police lieutenant in Midtown. He's the only who walks away from this whole mess with his integrity still intact. That son of bitch has some guts—I'll give him that."

"Yes, sir, he certainly does."

Sarah parked her cranberry-red Mustang in the 9th Precinct parking lot. Only Malone's Explorer and a handful of other vehicles occupied the parking lot. Her face was flushed from the cold winds as she climbed the steps to the front entrance. She went inside, passed through the metal detector, and approached the desk sergeant.

"Happy Thanksgiving, Sarah," said the sergeant.

"You too, Sarge. Is Frank upstairs?"

"I think he's the only one up there today. I'll dial his extension to let him know you're here."

"Please don't. I'd like to surprise him."

"Sure, Sarah, you know the way."

Sarah took the elevator up to the fourth floor. The doors opened. She initially saw no one. Midtown's Homicide Division was a literal ghost town. She followed the familiar path to Malone's office. He sat still at his desk, staring at his computer. Sarah stood for a moment in the doorway. Malone hadn't noticed that she was there. Rolled-up deli wrappers and a half-filled coffee cup sat on his desk.

"What's in the wrapper, Lieutenant?" she asked, interrupting Malone's thoughts.

Malone looked up, surprised to see her. "A turkey and Swiss sandwich on rye. After all, it's Thanksgiving."

Sarah moved closer. "I'm sorry I doubted you, Frank. I'll never forgive myself."

"Forget it; anyone would have reacted the way you did after seeing what you saw."

"No, I was wrong, Frank. It took Alex and Victoria Hamilton to point that out to me. It would have been a lot easier if I had just believed you from the beginning."

Malone stood up and came around his desk. "I don't care about any of that. You're here, and I know you believe me now. That's all that matters."

The two lovers embraced and shared a passionate kiss.

After they separated from their kiss, Sarah studied Malone's hardened face. "It's Thanksgiving, Frank. I'm sorry I didn't make anything. I didn't think today was going to end up like this."

"That's alright. I know a good Italian restaurant, and they're serving turkey today," he said, smiling.

Sarah looked into Malone's eyes, and she smiled too. "Is that the restaurant where a very wise waitress works?"

"Yes, it is," he promptly responded.

Malone dropped his Explorer off in his apartment building's garage. Sarah picked him up in her Mustang, and they drove to Tommy D's. The weather conditions were deteriorating quickly during the drive, but the couple barely noticed. They were preoccupied with their thoughts about their reconciliation. They entered Tommy D's and received a boisterous, warm welcome from Tommy.

"Yo, Frankie, Happy Thanksgiving!"

Rita came around the hostess station wearing a bright smile. She wrapped her arms around Malone and hugged him tightly.

Alex saw the commotion from across the dining room. She caught Malone's eye. They acknowledged each other with a smile.

"Where do you want to sit, Frank?" Rita asked.

"Anywhere in Alex's section."

Sarah excused herself and went to the restroom while Rita led Malone over to a table in Alex's section. Malone sat down.

Alex wandered over, smiling. "Well, well, well, look who got his girlfriend back."

Malone grabbed her hand. "Thank you for trying to help, Alex. I really appreciate it."

"What are friends for, Frank?"

When Sarah returned from the restroom, the two women hugged each other.

"How are you, Alex?" Sarah asked.

"Whatever I have going on, it's a lot better than dancing naked with a bloated stomach full of turkey and mashed potatoes . . . and believe me I know," she said, giggling.

"Maybe I'll learn more about that experience later in the evening," Sarah said, laughing.

"Well, it looks like the police lieutenant is in for a wild night," Alex remarked.

CHAPTER 26

Malone unlocked his apartment door and led Sarah into the living room. "Please have a seat, Sarah. I have something I want to give you."

He went into his bedroom to retrieve the engagement ring. He returned, hiding the box behind his back. "I have something I have wanted to give you for the past week, but things kind of went off the rails." Malone revealed the black-velvet jewelry box and placed it in her hand.

Sarah quietly gasped. "Frank, what is this?"

"Go ahead, open it."

Sarah opened the box and gasped again. The ring was perfect. It sparkled brightly against the black velvet. She studied it and then began to softly sob.

"What's the matter, Sarah? I thought it would make you happy."

"I don't deserve this, Frank. I doubted you, I didn't believe you. I am ashamed of myself."

"Nonsense!" Malone sat beside her. He wrapped his big arm around her shoulders. "You're human, Sarah. I know what you saw in those pictures. Any woman would be horrified. How could you not be? What matters now is that it is all behind us. I don't want us to think about that anymore. So, what's your answer, Sarah? Will you marry me?"

"Of course I will marry you, Frank." Then she paused for a moment. "My mother is going to have a heart attack," she said, laughing. "She figured at my age it would never happen."

Malone kissed her passionately. He poured her a glass of wine, and they talked for an hour about what was next for them. They discussed Naples, possibly adopting a puppy, and marriage plans. Later, they retired to the bedroom, where they made love to the point of exhaustion. They talked some more until they finally dozed off.

Later, at 3:23 a.m., Malone was awakened by a text alert. He grabbed his cellphone off the night table. He went into the bathroom to read the message: "Reference: Triple homicide, Willy's Tavern, 2100 Fairmont Street." Malone quickly splashed water on his face. He ran a comb through his hair and began dressing.

Sarah rolled over in bed. "Frank, what is it?" she asked groggily.

"It's work. I have to go in."

"Why, what's going on?"

Sarah was nestled under layers of blankets. Malone moved to the bed, bent down, brushed the hair away from her face, smiled, and kissed her warm lips. "Go back to sleep," he whispered.

A second text alert sounded. It was from Dolan, saying he would pick Malone up in ten minutes.

Ten minutes later, Malone was standing outside his apartment building in the bitter cold, shuffling his feet when Dolan arrived. He got in the Explorer. Dolan drove quickly away from the curb.

Malone pressed the talk button on his portable radio. "Lieutenant 21 to Dispatch."

"Go ahead, Lieutenant 21."

"Show Lieutenant 21 and Detective 119 en route to Willy's Tavern, at 2100 Fairmont Street, reference triple homicide."

"Acknowledge. Lieutenant 21 and Detective 119 . . . en route."

THE END

www.ingramcontent.com/pod-product-compliance
Lightning Source LLC
Chambersburg PA
CBHW071159100726
47908CB00002B/440